W9-BPL-158

Midshipwizard
Halcyon
Blithe

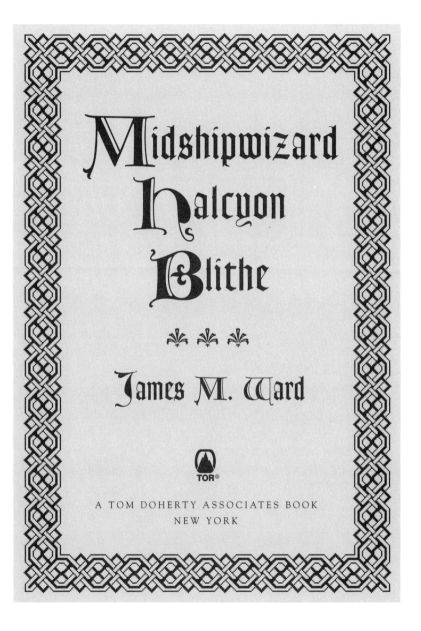

Midshipwizard Halcyon Blithe

❉ ❉ ❉

James M. Ward

TOR®

A TOM DOHERTY ASSOCIATES BOOK
NEW YORK

MIDSHIPWIZARD HALCYON BLITHE

Copyright © 2005 by James M. Ward

Edited by Brian Thomsen

A Tor Book
Published by Tom Doherty Associates, LLC
175 Fifth Avenue
New York, NY 10010

www.tor.com

Tor® is a registered trademark of Tom Doherty Associates, LLC.

ISBN 0-765-31253-0
EAN 978-0-765-31253-2

First Edition: September 2005

Printed in the United States of America

0 9 8 7 6 5 4 3 2 1

Contents

Acknowledgments

There were many people who helped me get this book to print and I would like to take this chance to thank some of them.

Brian Thomsen is an unusually talented editor and a good friend who made this novel ten times better by his efforts.

Mike Gray is a friend who took the time to give me great advice on every chapter of this book.

Craig Brain is a newfound comrade who was also very supportive in this effort.

Jim Fallone was nice enough to suggest I give this a try. Thank you for pushing me in this direction.

My wonderful wife, Janean, allowed me to take the time to write this book, and I credit her with all of my success since we have been married.

Finally, I'd like to thank my departed mother, who made me take two years of typing class in high school even though I complained about it, kicking and screaming all the way.

Midshipwizard Halcyon Blithe

PROLOGUE

✤ ✤ ✤

Arcania at War

"Damn all the gods above us, I've been feeling this twice-blasted storm in me bones half the night and here it comes." The dock-worker reached out and pointed with his hook for a hand at the storm clouds rolling over Ilumin Bay.

"Hook, me old friend, you've been complaining about storms for as long as I've known you. Here, take this to warm your salty bones," said the friend while handing Hook a tankard of hot rum.

"Pegleg, where did you get the coin for this?" Hook asked, forgetting all about the storm in the pleasure of sipping hot rum.

"It's the last of my prize money from that battle off of Easta two year ago. Settle me hearty, the Maleen fleets and our still-in-bed officers can wait a few grains of falling sand in an Arcanian hourglass for two old sailors to finish their grog." Pegleg hopped over to a crate under the cover of patched sail and motioned for his friend to follow.

Hook raised his namesake and shook it at the sky. "Let the Maleen navy come. Every dock sailor here has a missing leg or hand, but we'll still give the bastards hell. Those shapechanging fiends aren't going to get past Arcania's wall of ships in my lifetime."

Pegleg rolled his eyes at his friend's feisty mood and raised his tankard in salute. "With that said I hope you live forever, friend."

Hook knew he preached to the salty choir. "All right, all right." He sat by his friend on the crates they would be loading aboard frigates all morning. "It's weather like this and a battle with a first-rater that cost me this hand. You know they love nothing better than boarding and taking over ships. It was the Maleen captain of that first-rater that chopped off me hand as I spilled his guts on the deck in reply for his effort."

"Now don't go getting all glum-like. There's a wall of Arcania fleets between them and us. Even iffen those dark bastards do break through and land on these docks, there's you and me greeting um with a friendly smile and a cheerful stab." Pegleg drew out a slim dagger from a sheath on his wooden leg and cut some bread for himself, afterward raising the weapon suggestively.

Just then, the morning coach came around the corner and up to the docks.

Lately the coaches were crammed full with officers. Such was a sure sign that the fleet was ready to move out.

The two men walked over to see if coin was offered for unloading sea trunks.

"New fish," both of them said at the exact same time, and smiled at having the same thought. They stepped back under the awning to get out of the drizzle, and heard a loud snap of the fingers from inside the carriage.

The pouring rain all around them stopped.

The sun broke through the dark clouds and the pair of soggy dockmen became highly pleased to see they weren't going to get too wet in the loading of naval supplies for the anchored ships that day.

Leaping out of the carriage as if the seat had a spring ejecting him, the midshipwizard landed on the dock with the sort of energy only the young possessed. The two men could tell he was a wizard by his white shock of hair and white eyebrows. His brown-and-white midshipwizard uniform was so crisp it could be only the second time it was worn.

"Look at him, he's a midshipwizard fresh out of the academy, or I'm a sea bass," Pegleg whispered to his friend.

"Did you see the red in his eyes? There's demon blood in him for sure," Hook remarked.

"A big un, over six foot if he's an inch," Hook observed.

"Did I thank Uncle Frank for the gift of this sword?" the midshipwizard muttered to himself. (Fastening on his gleaming new naval sword, he patted it with the palm of his callused hand, deep in thought.) "I know I thanked Uncle Jim for the midshipwizard hat." (His sea chest magically floated at his command from the top of the carriage to the ground and followed him in an impressive display of arcane skill for one so young.) "Where is Uncle John's checklist of things to do on the first day?"

He searched his many pockets and finally found a small piece of parchment. Reading it quickly, counting to himself, he put it away for the hundredth time.

"Well." Still talking to himself, he looked around to see the two old sailors on the dock. "I've got six months of academy training under my belt. The good wishes of six different uncles and six brothers are all still ringing in my ears. I'm a sailor with prospects and I have to get to work."

He walked briskly over to the pair. Bright sunshine warmed him, causing him to smile in satisfaction.

"Men, I beg pardon for breaking into your breakfast." His voice was friendly and his smile was infectious. Pride almost burst out of every part of his uniform. "I'm Midshipwizard Halcyon Blithe with orders to report to the HMD *Sanguine* dragonship of the line this morning. Could one of you tell me how I get aboard her?"

Pegleg and Hook had the same thoughts flash through their minds. They could give him wrong directions. They could send him to cool his heels at the officers' billet. They could probably get him in lots of trouble, just for the sheer fun of it . . . however, the young man before them had a likable smile, he wasn't being pushy, and the red tint in his eyes warned them that it might not be a good idea to cross this new officer in the king's navy.

Hook, remembering other officers with those same red eyes, didn't want to take any chances. His hook pointed down the docks. "The *Sanguine*'s jolly boat rowed up to the dock an hour ago. I suspect they're waiting for you. All of them went for a bite to eat at the Blue Dolphin Inn, but are back on the boat now. Your craft is a hundred yards down that next pier. You can't miss it; it's the only lizard green jolly boat in the entire fleet right now. The *Sanguine* is at the mouth of the bay, you can just make it out in the distance. You might think about getting something to eat before you find her. The morning-meal bells have all rung on the ships at anchor and it's a long time till the lunch bell."

"Thank you, men. King and country come first, as you know. Your help is appreciated." Blithe squared away and saluted.

The two sailors got to their feet and saluted back. As the young officer walked sharply down the docks, his sea chest floated magically behind.

Pegleg spoke first. "I hope Fate is in a good mood when that one sees his first Maleen boarding action."

Hook smiled and slugged back the last of his rum. "I'd wager he falls into the bay when he tries to get on the jolly boat, but there isn't a man or boy on this entire dock that would take that bet."

The laughter of the two men drifted to Blithe's ears, but he paid them no mind.

"I know I'll have to serve a few years to earn the respect of such men," Halcyon said to himself. "But earn it I will, because I'm an officer with prospects, no doubt about it."

The clouds of the bay, magically commanded to disperse, did so. Nature found it impossible to ignore the demands of a powerful young spellcaster, but it would bide its time and exact payment for this storm's clearing.

The sun continued to shine down on the Arcanian Empire's newest midshipwizard . . . for now.

I

The Jolly Boat

HIS MAJESTY'S ARTICLES OF WAR: ARTICLE I

No officer, mariner, soldier, or other person of the fleet shall leave their assigned post during combat unless ordered by the captain of the ship or unless extenuating circumstances warrant the abandoning of the post. Such dereliction of duty will be reviewed by a board of court-martial. The penalty for such dereliction is death or other punishment as the court-martial board shall find suitable.

"Officer of the jolly boat, permission to come on board." Halcyon Blithe stood at attention at the top of the gangplank, saluting the officer of the jolly boat and looking down. The large-oared vessel held twelve sailors and a midshipwizard at the tiller. The wide twenty-foot-long vessel had lots of room for gear and men, as jolly boats worked the cargoes from ship to shore.

"What's your rank, Midshipwizard?" The lanky officer at the stern returned Blithe's salute, calling the question up at Blithe in a slow eastern drawl; his accent marked him as coming from Et Bay on the southern tip of Arcania.

The twelve brown-uniformed sailors in the boat got their oars in the water.

Blithe, coming down the planking of the quay, stopped short at the officer's question. His midshipwizard brown-and-white uniform proclaimed his officer status. For the life of him, he couldn't tell why the other midshipwizard would care about his rank. "Midshipwizard Fifth Class Halcyon Blithe with orders for the *Sanguine.* Why do you ask? Do I need to show you my papers?"

"Show me no twice-blasted papers, Middy. We've been waiting for you most of the morning. Sitting in the wet isn't my idea of fun. Haul yourself on board and be right quick about it. Didn't they teach you anything at the academy? Way the lines, ready the oars, look sharp now, men. I'm Midshipwizard Dart Surehand Third Class." He said the last emphasizing his rank, not needing to tell Halcyon it was superior to his own.

Blithe estimated that the officer in front of him couldn't be much more than his own sixteen years. Surehand was lean with long arms and legs, and his own brown-and-white midshipwizard uniform was almost as crisp as Blithe's. He had a long face filled with buckteeth.

The midshipwizard had unusually thick white eyebrows. Blithe noticed that the other officer's big hands bore no rings. The officer's sword, sheathed and lying on the tiller seat, looked well made and the handle showed itself well used, and there was a crest on the bell guard of the weapon, but Halcyon couldn't make it out from the gangplank. There were enough gems on the handle and sheath to mark its owner as a wealthy man.

The bored crew had carried out all of Surehand's orders before he finished barking them out. He went on, "I'm the jolly boat's commander, such as it is. Every vessel no matter how small, and this one isn't quite the smallest in the king's navy, has its commander. Why isn't your sorry ass in my boat yet?"

Halcyon deftly leapt aboard, unhitching his own fine new sword, and positioned himself in the stern next to Surehand. His sea chest magically floated between the benches and came to rest at the bottom of the boat.

Halcyon didn't quite know what to make of him, but he didn't like this Surehand's tone of voice.

"I'm rather fond of Article Fourteen myself, if you get my drift," Halcyon remarked, looking up at Dart to see what expression filled his face at the quip.

Surehand quoted the article with a questioning look on his face. "No person in or belonging to the fleet shall sleep on his watch, why would you like that one?" Dart asked, steering the jolly boat toward the opening of the bay.

They took a heading straight for the *Sanguine*, but it was quite a distance away.

"No, sleeping on watch is Article Sixteen; didn't they teach you anything at the academy, Midshipwizard Surehand?"

The "gotcha" look made both young men laugh, and the tension broke like a wave on the shore as both of them realized at the same instant that they could easily be friends.

"All right, I can never remember those first twenty articles of the ninety-nine Articles of War, I don't know why. When we aren't on duty together, call me Dart." He held out his big hand and Halcyon reached to shake it.

"Halcyon, Hal to my friends and I hope you'll be one."

Dart waved his hand in a motion to take in all the ships in the harbor. "The bay is filled with ships of the line. Ilumin is the major refitting center for the western fleets. The battered ships waiting refitting anchor on the south end of the bay. The ten over there now have seen hard use in the war. The ones anchored in the north end of the bay are ships of the line, waiting to join the fleet. Look and you'll see more fitted ships, at least thirty of the line with a host of supply ships and other merchantmen on that side of the bay, always a good sign the war is going well for Arcania when the ready ships far outnumber the wrecked ships."

"I couldn't help noticing the crest on your sword. How are you related to the king?" Halcyon had to ask.

Dart showed a pained expression on his face. "The king's my uncle and that's the last I want to talk about that. I'm working my way up the chain of command like any other swab. When I get my captaincy, it's going to be because I earned it in this war with Maleen and not because I'm the king's cousin. Some officers and men have made it clear they think my birth is more important than my skills. I make it a point to set their minds right. Speaking of cousins, I don't think you can throw a rock at any of these ships and not hit a commander that's not a Blithe. Are you related to all of those Blithes?"

Halcyon could tell that his new friend was sensitive about his royal birthright. He could well imagine what problems such heritage might bring. He had his own naval heritage to work around.

"My family has had a Blithe in the Arcanian navy for as long as there's been an Arcania, bless her and the king," Halcyon said. "Right now, I have five uncles commanding ships of the line. The sixth is the naval master of the Exchequer. My six brothers are all officers, lieutenants, and lieutenant commanders in the various fleets . . . though most of them serve in the southern and western fleets. My father was captain of the *Warsprite*, blown up last year off the coast of Drusan in the battle for Ordune."

"I heard about that battle and the *Warsprite* saving others as she died," Dart said.

"My families have always been in the navy and now it's my turn," Halcyon replied proudly. "My father wanted me to serve, but only as a midshipwizard. I came into my magical abilities just recently. Most Blithes start serving on board His Majesty's ships at twelve; all my six brothers did just that. I didn't come into my power until the day I turned sixteen. I've just finished my academy training, and this is my first duty. What are the other officers like on the *Sanguine?*"

He and Surehand looked ahead in the distance to their assigned ship. The head of the dragon was dipping up and out of the water.

The sun glowed off the green scales of the dragonship.

The rowers moved back and forth, as they slowly struck oars through the bay.

"Not a bit of that," Dart admonished his new friend, "in front of the crew." His head nodded to the twelve brown-uniformed sailors working the oars. "We officers never talk about other officers of the *Sanguine* or any other ship we serve on. Course, the *Sanguine* itself is a different matter. I could talk all day long about it and its excellent crew." The last comment pleased the men straining at the oars and many of them turned their heads to smile back at Surehand as they rowed.

"Please do, we didn't get much training about dragonships of the line at the academy." Blithe relaxed for the first time that morning. He enjoyed talking to Surehand, as if he had known him all his life.

"It's a beauty it is. Now, I know most ships are called she, but dragonships are different. All dragonships are males for lots of reasons. We don't ever call them anything but 'it' when we talk about them and we talk about them a lot. The *Sanguine* is three hundred and ten feet long from stem to stern. The dragon itself is two hundred feet long in its beam, the sea dragon's body that is. It's sixty-two feet wide and the ship hull adds another twenty feet for a maximum beam of eighty-two feet. It's just out of dry dock so those measurements are exact, but it will grow longer and wider in the next two years before its next refitting, they never stop growing, these sea dragons of ours.

"Dragons shed their skin every two years. That's why we were in dry dock. The new shed skin went into refitting the orlop hull. We keep the shed skin connected to the body so blood still flows through the flesh. We stretch it and make our hulls from it. Normally a sea dragon comes to the surface every two years to shed itself of its smaller skin, scraping it off on the rocks and trees the creature finds onshore. While shedding, it can't let the seawater hit its exposed vital organs. All sorts of parasites and disease can strike the dragon down during shedding. Its heart and liver are exposed to the air and sea; therefore, the creature never submerges during the entire process. Some smart Johnny decided centuries ago that capturing a dragon was possible while it shed its flesh. Now clamps hold the flesh to the huge veins pumping blood through the skin of the dragon. That flowing blood continues to feed that shed flesh and heals the rips and tears of battle.

"We've got good Arcanian elm for the decking. There's a layer of elm timber for the supports, and naturally we use the stretched shed flesh of the dragon for the hull and inner walls. All of the clamps used to hold the shed flesh to the body of the dragon are covered in special caissons of steel and padding, and every two years we come in and treat the new shedding flesh. We know it's time to shed its skin because the green skin of the orlop deck turns milky white. At that point, we've got thirty days to treat that skin in dry dock, after it turns white. If it takes longer than thirty days to reach dry dock, the whole ship slides off the dragon with its shedding skin and it escapes into the depths of the sea. The navy tries hard not to let that happen much.

"When we're through we have a ship that heals its own walls. We've only been using them for twenty years or so. Our versions of the dragonships of the line are the biggest and fastest of all the dragonships on the high seas."

"Are dragonships faster than other ships of the line?" Halcyon could barely contain his enthusiasm as the vessel got closer and closer.

"Fast. Most first-raters can do six knots cruising speed and eleven knots when the wind pushes them hard. Sink me if the *Sanguine* cruises at eight knots and on a good day races along at fifteen knots. It almost seems like we're flying when we go that fast. I've seen her hit those speeds several times and it's as if we're on a cloud. There aren't many privateers that can outrun her and we can come into the wind better than any normal ship of the line."

"I know I have a lot of catching up to do. Until last year I was going to go into the army." Halcyon suddenly filled with dread at his new posting.

"Don't worry about not knowing everything there is to know about sailing. You're fifth-class because you have to learn a few things yet about command," Dart said. "Someday you'll know everything and be the commander of your own ship of the line."

Surehand continued, "The ship carries sixty-nine thousand square feet of sail on thirty-two different sail configurations. You'll learn each and every one of them as all new midshipwizards do sail duty for their first year of service.

"There are one hundred blast-tubes and twenty double tubes on the three decks. Second Officer Master Andool Griffon loves her blast-tubes better than her life, so don't touch one of her tubes until she gives you leave. She's the best blast-tube officer in the fleet and Captain Olden comes from a blast-tube background as well.

"Wait a minute. It just struck me, sink me if it didn't. You're the seventh son of a seventh son. Are you a better spellcaster because of it?"

"I don't usually talk about that much, because I haven't really figured out all the things I can do with my magic. I've only been a spellcaster for eight months now. I seem to be uncommonly good at air magics. At the academy, I was the strongest with sea spells as well. Aside from that I don't know what else to say, except for one silly thing." Blithe looked down at his sea chest, embarrassed again.

"What's that, Midshipwizard, speak up, man, no need to be red-faced, we're serving together, man," Dart spoke in a friendly manner to his new friend.

"Rope seems to like me." Blithe said this last in a soft, embarrassed voice.

"You're kidding me, you're a rope speaker?" Dart was clearly amazed. "There aren't ten of those in the entire western fleet. Your fortune's made, Hal. Rope speakers are worth their weight in gold. They can tell when a rigging is about to break. They can make rigging stronger and order it to untangle itself when it fouls. Oh, the captain is going to be wild for you.

"I'm an earth wizard myself and a more useless spellcaster on a ship I can't imagine. I do fairly well at the blast-tubes because of my earth skills, but everywhere else that a midshipwizard should be doing well, I do horribly. It's gotten me written up several times, because I'm so fumble-fingered with the everyday spells of the ship. I struggle with every sea spell Lieutenant Commander Giantson tries to teach me."

"What's life like on board the *Sanguine?*" Halcyon asked.

"We are nothing if not regular on board ship. Every Airday afternoon all the midshipwizards take blast-pike practice. Helping with that practice is Marine Corporal Darkwater, a very large and impressive woman. She takes far too much pleasure in volunteering her unusually skilled services in the fine art of blast-pike use."

"A woman marine?" There was wonder in Blithe's question. It was clear he couldn't imagine a woman with the rough-and-tumble marines, who were the first sea troops in every battle and known for their deadly ferocity.

"Oh, I know what you're thinking." Dart smirked. "Wait until you see our good marine corporal. She's what one would call a special case, physically and literally, but never call her that to her face. She loves practicing with men, not because she's interested at all in the opposite sex. No, I think you will find that she greatly enjoys defeating men, especially men larger and stronger than she is. Unfortunately for you, there aren't many men like that on ship. She's one of ten females in the crew, with Master Andool Griffon the highest-ranking female and Corporal Darkwater the lowest ranker."

"Unfortunately for me, why do you say that?" Halcyon asked.

"Well, I noticed when you got on board that you are a tall fellow. Six foot two or three, I would guess," Dart said.

"And you would be right, so?" Blithe said, not having the slightest idea what Dart was talking about right now.

"Our good Corporal Darkwater is just under six feet tall," Dart said, clearly enjoying himself with the description. "She's going to ask, some might even say sweetly request, to be pitted against you next Airday, just because you are new and you are taller than she is."

"I'll acquit myself well, what does it matter if she's up against me?" Halcyon was growing more and more confused.

"Men, put your backs into it," Dart ordered. "The ship's getting ready to leave the harbor."

"How in the world do you know that?" Blithe asked.

"Listen." Dart cupped his ear with his hand.

Blithe did the same thing and he could hear a chantey being sung somewhere on the deck of the *Sanguine*.

Whiskey-o, Johnny-o
Rise her up from the depths below
Whiskey, whiskey, whiskey-o
Up the anchor from the sea must go
John rise her up from down below

"When they sing that chantey they're taking up anchors," Dart remarked. "We have one of the best chanters in the fleet in our crew. I know you've been around ships all your life, you being a Blithe and all, but you're going to hear some new chanteys from this fellow, I'll tell you right now. There's nothing like a skilled chanter to keep a crew working hard and happy. The whiskey-o chantey pulls up our anchors but it works just as well for rowing and I think we need to get a move on." Surehand broke into the chantey. It was one Blithe had never heard before.

Now whiskey is the life of man
Always was since the world began

The sailors started rowing faster to the beat of the chantey. They all joined in on the refrain.

Whiskey, whiskey, whiskey-o
Much faster the oars must row
John help us move this boat we row
Whiskey, whiskey, whiskey-o

The oars hit the water faster, following the beat of the chantey. Surehand's tenor rang out over the boat and the rowing men.

Now whiskey gave me a broken nose
And whiskey made me pawn me clothes

The sailors started in again, rowing their hearts out, and the jolly boat fairly flew over the bay. They were past all the other ships of the line now and in the distance the *Sanguine* started twisting around, responding to the leaving tide as its two anchors lifted up off the floor of the bay.

Whiskey, whiskey, whiskey-o
Much faster the oars must row
John help us move this boat we row
Whiskey, whiskey, whiskey-o

Surehand was even louder with the next verse.

I thought I heard Mr. Blithe say
I treats me crew in a decent way

Even working as hard as they were, the men all broke out into smiles, turning their heads back to see Halcyon's reaction as their chantey changed words a bit from the normal. Even Halcyon broke into the refrain of the chantey then with his own strong baritone.

Whiskey, whiskey, whiskey-o
Much faster the oars must row
John help us move this boat we row
Whiskey, whiskey, whiskey-o

Then they stopped singing and stopped rowing.

"Why did you stop?" Blithe asked.

"Because we've arrived," Dart said, raising his hand into the air and gesturing toward the *Sanguine*.

Blithe turned to see the side of the *Sanguine* filling his vision. The dragonskin hull was a glossy deep green. The blast-tube ports

filled his vision from stem to stern. Halcyon didn't know what to
expect from this new ship of his, but he had a large family of navy
men wanting him to do his best and he wasn't going to let them
down as long as he breathed.

"Go ahead. You go up the ratline first. There will be an officer
there to take your papers. Luck to you, Midshipwizard Blithe."
Surehand saluted his friend and held the ropes and metal that
made the ratline ladder for him as Halcyon went to join the crew
of the *Sanguine*.

※ ※ ※

Permission to Come on Board

If any letter of message from any enemy or rebel be conveyed to any officer, mariner, or soldier or other in the fleet, and the said officer, mariner, or soldier, or other as aforesaid, shall not, within twelve hours, having opportunity so to do, acquaint his superior or a commanding officer, or if any superior officer being acquainted therewith shall not in convenient time reveal the same to the commander-in-chief of the squadron, every such person so offending, and being convicted thereof by the sentence of the court-martial, shall be punished with death, or such other punishment as the nature and degree of the offense shall deserve, and the court-martial shall impose.

The ratline ladder took him across the green expanse of the creature's back onto a narrow set of stairs to the main deck. The outer skin of the creature showed many ropy veins, and the pulse of blood beat clearly through the scaly flesh of the sea dragon. The oddity of climbing an actual dragon was completely lost on Halcyon as he rushed to get on deck and be about the business of becoming a real seaman. As he arrived on the main deck, naval pipes sounded, telling the crew a new midshipwizard was on deck.

Being piped aboard was a new experience for Blithe. His chest puffed with pride as the young naval officer heard the pipes sound for him for the first time. *I get only three short blasts as a midshipwizard*, he thought to himself, *but they are all mine*, and he was proud of every shrill note.

He saluted the piper and then the first officer. Hundreds of men were about the wide deck and working in the rigging of the sails. The intensity of the frantic action didn't distract the conscientious Blithe from saluting the officer on deck.

"Permission to come on board, sir?" Halcyon asked.

"Permission granted. Midshipwizard Fifth Class Halcyon Blithe, I presume. I am Lieutenant Commander Dire Wily, the first officer of the *Sanguine*. Welcome aboard."

The officer introducing himself to Halcyon was huge. Standing almost seven feet tall, Dire Wily displayed a monstrous power in his muscular arms, axe-handle-broad shoulders, and massive legs. He paced around Halcyon, looking him up and down. He glanced at and quickly handed back the orders Blithe gave him. Wily had a huge scar from his right eye to his chin, and his dark blue eyes seemed to read the very soul of Blithe, making the young man very uncomfortable as he withstood the inspection.

The officer had the white hair of a wizard, but it was bristly short. Most wizards allowed their hair to grow long as a personal display of their magical power. In Arcania, it was said, the whiter the hair and the longer that hair, the more powerful the wizard.

Even Officer Wily's voice held a massive power few men could equal.

"Ah, Surehand, never mind the jolly boat, your rowers can handle stowing it away. I want you to hear this as well," the first officer said, positioning himself in front of Halcyon Blithe and waiting for the other midshipwizard to get on board.

Dart came abreast of Blithe and stood at attention as well.

"I call what I'm about to say 'the Speech.' I give it to all new men coming to serve on the dragonship *Sanguine*. It won't hurt you, Surehand, to hear it again." Commander Wily moved back and forth in front of the two midshipwizards as he spoke. There was something almost tigerishly powerful about the man, as if at any second he could spring on a foe and rip them apart with his bare hands.

Blithe, standing ramrod straight, knew he should be paying strict attention to the words of the second-in-command, but his mind was moving in a thousand different directions. Even with his eyes riveted to the front, there was so much to see of the *Sanguine*. The excited midshipwizard could barely contain himself. The hundreds of distractions of the ship made it impossible to listen to his superior officer with any degree of concentration.

"The Maleen Empire is awesomely powerful, and their deadly fleets move wherever they wish along any country's coasts. Their mainland armies have been nearly unstoppable." The commander's words came down like hammer blows on both of the midshipwizards, each forceful word blasting out a warning about Arcania's deadly enemy. "The men and women of our island country are in a losing fight for their very lives. Daily Arcanian forces meet fleets twice our size. Battling to the death has become the Arcanian way of life. Every ship we desperately manage to destroy is one less to reach the shores of Arcania, but that's not happening often enough."

Halcyon stood at attention, forced to stand still while this officer tried to warn him. The midshipwizard ached to become a part of the action of the ship. Even at attention with his head and eyes locked forward, he could see so many interesting things happening on the dragonship. Men were luffing the sails. Blast-tube crews worked on massive tubes, sliding them in and out of tube ports—he couldn't wait to help with that. Sailors and marines ran back and forth on the main deck, preparing the ship to leave, and soon he hoped to be giving the orders for that to happen.

First Officer Wily continued, "I've been on five other dragon-ships of the line in the last ten years, and had them shot out from under me in battle. If it weren't for the foolhardy bravery of other ships wisely fleeing those battles, I would have died. Those ships stopped to collect me; when I got on board each one of them I thanked them and shouted at them as well for their unnecessarily risking their ships." Officer Wily was glaring at them; his tone and body language showed him filled with some type of anger.

The two midshipwizards had no way of telling why the man in front of them showed such rage.

"Yes, I yelled at them because they stopped to save men when they had an entire crew on their own ship to save." Wily was roaring at them now. "We expect you to be brave. The king doesn't expect you to be foolish." Officer Wily got louder and his words were moving.

Other men, working around the deck, stopped to take in what he was saying. Many of those sailors and marines showed concerned expressions on their faces. None of them wanted to die at sea fighting unbeatable odds. The same thought flashed through all of their minds as the first officer spoke: Could the Maleen forces be that undefeatable?

Dire Wily continued, "Arcanian ships have run from battles. Who can fight terrible odds, I ask you now? The Arcanian navies are undoubtedly the bravest in the world. The national navies of Toman and Drusan gave up and they had thought themselves brave defenders of their homelands. Their ships now serve in the fleets of Maleen. Country after country has fallen to the forces of those powerful Maleen armies and navies." Placing his hat on his head, the first officer drew his huge sword.

Blithe, no expert on weapons, thought the first officer's sword seemed thicker and longer than the normal navy saber. He knew for sure he didn't like it pointed at his face. He ached to take a step backward, but he was at attention and would stay that way until ordered otherwise.

The tip of the weapon pointed right between Blithe's eyes, the big blade never wavering an inch, presented an impressive display of arm and wrist strength.

"Midshipwizard Blithe, you must ask yourself what you would do when facing death. Your enemy is powerful and more experienced. Blithe, are you paying attention!"

He wasn't paying attention, but naturally he couldn't admit that. Halcyon shouted back, "My enemy is more powerful and more experienced than myself, I heard that, sir!"

From the quarterdeck, a slow, calming voice spoke down to the three on the main deck. The words almost floated individually and each one had its own impact. "First Officer Wily, please stop scaring the new crew member and come up here, if you would." There was an odd deliberate tone to the voice, as if it had all the time in the world to do anything it pleased.

Blithe's fast-beating heart immediately slowed down. Even at attention, he felt instantly better.

"Aye, aye, Captain," Wily said as he sheathed his sword with blinding speed. "The king and this crew expect its officers to know when to fight and when to retreat from battles. See that you remember my words. Midshipwizard Surehand, show Blithe to his wardroom. Carry on, that is all."

"Aye, aye, sir." Both midshipwizards saluted and left the main deck.

Halcyon Blithe's glances marked everything.

He'd never been on a dragonship.

Everything was so green, from the hull to the walls of the forecastle and quarterdeck. The white elm of the decking made the dragon's stretched flesh even brighter green in the midshipwizard's eyes. Standing and gawking at the many tasks up and down and all around his position, Halcyon was too slow to move for his guide. Surehand had to pull Blithe down the stairs into the middle blast-tube deck.

As they went down into the darkness, Dart looked behind to make sure no one followed. "You are the luckiest officer on the dragonship *Sanguine* today; sink me if it isn't so."

Blithe looked all around, taking in the many blast-tubes of this new deck and the darkness made penetrable only by two open blast-tube ports, one on the port side and the other on the starboard side.

"Why do you say that?" Halcyon asked.

"That speech of Officer Wily's is at least twenty more minutes long. His words bring chills to a man's spine." Dart shivered. "That officer is talented; don't get me wrong. The problem is that he goes on forever about the Maleen and their many fleets and terrible armies. It half scares a person to death just to hear it all and I've heard it at least ten times. You, my friend, were saved by the captain himself, thus proving to me you've got some luck about you."

"Saved? I have no idea what you're talking about. An experienced officer in the Arcanian navy should warn new recruits about the danger they might face." Blithe smiled to see his sea chest still magically floating behind. Sometimes, when he lost concentration on the air spell causing the chest to float, it could wander. That wouldn't have been good on his first day aboard, he thought.

"You're right of course. Many say Commander Wily takes too much pleasure in describing the power of the Maleen," Dart said. "He goes on and on and on. Now, sink me if you can't respect a man who has had five dragonships shot out from under him in battle and has survived all of that without a scratch. Still and all,

I know the captain doesn't like to hear that speech, I've heard him say so. He's remarked on it several times. That was the captain's voice on the quarterdeck ordering us squared away. Both of them are good officers, fair men. Enough of that, you're in the middle blast-tube deck. The marines crew all of these blast-tubes and string their hammocks up to sleep here. The younger midshipwizard wardroom is at the center of this deck, with the galley, the armory, and the pantry."

The green walls were alive, Halcyon thought in wonder. He didn't know if he'd ever get used to that. He reached out and placed his palm on the wall, expecting it to be a lot warmer than it was. It felt cool to his touch. He showed his surprise in his wide-eyed expression to Dart. "It's cold; I expected the living flesh to be a lot warmer."

"Sink me, man, don't you know anything?" Dart chided. "The dragonship's entire skin from the quarterdeck and forecastle to the orlop deck is the same temperature as the water it swims through. That's why we never get duty in the north where it's cold. The blood flowing through those walls cools the ship, unless we sail down south. Makes the hot nights better, I'll tell you that."

The drumbeats of many feet boomed loud above them, and the trumpet blasts ordering the sails unfurled were clear even down where they were with a deck above their heads.

"You'll learn to get used to the noise above and below you as you serve on the *Sanguine*," Surehand said. "Your duty assignment will be the mainsail rigging every night. I've got foresail duty in the same night shift. They'll put you on the mainsail till they know what you can handle." Surehand moved through the dimness and around the blast-tubes and sleeping men in swaying hammocks as if he'd done it a thousand times.

It was all Blithe could do to keep up. He'd been on ships of his uncles and father when he was younger, but it was different now that he was serving on his own ship of the line. At least the decks seemed laid out the same on a dragonship as on a seventy-five-blast-tube ship of the line.

Surehand opened the hatch to the midshipwizard wardroom and they heard crying and shouting from within.

"The Articles, you idiot, are important. We live and die by the Articles. You don't know any of them, do you, boy?"

A thin, balding man with beady eyes was screaming at the top of his lungs at a crying twelve-year-old midshipwizard. The thin man stood over the boy and barked his words out, clearly intimidating the young midshipwizard.

Blithe took an instant dislike to the man.

Some might have hesitated at interrupting the clash between the older man and the young boy, but not Dart. Bold as brass he stepped into the room and saluted. This allowed the young boy a brief respite from the verbal abuse he was taking.

"Lieutenant Junior Grade Hackle," Dart said in a crisp military tone of voice. "I have the honor of introducing Midshipwizard Fifth Class Halcyon Blithe to you, sir."

The lieutenant turned to glare at the pair. He barely lowered the volume of his voice, clearly irritated at being disturbed from his browbeating of the sobbing boy beside him. "Blithe, is it? You're a big un, aren't you? Hand me your papers, boy." Hackle barked the order, showing a clear disdain for the young officer in front of him, as evidenced by the sour look on his face.

Blithe already had his orders in hand, saluting with his other hand.

Hackle didn't return the salute and so Blithe and Surehand had to stay at attention, still saluting, until the lieutenant junior grade was good and ready to gesture back.

Hackle was a head shorter than Blithe. There were wrinkles all over his face, and his flesh was pale, which struck Halcyon as odd considering that the tropical seas the ship must have commonly sailed in for the last year should have colored him up some as it did all the rest of the crew. All crews sailing the east and southern seas were darkened from the strong sun of those climates, making Halcyon wonder if this Hackle ever left the middle deck.

Lieutenant Junior Hackle completely scanned Blithe's orders, taking several minutes. The two midshipwizards watched him stumble over several of the phrases in the orders as his lips moved over every word. Finally, he threw the orders on the wardroom table and glared at Dart and Halcyon. The boy beside Hackle managed to take control of himself and dried his tears on his uniform sleeve.

"I am Lieutenant Junior Grade Hackle and the master of this wardroom. It is my duty assignment to turn midshipwizards like you into officers and gentlemen and it's a duty I take no pleasure in."

He finally saluted back to them, allowing the pair to come to parade rest in front of him. "You will find me a fair man, just like the captain up above. On this deck you do what you're told, by me, do you understand?" He was trying to be commanding, but his weak, thin tone of voice held nothing of the power of First Officer Wily or the captain.

"Yes, sir," Halcyon barked back through the bad breath of Hackle, as the man's face was inches away from Halcyon's own.

Hackle started pacing back and forth in front of the two, much as Commander Wily had up on the deck. Comparing the two men brought a smile to Blithe's face. They weren't anything alike, but imagining the two standing together was highly amusing.

"Your papers say you've just finished midshipwizard academy. Come into your magical powers late in life, did you, Midshipwizard Blithe?" Hackle sneered that question out.

"Yes, sir, I did, sir."

"Some say that makes you destined for great magical power . . . I care nothing about that." Hackle snapped his fingers in Blithe's face. "Maybe you noticed I don't have any magical powers."

Halcyon ached to give him back several clever answers, but bit his tongue. It just wouldn't do to have an improper attitude about a superior officer displayed on Blithe's first day aboard.

"In the king's navy most of its sailing men don't use magic. Keep that in mind, Blithe, and mind your betters," Hackle said as he whirled on Halcyon, trying to startle him.

Halcyon didn't move an inch. Dart was unmoved as well.

Hackle started up his pacing again. "We were just studying the Articles of War; Midshipwizard Fifth Class Tupper Haywhen and I were, that is. Mr. Haywhen wasn't doing very well. He gets three demerits for that. Blithe, on this ship all the midshipwizards must know all ninety-nine of His Majesty's Articles of War. Midshipwizard Fifth Class Blithe, what is the first Article of War?"

Halcyon spent less than a heartbeat remembering the article, took a deep gulp of air, and said, " 'No officer, mariner, soldier, or other person of the fleet shall leave their assigned post during combat unless ordered by the captain of the ship or unless extenuating circumstances warrant the abandoning of the post. Such dereliction of duty will be reviewed by a board of court-martial. The penalty for such dereliction is death or other punishment as the court-martial board shall find suitable,' sir."

A sour expression filled Hackle's face. It was almost as if he hadn't wanted Blithe to know the article in question. Hackle's tone became brisk. "Exactly correct. Your bunk is on the lower port side over there. You have the evening shift. Surehand will bring you up to speed on your duties at the sails. I will be making sure you serve well belowdecks. I expect my orders to be carried out fully and with speed. Do you have any questions, Midshipwizard?"

"No, sir," Halcyon replied.

"Well, get your gear stowed and check out your duty station. That is all." Hackle left the room, and the seven other midshipwizards forced to stand at parade rest all pulled out wardroom chairs and slouched down into them with sighs of relief. Halcyon was the largest of all of them. All seven appeared to be twelve to thirteen years old.

Dart made the introductions all around. "The twelve-year-olds on this side of the table are Tupper Haywhen, Jason Argo, Andorvan Mactunner, and Jock Woodson. The thirteen-year-olds are James Grunseth, Mark Forrest, and Ryan Murdock. All of you are midshipwizards fifth class right along with Halcyon Blithe here. Boys, this tall drink of water beside me is your new fifth-class midshipwizard, but you couldn't tell his rank judging from his size."

That got a laugh out of all of them, even the recovered Tupper.

Surehand started pacing back and forth and took on the same body stance that Hackle had just used. "Lieutenant Junior Grade Hackle says he's a fair man. Now, far be it from me, a midshipwizard third class, to disagree with a superior officer." Dart snapped his fingers in Blithe's face, in exact imitation of Hackle, and this got the boys roaring with laughter. "I'm thinking it would be a good idea if you all study the Articles of War a little bit more so that the good officer Hackle can't have the dubious enjoyment of getting under the skin of officers like Mr. Haywhen here. Do you all get my drift?" He snapped his fingers in Haywhen's face, getting everyone to laugh again.

Suddenly, the wardroom became deathly quiet, with only Halcyon continuing to laugh. He looked around to see what had made the others stop. All were looking at the other side of the wardroom and its other hatch. The hatchway filled with a bald man with large eyes and a dark swarthy look about him—a senior chief petty officer, judging by his duty uniform and badges of rank. He had a commanding presence even though all of the boys outranked him.

His voice boomed out into the wardroom.

"Mr. Surehand, if you are through copying the ways of your superior officers, I need a private word with the new midshipwizard. Ship's business, you understand, or I wouldn't stop you in your efforts, such as they are."

The petty officer's tone of voice made it clear that he didn't approve of Surehand's mimicking of a superior officer.

The boys all scrambled out of their chairs and dashed for the other hatch.

"Yes, Chief. Mr. Blithe, let me introduce Senior Chief Petty Officer Ashe Fallow. He's one of the men who make this ship run as well as it does. You will give your papers to him. He keeps all the papers of all the crew on board. When you receive new orders commissioning you to another ship, he will be giving you those orders. Carry on, Petty Officer." The last was said halfheartedly, as if it was difficult for Dart to give Fallow orders.

Dart left with the others and closed the hatch behind him.

Halcyon knew he wasn't to come to attention in front of this man, as Fallow ranked below him, but felt compelled to do just that. Blithe saw instantly that there was a controlled power in the man in front of him. The chief was bald, and his eyebrows were thick and dark; those features showed Halcyon that the chief wasn't a spellcaster.

The chief petty officer strode into the room. He displayed confidence and a businesslike attitude in his face and body language. "Permission to speak freely, sir?"

"Permission granted, Mr. Fallow." Halcyon was surprised to see the petty officer reach out his hand in invitation. Blithe clasped it in his own firm grip.

"That's a good handshake," Fallow said. "I would expect nothing less from a Blithe. For just this moment, let me speak frankly—man-to-man, so to speak." Ashe took his other hand and firmly gripped Blithe's arm as well. "I'm a Lankshire man born and raised, just like you. Your family has helped mine many times in the past, maybe for generations. I know it's a bit irregular for a ranker like myself to offer my hand. After this short meeting, you and I can be all proper from now on, but I wanted you to know I'm damn glad to see one of your da's sons serving in this fleet. I knew him well and served with him on several tours of duty. I was sorry to hear about his death."

Ashe Fallow's words moved Blithe. "My dad proved himself an able officer. I hope to serve half as well. Is your mother Lady Fallow, owner of the Seven Trees Inn?"

"No, that's my mam's sister. Our family lives a good ways from her at the south end of Lankshire County, but I know what your kin have done to support my aunt and our family. You can trust me to watch your back at need, boy. That's all I will say about that." He stepped back and saluted. "This is a good ship and you can learn a lot on her. Welcome aboard."

Halcyon smiled and saluted his fellow countyman. "I appreciate your kind words, Petty Officer Fallow. You may also count on my support at need."

Blithe happily moved into the bowels of his new ship.

III

✿ ✿ ✿

Crossing Swords at Sunrise

HIS MAJESTY'S ARTICLES OF WAR: ARTICLE III

The use of high magic is expressly forbidden on any of His Majesty's ships. If any officer, mariner, or soldier or other aforesaid uses high magic on board His Majesty's ship, every such person so offending, and being convicted thereof by the sentence of the court-martial, shall be punished with death, or such other punishment as the nature and degree of the offense shall deserve and the court-martial shall impose.

Frantic action filled the midshipwizard wardroom as boys scrambled to get ready.

Everyone bustled around belting on sabers and padded practice vests. Halcyon had just come off of four hours of sail duty, but he was just as energetic as the rest.

This would be the first time he'd get the chance to meet the captain face-to-face.

Dart came into the wardroom. As he saw the confusion inside, an amazed look spread over his face. He bellowed, "Come on, you slugabeds. Alvena and Jacom are already up there and all of you should be there as well. Get a move on!"

Clothes, vests, and swords flew in all directions as the other midshipwizards streamed out of the wardroom past Dart. Halcyon was last in line and gave Dart a friendly grin.

Dart smiled back. "It wouldn't do to have you late on your first day of swordplay. Get a move on, Midshipwizard."

"Aye, aye." Halcyon moved as fast as the seven boys in front of him allowed him to.

The dawn's light cast a pleasant glow on the full canvas above their heads. The ship was sailing east to the coast of Drusan to join the blockade of the Port of Ordune. To Blithe's way of think-ing, all that mattered little on this bright Fireday morning and the occasion of his first blade session on the *Sanguine*. *I've been prac-ticing with swords since I was ten*, he thought. *Now I have to show others what I've learned*. He hoped he was up to the challenge.

Most of the midshipwizards wore the same thing: a gray work uniform with one badge to mark their rank as midshipwizards. Each also wore a padded practice vest with thick sleeves to give some protection to his arms from dull sword strokes. Midshipwiz-ards usually wore a real blade sheathed at the hip, but dull and heavy practice swords were the order of the day for each practice session. Those racked practice weapons filled the port side of the forecastle.

Blithe noted Midshipwizards Alvena Merand and Jacom Boat-son dressed in white blade-practice uniforms, the same as the cap-tain's. Halcyon had worn such fencing gear himself when practicing at home with his uncles and brothers, but hadn't thought to bring one of those outfits in his sea chest. He wasn't pleased at this lack on his part and thought he would spend some time at a tailor's at the first port of call.

The other older midshipwizards were already at attention on

the deck, and Halcyon vowed to himself to be early to practice sessions from then on.

Six bells rang out over the deck, and the captain turned smiling at his junior officers. He stood six feet tall, the perfect figure of a naval ship captain. He had broad shoulders and displayed an easy gait as he walked back and forth on the forecastle deck. Captain Olden revealed sunken eyes, high arched eyebrows, and a short, sharply trimmed black beard, in stark contrast to his long flowing white hair, worn in a military braid down his back.

"We'll do a bit of review since we have a new midshipwizard in our group. Mr. Blithe, front and center." The captain spoke slowly, and his words carried well even in the brisk salty wind they all felt blowing over the deck.

Halcyon quick-stepped up to the captain and saluted. The captain just as quickly saluted back.

"I've already received good reports from Lieutenant Durand about you and your work, Mr. Blithe. Fellow officers, you will all be interested to know that Mr. Blithe here is a rope speaker. Rope speaking is a rare skill, the ship and crew are lucky to have such a crew member aboard. Mr. Durand reported there were several fraying lengths of rigging which revealed themselves to your talent. Keep it up, Midshipwizard Blithe. May I?"

The captain held out his hand, and his eyes looked on the sword at Blithe's hip.

Halcyon drew his weapon and handed it hilt-first to his captain. He openly smiled at the pleasant attention he was getting.

Taking it, Olden inspected the blade and then went through several blurringly fast maneuvers with the weapon, testing its balance.

"It's a good Lankshire blade." He lunged with Blithe's saber and retreated to his on-guard position. "One can tell quality by the blurring of the thousand folds of the metal in the blade's making. There are few weaponsmiths more talented than those found in Lankshire." His arm moved in maneuvers almost too quick to follow as he went through all the defensive positions of the standard naval saber while talking to Blithe. "I had the pleasure of serving with several of your uncles. I was sorry to hear of the death of your father in the battle of Ordune. But men die in the king's service and I'm sure you are justly proud of his notable career."

"I strive to be half the man he was," Halcyon replied.

"Quite right, Mr. Blithe. Well said. If I don't miss my guess, Rear Admiral Frank Blithe, the now commander of the *Sea Dragon*, gave you this blade and taught you a few things, didn't he?"

"Yes, sir, he did," Halcyon replied smiling.

"Well, we will see that you put those lessons and the ones I'll be giving you to good use." The captain stopped his maneuvers and looked Halcyon straight in the eyes. He wasn't smiling now. "Mr. Blithe, your family history is long and respected in this man's navy. That respect puts a great deal of weight on your shoulders. The fact that I like and admire several of your uncles does not mean that any of your actions will be viewed more favorably than those of any other officer on my ship. I expect you to work harder than most because you have a proud history of men and women named Blithe giving their lives in service to king and country. All of your ancestors are watching you now. Do your best for them and yourself. Have I made myself perfectly clear?"

Halcyon Blithe wasn't sure what type of response to give to the captain. The midshipwizard didn't want the respect for his family to give him any advantages on board the ship. He just wanted to do the best job he could. There was a lot he could say about his family and what he hoped to accomplish. At that moment, he didn't think the captain or the other midshipwizards wanted to hear those words.

"I understand your meaning, sir," Halcyon said, tipping his head in acknowledgment.

The captain grinned again and handed the hilt of Halcyon's sword back to him.

"Jolly good then. Sheath it and return to the line. Carry on."

"Aye, aye, sir," Blithe replied.

"Before we begin stretching, I want to speak on Maleen shape-changers and what you need to think about when battling them. Our duty station takes us into blockade action in front of the Port of Ordune. The enemy fleet will have shapechangers among their officers and marine battle units. Most of you should know by now that blows to the head, arms, and legs of a shapechanger have little effect."

"Sir." Jacom Boatson raised his voice. "How do we recognize a Maleen shapechanger among the rest of the enemy? Won't they look like a human?"

"An excellent question, Midshipwizard Boatson," the captain replied. "In the heat of battle, shapechangers quickly reveal their true nature. Look to their hands and face. Their hands sprout huge patches of hair and their face sprouts two more eyes. I haven't seen it myself, but I'm told this always happens as they fight for their lives. So, remember, you must concentrate your blows toward the trunk and neck of a shapechanger's body. Later in the practice session today, we will contend with each other and only allow body hits to score points. Let's begin stretching, everyone. Blithe, you watch Mr. Haywhen and imitate him."

Blithe saw them all go through the oddest gyrations, with even the captain participating. He'd never witnessed such goings-on. His expression of amazement must have shown on his face as the captain watched him.

"Officers," the captain said, moving back and forth in front of the two lines of midshipwizards. "The dawn finds your muscles particularly cold and stiff. Before practice and indeed before any battle, one should stretch one's muscles. Cold arms and legs don't serve as well once the action begins. These maneuvers might seem silly to you, but I assure you they are a good idea."

After what seemed like forever to the excited Blithe, the last of the arm-twisting and leg-stretching was over. Halcyon knew there were parts of his body that needed some strengthening. His whole left side ached and he hadn't even swung a sword yet.

"Don battle helms," the captain said while putting on his own. "Take a racked practice sword, and pair off. The largest of you match up with the shortest."

As the midshipwizards gathered their practice materials, the captain kept up his dialogue. "You all have sheathed swords at your hips because you have to get used to dealing with sheaths during battle. They can get between your legs and hinder you in other ways unless you keep your wits about you.

"On board the *Sanguine* during this practice, we pair off with the tallest midshipwizard facing the shortest midshipwizard. Can you tell us all, Officer Blithe, why we do this?"

Halcyon already noticed that he was the tallest of the group. Until now, it hadn't bothered him at all, as he thought his height would give him an advantage in swordplay.

Halcyon caught off guard couldn't think of a single reason why he should face the shortest of the others. He stood there with his mouth open.

"Midshipwizard." The captain's voice was reproachful. "Timing is important. You will find your enemy won't wait for you to come up with good answers on how to kill him. Everyone is now ready and Mr. Haywhen faces you Mr. Blithe. Officer Haywhen, why are you paired with Mr. Blithe?"

Tupper Haywhen shouted out, "In the heat of battle I will have to face men larger than myself. I must get used to this fact and deal with it or die. Also, large men just as often have to face much shorter opponents and they should know how to manage the smaller target area, sir!"

"Quite correct," the captain said, standing at the bow of the ship, positioning himself at the top of the group. Raising his hand, he magically caused a log to hurl itself into the sea. "Mr. Blithe, be good enough to strike that wood with your magic."

Floating in the water not thirty yards away, the log appeared to be an easy target to strike. Halcyon raised his hand and, using magical resources, blasted the log with lightning. The bolt arched out from his hand, struck the log, and caused it to burst up into the air. It splashed back into the water about fifty yards away.

"Jolly good, Mr. Blithe, again, if you please," the captain ordered.

Once again, Halcyon blasted the log, now sixty yards from the ship, and again it rose into the air. The burnt wood hit the water roughly seventy-five yards away.

"Make an effort one more time if you please, Mr. Blithe."

Halcyon knew that the log was probably out of range and his inner resources of magic were almost gone, but an order was an order.

He tried again, opening up his hand and using all his willpower.

A weak small charge of magical lightning did indeed strike the log and splinter it.

All the other midshipwizards gasped at the display of power. A typical midshipwizard couldn't send out more than a second blast of magic in an hour's span of time.

"Well done, Mr. Blithe." The captain's tone was a praising one. "That display of magical strength impressed all of us. I suspect our Lieutenant Commander Giantson will be equally impressed during your wizard training session. Your talents will serve you well in battle. Now, you all see that our Mr. Blithe is quite out of arcane energies and stands arcanely defenseless. Any one of you could now attack him, causing Mr. Blithe great harm. Indulge me, sir; I'm going to throw mystic bolts at you. These will only sting if they strike you. Defend yourself."

The captain didn't even give Blithe a second. He began gesturing and hurling spikes of energy at Blithe.

Halcyon was able to move his practice sword to intercept the blasts. From the on-guard position, his sword moved into the prime defensive position, covering the left side of his body and stopping a spike with the metal of the blade. His sword flashed to the second position, covering the right side of his body and striking the second bolt. In quick succession, the saber moved to tierce, then quarte, and then to quinte to block magical spikes; the final one aimed at his head. He blocked all the magical spike attacks even though he was dog-tired from his own spellcasting.

"Huzzah." Many of the other midshipwizards raised their blades, cheering Blithe's impressive display of swordsmanship.

"Well done, Blithe, jolly good." The captain's words praised Halcyon. "There are few here who can catch all of my bolts. As wizards, we can kill men with our magic, but that magic doesn't last us long in the heat of battle. Common wisdom says that Blithe here won't be able to cast spells for at least an hour. What does he do then? He must rely on his good right arm, of course. In the weeks to come I will have you battle left-handed as well as right-handed. In the heat of the boarding action, you must be able to defend yourself if your right arm takes a wound. We practice with the sword because it's a gentleman's weapon and in the king's navy we are all officers, gentlemen, and gentleladies." The captain nodded in the direction of the females in the mix of midshipwizards.

"There are advantages in its use over a blast pike. We'll deal with those advantages in later sessions."

Two lines of twelve midshipwizards faced each other across the forecastle. There were oars and ropes lying on the deck between them. Debris twisting about wasn't usually tolerated on a warship. Just then, Blithe noticed that the longboat and jolly boat were gone.

"On guard!" the captain shouted.

Twenty-four bodies turned sideways. Right legs positioned in front of their left ones with their right foot pointed straight at their opponent. The left leg positioned behind the right, with the left foot at a ninety-degree turn to provide stability. Constantly maintaining about a shoulder's span of distance between the feet was the norm for bladework. Chest and head were straight up and down with no leaning toward the opponent. The saber wielder's left arm bent and the left fist remained constantly positioned on the hip at the belt line. Each of the weapon hands held the practice saber easily in front of their bodies.

The captain walked up and down between them. "Mr. Surehand, move that left foot. Mr. Grunseth, stop leaning. Mr. Murdock, widen your stance, it should be as wide as your shoulders. Try to remember you are a good-sized king's officer."

Halcyon stood on guard. From the age of ten, he'd taken instruction in several different types of swords, but especially the naval saber. He enjoyed the use of the blade, and he'd taken to practicing with it a lot, as he never thought he would come into any magical skills when at twelve and thirteen he hadn't grown the white hair that all his brothers grew when they reached the age of twelve.

"The naval saber is a military weapon with a history going back as long as there were warships," the captain said with relish. He drew his own practice saber and advanced quickly down the line between the midshipwizards. His eyes caressed the blade and there was a clear love of the weapon shining on his face.

Halcyon knew that each of these practice blades would be the same. The grip lay under the protection of a large bell-shaped guard of thick steel. Through the ages, guards of that style protected the hand and could smash the body and face of a foe at need. The blade was thirty-four inches long with a thick triangle shape to the entire length of the weapon. Holding the blade

straight out from the body, one could see the flat end of the triangle. This dull end of the blade edge was at the bottom of the
weapon. Forte was the name for the lower third of the blade by
the hilt. That section of the weapon handled the parries. Foible,
the top third of the blade, was the portion making the attack.

"The saber in your hand is perfect for hacking at the enemy
with its long edge," the captain explained. "Experienced officers
can get a lot out of using the point of the weapon as well." Coming to the end of the line, he turned and shouted, "Lunge!"

They all lunged and held that position so the captain could
check the final positions of their bodies. They were all supposed
to have their right knees bent at a ninety-degree angle while their
left legs trailed straight back behind them. All of them were
letter-perfect and needed no correction from the captain.

"Retreat, on guard," the captain ordered.

They all took a step back and assumed the upright guard position with their saber tips aimed at the hearts of their opponents.

Now, at the other end of the line, the captain continued
speaking. "In practice we use a special battle helm and wear a
gauntlet. Even a dull weapon can cut open the top of the hand or
take out an eye. Your weapon's guard only protects part of your
hand, and clever bladesmen can cut that hand if you are not careful. In battle, I strongly urge you to continue the use of the gauntlet. Your hand sweats and a good leather-backed gauntlet can
mean the difference between keeping the weapon and losing it in
battle. Advance, cut, retreat!" The captain shouted maneuvers
they were all supposed to execute.

Twelve bodies took a quick step forward, made a cut with their
blades as if their foe were in front of them, and then took a quick
step back. Each had to navigate around the equipment and rigging lying on the deck. There was still ten feet of deck space between each of the paired saber wielders.

The captain's reassuring voice was oddly easy to hear even

with battle helms on their heads. He again walked between them. "Some say mastering distance between your blade and your foe is all-important. Some say bladework, some say defense and offense of the weapon are the key. I say footwork is the life's blood of perfecting the naval saber and fighting on a ship of the line. We're not dandies in a fencing school. The weapon you hold in your hand is all that's between you and your deaths at the hands of the enemy. We use it on a rolling deck in the heat of battle. Rigging comes crashing down; tight quarters often fill a deck with friend and foe. Blasting-tube fire can cover a deck in wreckage that the fencer must fight around and through. You are tasked to move through all this and fight for your life. Footwork is everything." He'd gained the other end of the line. "Advance, advance, retreat," he ordered.

The group came forward twice, and then moved back a step. Clawson and Murdock tripped up on whatever was in front of them. The captain shook his head at the two midshipwizards as they recovered and returned to their on-guard positions.

"Mr. Clawson, Mr. Murdock, I trust you both realize," the captain chided, "if you can't manage your footing in a practice session where everyone is your friend, you certainly can't manage in a real battle. Let's continue.

"The thrust is more efficient than the cut. Why, you ask? Watch," the captain said while smoothly turning and lunging at a practice dummy placed against the mast. His tip dented the heart of the straw-filled target dummy. "I can pierce his heart before his cut reaches me. However, I have to make sure that my dead opponent doesn't score with that cut anyway. It's not enough to lunge; I have to recover quickly as well. Retreat, retreat, lunge, recover, on guard!" he ordered them all into motion.

The forecastle was barely wide enough for the orders the captain issued. Halcyon had trouble with them at first, because he'd never been asked to retreat and then lunge before. He noticed that Tupper didn't have any trouble with the maneuvers.

The captain talked to his sword, clearly admiring the blade as he spoke. "You will experience the cut most often of all the possible sword strokes. Such cuts move best with the upper third of the edge of the saber blade. The sword hand and blade extend toward your opponent. At the moment of contact, the cut completes itself with a downward dip of the thumb and wrist. The snapping action of the blade moves best with a firm follow-through. Try not to be too heavy with your motion so that you aren't unbalanced at the end of your effort. It's not good enough to strike your opponent and then take a cut in return. Dying on your opponent's blade as you kill him isn't the best use of your time or the king's blade." He didn't wait for the laughter to die down at his quip. He just continued talking. "You must always think three moves past your next effort. Advance, cut in second, advance cut in prime," he ordered.

Halcyon's advances were longer than everyone else's. His steps took him right in front of Tupper. He'd hoped his strides would be a little intimidating to the much younger and shorter boy. Tupper just smiled and tapped Blithe's shoulder with the tip of his own blade.

"Retreat, retreat, retreat, on guard." The captain ordered the two lines of fencers far back from each other with his instructions. "When defending with the blade, never use the flat if you can avoid it, as this type of action creates a weak parry that can become a mortal thrust all too easily. I'm of the opinion that the tierce parry to the left and the quarte parry to the right can handle almost all attacks made against you. Officer Merand and Officer Boatson disagree with me and come from saber schools insisting on the use of all five parries. You will take some instruction from them in the other parries just to please them. Retreat in tierce. Retreat in quarte," he ordered.

Suddenly trumpet blares commanded sail crews to tack to port. Riggers got among the spars and sailors moved on deck to shift the sails. Officer Wily's orders, even from the quarterdeck on the other side of the ship, floated to them carried on the wind. Usually such orders came from commanders beside the wheel on the quarterdeck. Sailors were moving about the forecastle now as they went into the rigging of the foretopsail and topgallant.

"Don't concern yourself with the crew," the captain noted. "They know enough to ignore us as they tack the ship. I've ordered a few wide ship maneuvers so that we can practice today with a heaving deck under our feet. It should make life very interesting for all of us. Now then, where was I? Oh yes. The moulinet is a circular movement of the blade with the forearm. First toward the body and then away from the body, designed to be an attack at an opponent's head after they have attacked and are off balance. Advance, moulinet," the captain ordered.

Halcyon wasn't familiar with the term and didn't know exactly what to do. He watched Tupper performing the saber stroke, but still couldn't follow it. He didn't want to stop the captain and ask how to do the passage of arms. He would ask Tupper as soon as they had a moment. The captain was going through the session faster than Blithe liked.

"In counterattacks," the captain explained, "the stop-point thrust is best, of course. Any opponent displaying wide movements of his arm and blade is ripe for the stop thrust. You extend your saber-blade point forward into your opponent's attack without lunging. Your reach can strike any target, but slicing the sword arm of your opponent is, of course, devastating. Point control is the key to this counterattack." The captain was in the middle of the group now, and he did the maneuver without lunging. The angle of his arm made it clear that he would have been striking his opponent's arm if there had been someone in front of him.

The ship was pitching at an angle now as it tacked to port. Some of the things on the deck started shifting.

"Well, we've had enough of me talking," the captain said, smiling. "Let's get right to bouting, shall we. Officer Merand, please refere Mr. Blithe and Mr. Haywhen on your side of the forecastle, and I will take Mr. Surehand and Mr. Spangler on my side. The rest of you act as spotters."

Midshipwizard Alvena Merand was one of the female officers of the ship. Her quarters were with the other women crew in the middle of the lower blast-tube deck. As the first-class midshipwizard, she was in charge of the general training of all the other midshipwizards. She was a no-nonsense officer, not displaying any sense of humor.

In a ship filled with men, the sound of a woman's voice was odd to Blithe's ears. Halcyon didn't let her face and figure move him; after all, she was the officer in charge.

Merand's commanding voice was different from her tone when not on deck. There was no softness or femininity in her attitude now. "Mr. Swordson and Mr. Clawson, you spot to the port. Miss Driden, Mr. Getchel, you both work on my side. I will referee the match from starboard center. The rest of you stand out of the fencing lane. Mr. Blithe, on this ship the bout is to the first saberist to score three touches with their blade. We stop between every touch in these practice bouts. Swordsmen to the ready," she ordered.

Blithe and Haywhen saluted each other, and the tips of their blades touched, marking off the proper starting distance. Halcyon would have never admitted it to anyone, but he quite enjoyed looking down at the much shorter, twelve-year-old Haywhen. He wasn't thinking of anything but the advantage he had in height and reach when Midshipwizard Merand's order caught him off guard: "Begin!"

Tupper's lunge was past Halcyon's guard, and his saber point struck Blithe's chest before Halcyon could move a muscle.

"Touch!" The four line judges all marked the hit at the same time.

Under his battle helm, Halcyon turned beet red, embarrassed to have done so poorly in his very first bout.

The words of his uncle Frank came to his mind: "You are going to lose lots of fencing matches. You're young yet, so don't worry about any of them. However, never lose one because you thought you were better than your opponent. Respect anyone who has a blade in front of you and you'll live a lot longer."

Turning from the touch, Blithe walked several steps back to focus his mind and collect his thoughts. He knew that touch would never have happened if he hadn't been thinking about his advantages.

"Swordsmen to the ready." The order reached through Halcyon's thoughts.

He turned, vowing to prevent Tupper from taking another touch. Their blades met and they assumed the on-guard position. Tupper shifted his blade and held it much lower than the usual guard position. Halcyon had never faced a weapon held that low before. He adjusted his guard lower to match, but the new defensive position felt awkward and made him lean forward a bit. Before he could change his position to what it should be, Merand once again shouted, "Begin!"

This time Tupper feinted low where Halcyon had his weapon. Tupper then quickly shifted above Blithe's blade to score yet another touch, this time to Blithe's forward-leaning helmet.

"Touch!"

Halcyon was deeply embarrassed. He hadn't expected Tupper to be that good or that fast. He steeled himself to use all of his advantages. This time he would extend his saber to its full length when they started. He planned on using his much greater reach to push back young Haywhen. With a few passes of the blade, he hoped to be able to see what Tupper was doing and counter it.

"Swordsmen to the ready," came the order again.

They both came on guard. The big friendly grin on Tupper's face caused Halcyon to grin as well, even though he badly wanted to win this match.

"Begin!"

Halcyon extended his arm and blade full-out, expecting Tupper to backpedal a little. The smaller opponent was having none of that. Haywhen shifted and extended his own blade, using his short stature to take his tip under the bell guard of Halcyon's weapon and into Blithe's hand.

"Touch and bout."

Tupper had his helm off and had held out his hand before Halcyon had even taken his blade back from its extension.

"My family comes from a long line of duelists," Tupper said matter-of-factly. "My dad and grandfather started teaching me the blade before I could walk. Better luck next time, hey, Hal?"

Blithe took off his own helm and shook Tupper's hand. "I think I'll need more than luck, Tupper. Well done."

"That's the spirit, Mr. Blithe." Alvena pushed him to the port side. "No time to lick our wounds; we have lots of people to run through their paces. You'll see Mr. Haywhen beat most of us today—but not me, of course." She said this last with a deadpan expression on her face as she moved back into position.

After a moment to think about it, Blithe laughed, believing that Midshipwizard First Class Merand had actually made a joke.

IV

✿ ✿ ✿

𝔑ight 𝔚atch

HIS MAJESTY'S ARTICLES OF WAR: ARTICLE IV

All the papers, charter parties, bills of lading, passports, and other writings whatsoever that shall be taken, seized, or found aboard any ship or ships which shall be surprised or taken as prize, shall be duly preserved, and the very originals shall by the commanding officer of the ship which shall take such prize be sent entirely, and without fraud, to the court of the admiralty, or such other court of commissioners as shall be authorized to determine whether such prize be lawful capture, there to be viewed, made use of, and proceeded upon according to law, upon pain that every person offending herein shall forfeit and lose his share of the capture, and shall suffer such further punishment as the nature and degree of his offense shall be found to deserve and the court-martial shall impose.

"Stand to for billet inspection!" Hackle said, grimacing at everything and everyone.

In the last few days, Aber Hackle had shown an increasing irritation with all the midshipwizards, and it was Halcyon's doing. He'd been drilling all of them on the Articles of War, and in the last week no one made a mistake.

Halcyon and Tupper spent hours on their last three sail shifts practicing reciting each of the Articles to get them letter-perfect. The pair would move around the mainsail lines, maintopsail lines, and main topgallant lines reciting the Articles one by one as they checked the rigging for wear and tear.

Halcyon stood at attention with the rest, but his mind recalled all the times he and his father had recited the Articles of War together. For Halcyon's part, he knew all ninety-nine Articles because his father made a game of reciting them every time he returned from a tour of duty. At the oddest times when father and son were together, one or the other would call out a number, and whatever the other was doing, he had to stop and recite the proper Article of War. Halcyon loved calling out numbers when his father was eating or in the middle of mending their drydocked sailboat. For his father's part, whenever Halcyon found himself tucked in bed and half asleep, a number called out by his father forced Halcyon to recite the proper article.

Halcyon was pleased to note that after a while Hackle stopped asking him to recite articles and the junior lieutenant began scrutinizing Blithe's uniform and equipment instead. (There wasn't much there for Hackle to complain about either.) What Hackle did frequently berate Halcyon on was his lack of seamanship skills. There were big gaps in Blithe's knowledge of sailing tactics, and Hackle soon started questioning him in areas he'd just barely studied at the midshipwizard academy.

It was just short of ten bells and the start of the late watch when Hackle in his inspection dumped Blithe's sea chest all over his bed. Clothes and equipment spilled out.

Blithe turned on Hackle, anger clear on his face and in the tilt of his body. Halcyon didn't have the slightest idea why the lieutenant would do such a thing.

Unfortunately for the midshipwizard, when he was angry everyone could tell.

He raised his voice to Hackle. "Sir, it was my impression that a sailor's sea chest was private. You've no right to dump mine out." Only the reserve of his family traditions kept him from striking out at the stupid grin on Hackle's face. Unfortunately for him, his birthright made his eyes glow red when he was angry.

A stunned Hackle observed this condition for the first time and began smiling in unpleasant glee. "Stand at attention, boy! I care nothing for your red demon eyes." Lieutenant Junior Grade Hackle smirked at Blithe as the young man obeyed. "I can see now why you make such a deficient officer. You aren't human, are you, boy? Well, that explains everything, it does. Do you know what the penalty is for striking a superior officer?"

Blithe tried to calm down, but he wasn't used to injustice and didn't suffer fools easily. He was able to quote the penalty. "Fifty lashes, loss of rank, and thirty days in the brig, sir."

The other seven boys stood at attention by their bunks. This was required of them every time Hackle felt like inspecting them or instructing them in the ways of officers. It didn't matter if one or two of them had just finished working eight hours at the sails. They had to stand at attention no matter how tired they were. Blithe looked to them for support. Some of them showed fear, visibly upset at the idea of him not being human.

"Wrong again, Mr. Blithe. In times of war, a time our country finds itself in right now, the penalty is death by hanging. Now, as I see you have no contraband in your pitiful things, get them cleaned up. Your eyes glowing red when you get angry is a bad habit you have. That glow gives you away, Blithe. It's a big advantage for all who deal with you. By the way, do you know what happens if you use your demon magic on a fellow officer, an officer like myself who has no magical ability?"

Halcyon's glowing red eyes returned to normal and his face grew pale as he realized he'd been contemplating using magic on Hackle. "Death by drowning, sir." The last uttered in a whisper as its import hit home to Halcyon.

Tupper spoke up in an effort to relieve the tension of the wardroom. "Mr. Blithe has the duty tonight, Officer Hackle. We need to get up there before the next bell."

Hackle spun and snapped his fingers in the face of Tupper. "Indeed you do, Midshipwizard. That's five demerits for speaking out of turn. Under my command, you will all learn discipline. You both will, of course, go when I order it, but you are correct."

He turned back to glare at Blithe. "We will speak of this again, Mr. Blithe. That will be six demerits for the messy sea chest and four more marks for your poor display as a gentleman and officer. Those ten demerits go in the captain's book, my lad. As you know, for every ten marks in a week you get an additional four hours of ship duty. You will begin serving that four-hour duty after you finish your work shift this evening. Carry on."

He left the wardroom, and the other midshipwizards hit their bunks, not wanting to lose any more sleep that night. Tupper and Blithe got ready for their duty. They moved through the pitch-black middle gun deck and heard the sounds of hundreds of snoring marines in their swaying hammocks. After just a few days, Halcyon could move anywhere belowdecks, even in the dark. He'd made the ship his own and could feel his way through the passages.

Tupper moved right along with Hal and asked him a question as they maneuvered toward the stairs to the main deck. "Hal, do your eyes always glow red when you get angry?"

Ashamed, Hal quietly answered back, "It's my demonic heritage and I'm not proud of it. Somewhere in our history, a Blithe mated with a demoness and the family's curse of bad blood has continued for centuries. I try to keep my anger in check. The glow doesn't mean anything; it's just something I have to live with."

"It's freaking amazing, if you ask me. Oh, I wouldn't wish it on my worst enemy, but it's a sight to see. I'll tell you that for sure. You're going to scare to death the first foe you face sword-to-sword. Those eyes of yours are deathly odd, I'd say."

"There are other families with the same condition, even royal families," Halcyon reasoned.

"Not enough of them to make everyone comfortable with your condition. I'd be damned careful and try not to get angry if you can help it," Tupper observed.

Coming up on deck, they went to the quarterdeck and the wheel to relieve First Class Alvena Merand. He and Tupper saluted her. "We're logging in before the eleventh bell, ma'am."

The cool-as-ice Merand looked down her nose at them. "Both of you get your names in the wheel log. Tupper, you take to the mizzen topgallant and relieve Anne Driden. Mr. Blithe, I'm giving you the deck, and stationing you at the wheel with Able Seaman Hunter here. He's forgotten more about the sea and its ways than you or I will ever learn. Listen to what he has to say about the wind and weather tonight. Come to your station an hour earlier tomorrow night and I will quiz you on what you have and haven't learned. You are the duty officer tonight because nothing is going to happen on your shift. If anything does happen out of the ordinary, you send a sailor to fetch me out of bed and don't do anything stupid. Carry on."

"Yes, ma'am." They both saluted her away and signed on as officers of the night watch. Tupper waved to Halcyon as he climbed the rigging into the mizzen.

"Able Seaman Hunter, what's our course and speed?" Halcyon

did his best to sound official, even if he wasn't feeling that way in front of the experienced sailor at the wheel.

Hunter stood a head shorter than Blithe, about five foot, eight inches or so. He had dark hair in a long sailor's braid, and his face was wide with a big nose and eyes sunk far into his skull. They were large eyes, and Blithe noticed that the seaman didn't smile much. Hunter had a solid chin and a thickly muscled neck. The hands he put on the ship's wheel were large and knotted with muscle. The man didn't move quickly, but every movement seemed sure and steady.

His voice was deep and gravelly with a west-side-of-Arcania burr to it. "To answer the question I can see you're thinkin', I've been in this man's navy twenty-two years. There isn't much I ain't seen on any ocean or in any port. Midshipwizard First Class Merand's going to be a good officer, you didn't ask but I thought I would give my opinion on her. She and I get along just fine and she has me lesson the midshipwizards, like yourself, on weather and the wind. It's the only thin' I likes to talk on. Our speed is ten knots on a due-northwest course, sir.

"The *Sanguine*'s just moved through a big batch o' seaweed and he's fed well for most of an hour. The crew won't have to feed him tonight. So if you've a mind, Midshipwizard Blithe, what would you have me talk about, the wind or the weather?"

Blithe didn't want to appear stupid, so he had to ask, "I didn't know they were different things. Isn't the wind part of the weather?"

"One might think so, but sailin' the high seas one must know what the wind is doin' and goin' to do," Hunter observed. "Often what the weather is doin' or goin' to do is different from the wind's touch on the ship. The moon is up, so look out at the water. What do you scan of the waves you see over the bow?"

Blithe was a bit uncomfortable being questioned, but he looked out and answered as best he could. "I see long waves with a few whitecaps. I feel what I would call a moderate breeze at our backs. It's filling the sails well."

"That's a force-four wind you're describin'. Every time you see long waves with a few white tops, the wind is a force-four. There are twelve different types of wind and all of them mark the sea in their own way. Why don't you take out your little notebook and jot down what I tell you." Seaman Hunter looked at Blithe through the pins of the wheel as another sailor on the quarter-deck rang out the time at eleven bells.

"How did you know I had a notebook?" Blithe had purposely not taken out his notebook, not wanting to look like a young schoolboy in front of the sailor.

"Midshipmen and notebooks go hand in hand," Hunter replied. "I've never seen a midshipman, wizard or not, who didn't have a notebook for everythin' they learned. It's a good thin' when you're young like you are, but you'll not need it in a few years when experience has taught you what you write down today. Work off of the chart box behind the wheel. Midshipmen have been writin' there for more years than you are old. Are you ready?"

"Ready and willing," Blithe answered back.

"Force-zero wind would have the dragonship becalmed and the sea appears smooth as glass. Not a happy time for sailors; we usually have to row ourselves out of that. There was a time not a hundred miles off the coast of Elese that I had to row for five days before the wind picked up. I still bear the scars on my hands from that one." Seaman Hunter grimaced at the thought of that long-ago time.

"Force-one wind makes the sea show small ripples in the water. Force-two winds make short waves in the sea with no crests. Force-three wind creates wavelets with a crest or two. I'm not goin' too fast for you, am I?"

In the darkness, even with the moonlight, Halcyon couldn't see Hunter's face, but he could tell there was a grin from his tone of voice as Blithe tried to keep up. "No, Seaman Hunter, I've got it all. Who named these conditions?"

"Long ago, an Admiral Sir Francis Beaufort noted all of these and we've been usin' his system ever since. Force-four wind makes longer waves in the sea with some whitecaps crestin' those waves. It's odd how long we've had the current wind in our sails; mind you, I'm not complainin'.

"Force-five has moderate waves with lots of whitecaps," Hunter said. "That's the best wind for sailin' and it never lasts long enough if you ask any sailor. Force-six winds present a strong breeze with large waves, lots of whitecaps, and some spray hittin' your face. We often look to thin the sails some on the spars in that wind. It's also miserable to try movin' into a wind like that, but the *Sanguine*, bein' a dragonship, can maneuver better than wooden ships, if you get my meanin'. I'm kind of surprised you don't know some of this, you bein' a Blithe and all, beggin' your pardon for my sayin' so, Midshipwizard."

Blithe turned a little red at the words. "No pardon is necessary, Mr. Hunter. When I didn't become a wizard at twelve and thirteen, my family thought I should consider the army for a career. Blithes in the past who haven't had magical power have all gone into the army. That's what they were training me for when at sixteen, my hair turned white and I gained wizard abilities. I would have joined the army on my seventeenth birthday, but my family was proud to be able to send another midshipwizard son into the navy. It's been a mad scramble in the past eight months to give me the little I know about sailing. I managed to pass the academy training, but just barely. Now I strive to make myself a better sailor and officer. I know some things about the sea and sailing, but it's all from small craft on lakes and in the bay by our family castle. We are on force-seven winds."

"Quite right, Mr. Blithe." There was a new tone in Seaman Hunter's voice. It wasn't quite respect, but the tone was more diffident. "Force-seven is a near gale. The sea fills with waves and breakers where the white foam at the top blows downwind in long streaks. It's impossible to stay dry in that type of wind.

"Force-eight is a gale with high waves and large crests and the foam fills your vision wherever you look. We always take most of the sails in and only use the staysails by themselves because they are the nearest sails to the deck and easiest to take in at need.

"Force-nine winds are when you wizards come into your own and help save ships with your magic. The sea has high waves with long foam streaks and often the crests roll over with the wind. The spray is so thick it's hard to see. That's not the worst of the winds, but it sure feels nasty on your face.

"Force-ten winds give us storms to remember. The waves come at you ship tall with long hangin' crests. The sea looks white and each wave tumbles down on itself and you think you're goin' to die."

Blithe couldn't believe what he was writing and wasn't looking forward to his first storm. "It's gets worse than this?"

Seaman Hunter chuckled. "Oh yes, violent storms are force-eleven and the waves can hide ships of the line. Every wave edge fills with froth and shows lots of foam. There's only one type worse and that's force-twelve winds, the hurricane. When the sea turns completely white in foam, you can kiss your sorry ass good-bye, beggin' your pardon again, sir. Your chances of livin' aren't good. We turn in to the waves at force-ten and we hope we survive at force-twelve. I've only been in two of those and I'll be fine if I never see a hurricane again. That takes care of the wind. All of those you just need to memorize. Every time you come out on deck look to the sea. Note what type of sea conditions you have to deal with for your shift."

"Yes, Seaman Hunter, I'm sure I can remember these," Halcyon said, looking at his notes.

"The way to tell what the weather is goin' to be like is sort of silly," Hunter said, "but me mam taught me the sea rhymes and they've always been good enough for me. You ever heard of Red sky at night, sailors delight; red sky in the mornin', sailors take warnin'?"

Blithe couldn't believe what he was hearing. "You don't mean to tell me those silly little children's songs are how you tell what the weather is going to be?"

Hunter started laughing so hard he was slapping his knee in pleasure. "Now, I don't expect you to go spoutin' the rhymes to the captain, but you'll know when it's goin' to rain right enough, by rememberin' my rhymes. Let's not scoff at the wisdom of children and you just keep writin'," Hunter said. "The first one is Red sky at night, sailors delight; red sky at mornin', sailors take warnin'. It usually works every time. We've had a red sky every mornin' for almost a week now and I don't know why it hasn't rained, but that's the way the weather and fate is sometimes."

Blithe knew exactly why it hadn't rained, but he wasn't going to say that it was his air-magic skills keeping the breeze fair and the weather sunny. He didn't want a storm on his first tour of duty and fully intended to keep up the spell until they reached a port of call, no matter how long that took.

"The next is when the sky makes a change, the weather will be strange," Hunter told Halcyon. "The third one is mackerel sky and it's twenty-four hours dry. I particularly like that one."

"What in the world is a mackerel sky?" Blithe just had to ask the question, because he knew it couldn't be a fish-shaped cloud.

"It's a sky filled with dark wavy clouds, where the sunlight or the moonlight breaks through to the waves below," Hunter replied. "The clouds are high up and they might seem like they are rain clouds, but they never drop any water. The wind is always good under those clouds. The next is dew on the decks, the wind's from the sea; no dew on the decks, the wind's from the land."

"That doesn't rhyme and why do I care if there is or isn't dew on the decks?" Blithe was writing everything down, but this last one didn't make any sense to him.

"Put the notebook down for a moment," Hunter said, "and come put your hands on the wheel. There's nothin' much to han-dlin' the wheel on a night like tonight. All you have to do is make sure it doesn't spin. The *Sanguine* has just fed so it isn't pullin' against the rudder rig."

Halcyon secretly filled with joy at the chance to take the wheel. His hands went where Hunter's hands had been before. The wood of the wheel was cold to his touch. He could feel the massive circle of wood trying to pull to the right, but his hands re-sisted the tug. The effort took more strength than he'd imagined.

Seaman Hunter noted the smile on the midshipwizard's face. "It takes four men and sometimes as many as six to hold the wheel in big storms. The wind's a point or two off our course so it's pullin' a mite."

Blithe's academy training had him do watches at ship's wheels, but this one was a first-rater's wheel and much larger than the wheels of the sloops he'd manned at the academy or the ketches his family used in their merchant trade. The steering device stood seven feet tall and there were two huge wheels so that multiple crew members could work the wheel in heavy seas. Blithe counted thirty belaying pins fastened to each wheel.

Seaman Hunter looked at Halcyon as though he knew what the young officer was feeling. "I'm not too old to remember the pleasure of takin' the wheel on a first-rater durin' my first tour of duty. The experience is even better on a sea dragonship of the line. The wheels attach to lines of special pulleys under the deck. On a normal warship, the lines connect to huge rudders, massive things under the water at the stern. Our dragon has huge fins and this wheel rigs to those fins. Normally the sea dragon responds to simple turns of the wheel, but sometimes when it's near the shore or durin' high seas the dragon's instincts want it to go one way and we want it to go another. That's when it takes four to six strong men to force those fins to go our way."

Seaman Hunter moved behind Halcyon and kept talking. "I would ask you to close your eyes now and don't open them until I tell you. Can you do that, Midshipwizard?"

"Sure, but why?" Halcyon questioned.

"Never you mind, just close your eyes," Seaman Hunter responded.

Halcyon closed his eyes.

Hunter went on, his tone becoming more urgent. "Now, imagine the fog is thick and you can't see a thin'. You're at the wheel and the thousand members of this crew are dependin' on you to get them through this fog alive. You can't see an inch in front of your face. There's a force-four breeze movin' the fog and the ship at a quick pace. Do you need to worry about the land?"

"I don't know. I can't see in the fog." Blithe stood confused by the question and didn't like the idea of the entire ship depending on him.

"If you bottom out the belly and guts of the sea dragon and crash onto the breakers off a shore you lose the ship and maybe the lives of all on board," Hunter said. "The dragonship's movin' faster and faster in the wind. You can hear the sound of waves crashing somewhere. Where is the land?"

"I don't know." Some of the desperation of Hunter's voice infected Blithe.

"Not knowin' is death. It's your decision to turn to port or starboard. We are movin' to port right now. Where is the land?"

Blithe tried to calm down, but the urgency in Hunter's voice just wouldn't let him. "It's foggy, I won't know until it clears."

"It's not goin' to clear anytime soon. You could be dead in heartbeats. The answer's at your feet, boy. Where is the land?"

The decks were moist from the sea breeze. Halcyon knew they

were far out to sea. Suddenly the nonrhyming children's song he'd just learned came to mind.

"We are safe as the dew is on the deck, aren't we, Able Seaman Hunter?" Halcyon asked, having just figured out the answer.

The chuckle was brief and good to hear. "I'll take the wheel again, Midshipwizard. You should return to your notebook. We've a few more to go through."

Halcyon's heart was still beating quickly at the thought of all the lives of the ship's crew hinging on his decisions at the wheel. That was something he would have to reconcile himself to if he was ever to gain a command.

"Let's see now, oh yes, when the wind blows the foam you better head home," Hunter intoned.

Blithe had a tough time imagining that, but he didn't ask.

"A halo around the moon means rain or snow. The larger the halo the nearer the rain, don't you know. An odd thin' that, because we've had a huge halo around the moon for almost a week and it hasn't rained."

Blithe hid his face, knowing the magical reason for that, but not wanting to say.

"The seventh one is rainbow to windward means rain is comin'; rainbow to leeward means rain is endin'. I know that one doesn't rhyme either. Just write it down," Hunter ordered. "My mam's favorite was the higher the clouds the thicker the heather and the finer the weather. My favorite one, and don't ask me why because I don't know, is when smoke descends, good weather ends. Are you gettin' all of these?

"The last one to write down is seagull, seagull sittin' on the sand; it's a sign of rain when it's at hand.

"That's ten and if I know my first-class midshipwizard, she will want you to know all about the twelve types of sea breezes. I would try to commit those to memory if you can by tomorrow night. The rest will come to you soon I'm sure," Hunter continued. "Order the men on the mizzen down for tea and I'll get you a cup as well when one of the sailors relieves me at this wheel."

Halcyon shouted out, the crew responded, and the rest of the night went as expected.

V

⁂ ⁂ ⁂

Oiling Duty

HIS MAJESTY'S ARTICLES OF WAR: ARTICLE V

No person in or belonging to the fleet shall take out of any prize, or ship seized for prize, any money, plate, or goods, unless it shall be necessary for the better securing thereof, or for the necessary use and service of any of His Majesty's ships or vessels of war, before the same be adjudged lawful prize in some admiralty court, but the full and entire account of the whole, without embezzlement, shall be brought in, and judgment passed entirely upon the whole without fraud, upon pain that every person offending herein shall forfeit and lose his share of the capture, and suffer such further punishment as shall be imposed by the court-martial, or such court of admiralty, according to the nature and degree of the offense.

"They didn't talk about oiling duty at the academy." Blithe grimaced as the three of them went down into the orlop deck. "I've used sand and iron plates and holystoned a deck. I've painted blast-tube ports yellow and the rest of the sides of a ship black. To my mind, this must be one of the oddest duties in the navy, isn't it?"

"Just because only dragonships of the line have to do it, doesn't make it odd," Tupper said.

"What's the reason behind wearing special oiling clothes?" Blithe asked.

Alvin Condord was the sailor assigned to help the two midshipwizards. He looked to be almost twenty years old. A small man with quick eyes and hands, he was leading the way down into the darkest part of the ship. "We don't wear our regular work uniforms because oiling the old dragon is a messy business," Seaman Condord answered. "The creature likes the feel of the tannin oil on its skin, but the liquid's dark and nasty-smelling stuff. The tannin oil keeps the sea dragon's flesh from cracking in the sun and saltwater. Normally, it swims under the sea and keeps moist, but it can't do that when it becomes a ship of the line. Every time its flesh cracks, the dragon starts to bleed and that can kill our ride home. The tannin oil permanently stains everything and so we wear these large uniform aprons to oil the dragon's skin. Once a year and usually when we are out to sea, we oil down the outside of the ship."

Racked against the wall at the bottom of the stairs were large squares of heavy cloth with holes in their middle. Condord picked one up and poked his head through the hole. He looked comical with his long arms sticking out the sides of the fabric.

Blithe picked up one of the oiling uniforms and crinkled his nose at the oil smell. Waves of tar and burnt wood odor mixed together, assaulting his nose.

"The smell won't bother you after a few minutes," Seaman Condord remarked as he moved farther into the bowels of the deck chamber. Moving quickly, he didn't seem to mind the darkness at all.

"These are more like blankets with holes in them than uniforms." Halcyon grimaced.

"Never mind how ugly they look," Tupper advised. "When the oil splashes on you during the duty, you'll like the fact that you can hang your blanket on a peg and not have to get it washed."

The two midshipwizards shucked off their shirts and put on the oiling clothes. Blithe felt a strange prickly sensation on the skin touching the oiled cloth.

"Anyone else feel a tingling on their skin under these things?" Halcyon asked the other two.

"The tannin oil does that to some, pay it no never mind," the seaman told him. "Everyone eventually gets lots of this oil on their bodies and it's never hurt anyone yet."

In the darkest part of the orlop deck under the bow of the ship, Tupper raised his hand and cast a magical glow, revealing the barrels of oil and the harnesses needed to carry the barrels up out of storage.

"I've got to learn that spell," Halcyon remarked.

"Giantson taught me last year; you'll pick it up in his classes during this tour of duty," Tupper said.

Condord had a worried expression on his face. "I don't know why the lieutenant only sent you two; normally we have four midshipwizards on this duty."

"That's our Hackle," both of them said at the same time, as they smiled like simple fools.

"I know I've asked this question before, but no one knew the answer then. The stink is even worse here. Condord, do you know what this oil is made of?" Tupper was holding his nose as he asked the question.

"That would be the fish oil and the tannin root combined together. They take whales and render down their fat for the oil. I did duty on a whaler for a year before the press gang presented me with the great pleasure of serving on the *Sanguine*," Condord said, smiling toward the other two. "In this oil, they put in some type of magical tannin root to keep it from dripping off the sides of the dragon whenever it rains. The crew has oiled the sides of the sea dragon all day today. They finished the stern this morning. The old dragon has been purring like a kitten; it likes the oiling, it does." The seaman's smile revealed that he had no front teeth.

They rigged up the large barrel in a halter with two long staves of wood to carry on their shoulders. Blithe would bear the weight of the two poles on his shoulders at the front of the barrel. The other two, smaller men would each take an end at the back. Carrying the heavy barrel would allow the two midshipwizards to use their air spells, causing the other barrel to float in front of them with no effort to their bodies.

"The tingling is getting worse on my skin," Blithe remarked.

"Your flesh is probably reacting to Hackle turning us into donkeys," Haywhen grunted as he climbed up the steps behind Blithe. The sound of his voice labored as he barely managed the weight of the barrel pole.

For just a moment, the naive Blithe wondered if Hackle could turn them into donkeys, and then he realized that Tupper was making a joke. *Besides, Hackle has no magical powers*, Halcyon thought.

"That tingling's a good sign, Midshipwizard. They say only dragon speakers can feel the magic of the oil. Have you tried talking to the *Sanguine* yet?" Condord asked.

"I didn't know anyone could talk to a dragon," Blithe replied. "It's odd enough that ropes speak to me. I don't know that I like the thought of dragons being able to shout at me as well."

The barrel floating in front of them started bumping against the steps between decks as Halcyon lost a bit of his concentration. He moved faster up the stairs and focused on the floating barrel, trying to increase its enchanted speed up the passage. The heavy pull of the barrel he carried made the effort of arcanely floating the other barrel an easy task if his mind stayed focused.

Tupper spoke up. "The captain can talk to the sea dragon, and so can Blast-Tube Master Griffon. I'm also told she can talk to other large sea creatures."

"She can, can she. Now that's interesting to know." Blithe wondered if he could speak with the dragon. If the captain and Griffon could, then maybe it was worthwhile to have that talent.

"Get a move on, you slugs. The glow of the moon won't last all night." Up above them on the main deck Lieutenant Junior Grade Hackle shouted down at them.

In a voice too soft for anyone up above to hear, Tupper said, "The man is brilliant, he should be an admiral at least, our Hackle."

Blithe wondered what misery would bring Hackle out into the fresh air when it wasn't even his watch. As they brought the barrels on deck, other crewmen took up the two loads, placing large spouts in each, and racking them on the port side. Crew members immediately started pouring the thick oil into large canvas buckets.

The first thing Halcyon did when he got on deck was look to the sea, noting the wind speed. It was still force-four, as the tiny wavelets had only a few crests. Halcyon couldn't help smiling, knowing his spell on the weather above the ship was working nicely and wasn't straining him at all. There was a slight pushing against all of his senses. He thought the pressure must be the force of nature wanting to set the balance against his clear-weather magic, but it wasn't anything that he couldn't handle with his mind.

Halcyon looked up to see the dragon head twisted around to watch the oiling process. An odd trilling came from the nostrils of the sea monster. It sounded strangely content to Blithe's ears.

Tupper, Condord, and Blithe saluted Lieutenant Solvalson, who commanded the oiling duty.

"Tupper and Condord, you've done this job before, you load up the scaffold while I instruct Halcyon here on the duty," Lieutenant Solvalson ordered as he carefully picked up a large brush and kept talking as he held the brush well away from his body.

He dipped the brush in the oil bucket and then stroked the full brush against the inside railing made of dragon flesh. The scales started instantly swelling with the oil and took on a healthier-looking sheen.

"We brush the skin of the dragon with this specially treated oil," Solvalson said. "Not only does it keep the skin from cracking, but the magical elements in the oil help the dragon grow and heal itself quicker. That's one of the reasons our dragonships of the line are larger than our enemy's version of the same ships. This oil also allows the creature to eat less and still grow strong, so we have to feed it only a third as much as our sea dragon counterparts found in the enemy's fleets. One coat of the oil on the outside of the ship does wonders for the big monster. You can hear how happy he is by those loud purrs. Any questions, Blithe?"

Halcyon didn't see any problems with the work and said so. He did wonder why Hackle was filling an unusually large bucket with the oil. He couldn't imagine the lieutenant not ordering such work done by someone else.

Suddenly, the main halyard line of the foresail revealed itself to him. Blithe was new to rope speaking but was getting a feeling about the condition of all the *Sanguine*'s lines. He didn't know how he knew, but he just knew that the core of the halyard line on the port side of the foresail was weak with salt rot. Now that he was looking more carefully at the line, there was a blue glow revealing itself to his senses.

"Get a move on, Blithe, this duty needs to be done before the moon sets," Solvalson ordered.

"Sir, you're going to want to speak to the officer on deck. I can tell the foresail halyard needs replacing. It's cored with sea rot, it could snap at any minute," Halcyon advised.

"Really?" There was doubt in Solvalson's voice.

"I'm a rope speaker, sir. I don't know how I know, but I know that line needs replacing right now," Halcyon suggested.

There was no doubting Blithe's sincerity.

"I'll get the watch crew on that. You just do your oiling duty. Carry on," Solvalson ordered as he moved toward the forecastle steps.

Tupper and Condord were already over the side and on the scaffold waiting for Halcyon.

As he threw himself over the side and onto the platform, Tupper asked him a question. "Hal, have you ever had someone talk to you about Shidon the deity and his ways?"

"That's an odd question, Tupper," Blithe replied. He got over the rail and planted his feet on the side scaffold. There was a bucket of oil and a brush on his end of the planking. The crew up above winched the scaffold down to where the last duty crew had stopped. There was a section of bright and oily scales and right beside that section the sea salt had clearly turned the green of the dragon skin white.

Blithe started spreading on the oil. "Let's see, Shidon is the god of the sea. I've heard him called the protector of sailors and the bringer of fair and foul weather. He's not a deity most Arcanians worship, but most seamen give Shidon a small offering every time they leave a ship. Why do you ask?"

As the scaffold was winched lower on the side of the ship, Tupper and Condord positioned oil buckets at the middle of the platform between themselves and Halcyon. There were big grins on their faces. They began brushing on the oil, but constantly looked over to where Halcyon was.

Hackle was above them, bending over the railing of the dragonship. He shouted down to them, "Blithe, see where the other work detail stopped brushing on the oil. Begin there and get a move on."

Blithe brushed faster, but had to stop as the dragon head came into view. The creature was awesomely huge, and while Blithe knew the dragon's training kept it from swallowing him in one bite, the huge beast still made him uncomfortable. The tingling on his skin increased the closer the dragon's head came toward him. When he was on deck or below, the nature of their dragonship of the line wasn't so apparent, but right here with the dragon's breath on his neck, the creature's great size was daunting.

"Shidon's ways are strange to those not of the sea." Tupper started brushing on the oil at his position and was somehow able to ignore the huge sea-dragon head just a few feet away. The creature watched every stroke Tupper made on its side. "I'm sure your family wouldn't have talked about what happens to new crew members on various voyages around Arcania. Every ship has its Shidon traditions. When we sail down off the shore of Elese all the new crew members have to swim under the ship. It's a sort of birthing ceremony. There are lots of different Shidon things that get done to the crew as they sail in the different oceans of the world."

Tupper was going on and on about Shidon tricks, but Halcyon wasn't paying attention, as the sea dragon was watching him intently now. The dragon's head was huge. It could eat him with one gulp. Blithe could feel his heart beating faster. He couldn't help himself, he had to constantly look over his shoulder at the dragon and wonder if the creature would eat him.

"Not eat."

Halcyon's head rocked back as the strange thought struck his mind. "Seaman Condord, did you say something?" Halcyon asked. However, the midshipwizard knew the answer. It was the dragon thinking into his mind. Halcyon's whole body tingled now, not just the parts touching the oiled cloth. When the dragon's thoughts hit him, Blithe felt himself in the mind of the creature.

There was a big smile on Condord's face, but he shook his head.

Tupper kept going on and on about Shidon things. The midshipwizard nervously babbled, but with a dragon not ten feet away, Blithe wasn't surprised.

"Oil on head."

Blithe glanced at the dragon to see it looking up to the deck above. Blithe tore his eyes away and looked up as well. He saw a slug of oil rush into his face, poured from above as Hackle shouted with glee and tipped over the huge bucket.

Blithe slammed down on his knees, hitting the scaffold boards hard. He coughed out oil and tried to rub the thick liquid from his eyes.

With a restraining hand, Haywhen made sure his friend didn't fall off the scaffold. In a sad voice, he told him what was happening. "It's called the oiling of Shidon. All new crewmen get it when they do their first oiling duty. Sorry, Hal, we weren't supposed to warn you."

With his eyes tightly shut against the oil and his throat sputtering, Halcyon wasn't listening to Tupper. In fact, Halcyon wasn't in his body at all.

"I tried to warn you," the sea dragon thought to Halcyon. The creature's dragony mental voice was much clearer and seemed to be speaking in full sentences now.

Blithe found himself looking at the side of the ship. He could see Tupper, and Condord, and there was his body on his knees on the scaffold. The scene was all in different shades of sea green, which was just as odd as being able to look at himself from a distance.

"The oil lets us share thoughts. I can go inside your mind and you can go inside mine. Right now we are sharing my body as yours is in pain."

Blithe understood the sea dragon clearly. Looking at the ship, he saw the crew roaring with laughter on deck as they looked at his oiled body.

"You won't be able to hear me very well when you aren't all oiled up. If you practice, our speech together will get better," the dragon advised.

Blithe could barely think. The sea dragon's feelings and heartbeat were part of Blithe now. He could feel the dragon's fins working the water, its tail moving back and forth. He could feel its hunger and its sense of smell telling it there was a patch of floating seaweed just a mile away.

"Olden and Griffon are nice, but they don't speak to me much. It's good to have another of your race to share minds with from the shell on my back," the dragon said.

Halcyon had a dragon's perspective of the ship. It called the *Sanguine* its shell. Then Blithe could see Officer Wily gesturing from the deck, and Blithe's body filled with a blue glow. The oil left Blithe's hair and skin and splashed against another dry part of the dragon's side.

The sea dragon's tone of voice was sad now. *"Please try talking to me, especially at feeding time. Your mind goes back into your body now, as the oil's influence goes away."*

There was a jolting shock in his mind and body, and his thoughts once more filled his own mind. The scaffold rose to deck level and crew helped him off and slapped him on the back in happy companionship.

"Are you all right, Mr. Blithe?" asked Officer Wily.

Opening his eyes fully for the first time since the oiling, he saw the friendly faces of the crew all around him. There wasn't a speck of oil on his body. "I'm fine, sir. Thank you for removing the oil, sir," Halcyon said.

There was a strange cloth patch in Wily's hand. The patch was an image of the sea dragon. "You've become a member of an elite group, Mr. Blithe. With your dunking in the oil, you are now a

member of the sea dragon brotherhood. Place this patch on your
duty uniform with pride. Some people like to leave the oil on the
crew member until it eventually rubs off. I think being clean after
an experience like that is a better idea," Officer Wily said while
handing the patch to Blithe.

"*Brother Dragon is small for one of my kind.*" The dragon's
thoughts caused Halcyon to look up at its head.

Blithe could see the dragon's head twisting to look down on
the deck. Halcyon smiled and waved up to the creature.

"Mr. Blithe, since you're up here for a moment, help with the
changing of that halyard line. Lieutenant Junior Grade Alberta
Fosentat is the watch officer for the foresail. Lend your skills to
her," Wily said, giving the order and walking off to the quarterdeck.

Blithe hadn't worked with Fosentat yet, but he knew who she
was from wardroom meals. He stepped up to her and saluted.
"Ma'am, Midshipwizard Blithe reporting for this duty."

Fosentat was short, not more than five feet tall, but there was a
commanding manner about her. "Excellent, Mr. Blithe. I hope
you have fully recovered from Mr. Hackle's dousing. It's possible
he takes too much pleasure in that Shidon tradition. To the
point, I'm glad to have your rope-speaking skills aid us with the
line. You take the lead on the rope as we raise the foresail and replace that line. The chanter will sing the beat."

The duty was easy, as ten crewmen were at the halyard ready to
pull and men were in the rigging ready to luff the sail.

The chanter started singing and everyone pulled in time to
the tune.

Up jumps a crab with his crooked legs
Saying, 'You play the cribbage and I'll stick the pegs
Singing blow the wind westerly, let the wind blow,
By a gentle nor'wester how steady she goes.'

The deep voice of the chanter rang out clear in the moonlight. He started the second verse, and the men pulled on the halyard with a will, singing with him.

Up jumps a dolphin with his chuckle head
He jumps on the deck saying, 'Pull out the lead!
Singing blow the wind westerly, let the wind blow,
By a gentle nor'wester how steady she goes.'

Halcyon was enjoying the tune and the work. He didn't mind the duty as the rope moved through his hands. He could sense the rope's entire length as it went through the block and tackle and moved up the foresail. He didn't know the tune, but started singing the chorus with the men after the chanter finished singing the first two verses.

Up jumps a salmon so bright as the sun
He jumped down between the decks and fired off a gun!
Singing blow the wind westerly, let the wind blow,
By a gentle nor'wester how steady she goes.

He could feel the rope start to twist in the tackle. It would foul up in the next couple of pulls. He exerted his will on the rope and felt a power flow through his hands, into the rope, and up to the tackle, not allowing the rope to twist up as it pulled through the metal pulley. He never lost a beat in the song and the rest of the crew never knew he was helping with his power, allowing the work to continue moving smoothly.

Up jumps a whale, the biggest of all
He jumped up aloft and he's pawl after pawl!

Singing blow the wind westerly, let the wind blow,
By a gentle nor'wester how steady she goes.

Up jumps a herring, the king of the sea,
He jumps up on deck saying, 'Helms alee!
Singing blow the wind westerly, let the wind blow,
By a gentle nor'wester how steady she goes.'

There were more verses to the song, but the chanter sang the ending yodel and the men stopped pulling. The rope threaded out of the sail and some of the crew members sat in the middle of the deck with the old halyard rope coiled all about them. They started unraveling the scans of its length to make smaller lashing. Nothing was ever wasted on board ship. Even rope with rot turned into smaller and still useful strands.

"Blithe, fine work that. You were right. That entire length was filled with rot at its core," remarked the junior lieutenant. "I don't mind saying you saved us a bit of work there. Check out the length we are using to replace the halyard. It makes no sense to put a possibly bad line up after we just took a bad one down. Then I think you should take the rest of your duty and check out the lengths we have stored in the orlop deck."

"Aye, aye, ma'am." He saluted and started looking over the new line. He didn't see anything there that was going to cause trouble. "Start threading the line. It won't give us any problems."

Looking over the railing at the dragonship's side, he saw his friend Tupper and the seaman halfway down the side of the ship. Their oiling duty was going fast.

The sea dragon watched the work and purred. It looked up once and winked one of its huge eyes at Halcyon. The midshipwizard now knew that the oil was giving the dragon energy and making it feel great. Up until then Halcyon feared the creature's size and power. Now he felt he'd made a new friend and couldn't wait to try mind-speaking with it again. He took a lantern from the side of the ship and went belowdecks. He hadn't learned illumination spells yet, but when he got down into the hold he wouldn't need light. His talent of rope speaking worked just as well in the dark as in broad daylight.

Even from his position deep in the bowels of the ship, he heard another verse of the chantey and knew exactly what they were doing on deck as they used the new halyard to reluff the foresail.

Up jumps a shark with his big row of teeth,
He jumped up between the decks and shook out the reefs!
Singing blow the wind westerly, let the wind blow,
By a gentle nor'wester how steady she goes.

The entire middle of the orlop deck held a huge mound of coiled rope in all sizes and lengths. He slowly walked over the lengths of line and could feel the rope telling him it was whole and strong. There was only one section of rope, located beside the port wall, that had a light dusting of mold all over its length. The mold hadn't done any damage and would probably blow off when the sun and fresh air hit it, but he would report it just the same.

The idea of speaking to sea dragons was a new one for Halcyon. As he moved from rope section to rope section, he wondered if he could speak to land dragons as well. He'd seen such creatures flying high in the sky, but never dreamed he might actually be able to talk with one of the grand creatures.

❧ ❧ ❧

VI

Blast-Tube Drill, Lesson One

HIS MAJESTY'S ARTICLES OF WAR: ARTICLE VI

If any ship or vessel be taken as prize, none of the officers, mariners, or other persons on board her shall be stripped of their clothes, or in any sort pillaged, beaten, or evil-entreated, upon the pain that the person or persons so offending shall be liable to such punishment as a court-martial shall think fit to inflict.

A junior seaman stood on the quarterdeck at the ship's bell. He watched the hourglass slowly shifting down the grains of sand in the glass hanging by the wheel. In a few moments he would be ringing the bell six times to sound the morning watch.

The *Sanguine's* blast-tube crews all stood at attention at their firing stations on every deck. Blast-tube practice happened whenever Master Andool Griffon felt like it, and she felt like it this morning at dawn.

By rights, Halcyon should have been tucked in his bunk after just getting off the night watch, but he stood at attention with the rest because there was no way he was going to miss his first blast-tube practice. *Besides,* he thought, *who can sleep with tubes blasting all over the ship.*

Since this was his first practice, his bunkmates were groaning as five of them were at attention around his blast-tube. Normally, the midshipwizards spread themselves through the ranks of the blast-tube crewmen. They supervised and filled in when tube crew members fell with wounds or needed help. Since Blithe was new to the tubes, five of his midshipwizard mates had to serve on his battle station with him.

Master Andool Griffon walked the quarterdeck shouting commands loud and clear. Her boots made crunching sounds as she moved up and down the sandy deck. She was the only one in boots; all the rest of the crew were barefoot. Sand lay all over each deck to help with footing.

A tough commander, she had fiery red hair done in a long war braid down her back. There was a dagger sheathed and worked into that braid. Some said she came from dwarf stock, since she stood only five feet tall. No one said that to her face.

All the rest of the crew stood at attention.

Her words rang out over the crew. "We have one hundred and twenty-two long and double blast-tubes on this ship, and by the dark god that made me, they better all fire before that sixth bell tolling the morning watch or I'll know the reason why."

A large double-bladed axe strapped to her back showed how she would meet an enemy boarding party. She wore the weapon only at practice or during combat. The handle of the thing hung down almost to the deck from the middle of her back. Blithe didn't have the slightest idea how she could effectively use a weapon that large. Her black blast-tube uniform fit loosely over her frame, but he could see well-defined arms and legs under the cover of the uniform. He didn't even allow himself a second to think about the fact that she was a woman. Blast-tubes and their workings were often the subject of Blithe family meals when his father, brothers, and uncles were home from the war.

Andool continued speaking. "Those same blast-tubes throw over fifteen hundred pounds of iron shot at our enemy. Most blast-tube shots miss their targets. Our ship throws them faster and aims better than any other ship of the line in the Arcania fleet, because I command it so. We're going to miss, but not often and not when it counts."

There was a steel edge to the tone of her voice. She walked to the stairs by the forecastle. "The Maleen enemy fleets fire their shot at the top of the sea's roll. They do this to demast Arcanian ships and slow us down. The Arcanian admiralty disagrees with any battle tactic that slows Arcanian ships down, and for once I agree with our admiralty."

This got a chuckle from the crew lined up on both sides of the deck. Agreeing or disagreeing with the high-and-mighty admiralty wasn't something any of them could even think about doing.

"The Arcanian navy, our navy, fires its shots at the bottom of the sea's roll. We want to kill our foes at the water level, not toy with their rags and sticks." There was a wicked, bloodthirsty grin on Andool's face when she said this last. "Our shots are meant to kill the enemy firing at us. If I catch anyone firing their tube on the top of the sea's roll, I will personally flog them myself, if they live through that battle. That same instruction is being given, even now, to every tube crew on the decks below."

Just as she was turning to walk up the other side, Dart elbowed Blithe in his ribs. He looked over and heard Dart whisper to him, "Cold as ice, that one is."

Halcyon was so tense he couldn't even respond with a smile. The blast-tube process ran repeatedly in his mind. *Step one, roll the blast-tube back, and open the blast-tube port of the ship. Step two, sponge in the rammer to cool the tube and load in the jar of blast-tube gel. Blue jars are for long range, white jars are for medium range, and red jars are for short range. Step three, roll the tube to the port, and take aim on the enemy. The windage wheel raises and lowers the tube in its caisson. Step four, order the hot spike driven in to fire the tube. Watch out for the back blast.*

Halcyon was to be the aimer to begin this exercise, and he wanted to do everything right. Besides the firing steps, he also had hundreds of battle stories on firing blast-tubes that his father, uncles, and brothers had told him over the years to bolster up his confidence.

Andool's voice carried well on the wind, even when she was on the other side of the ship. "Lieutenant Commander Giantson will now use his magic to make targets for you all. Look out for his illusionary ships and prepare to fire sometime during the ringing of the sixth-hour bell. Anyone may fire with the ringing of the first clang of the bell. May the dark god help those who haven't fired when that sixth clang rings out. After the first salvo, stand ready at your tubes and I will come among you and evaluate your effort. Carry on."

A magical haze appeared off the port and starboard sides a good distance away. In each of the two hazes, a huge Maleen first-rater appeared with its blast-tube ports open and the wind filling its sails. Halcyon had no idea how far away the image was, but hoped it was at long range for the tube. He knew the tube could throw a shell a mile when the weapon was hot from former blasts. He also knew the weather conditions well enough now to note that the enemy ship wouldn't have had its sails filled with the force-four winds, considering the course that illusionary warship held as the magical image bore down on the *Sanguine.*

The big sea dragon roared out its defiance at the two illusionary ships, not knowing that the enemies in the distance were magical spells. Sea-dragon training caused it to rush into battle and it responded to the turn of the wheel to show its sides to the enemy.

A voice shouted in Blithe's ear. "Mr. Blithe, do you plan on firing this tube anytime soon?"

Halcyon jumped and turned to face Senior Chief Petty Officer Fallow. "Chief, I do indeed intend to fire this tube."

"Mr. Surehand is the senior commander of this duty station, but the aimer, that's you; the aimer shouts out the orders. Let's show them what a Lankshire man can do, shall we?" His grin was friendly, but his tone of voice was not. He was challenging Halcyon to do a good job.

All the midshipwizards stood looking at Blithe for instructions. They had large cloths tied around their heads to cushion the effects of the blast on their ears. Halcyon reached into his pocket and took out a mass of beeswax. He warmed the wax in his hands and watched the other crews shouting and working their tubes. Blast-tube crews moved all about the decks rolling back their blast-tubes.

Dart asked, "What are you going to do with that?"

"Never mind me. I'd say that target was seven hundred yards away, what would you say, Dart?" Halcyon put one-half of the wax in his right ear. He noticed that Ashe Fallow hadn't wrapped a cloth around his head. The chief smiled as Blithe put in the beeswax. Blithe hadn't brought a cloth. The wax was another bit of advice from his family and he noticed that the chief had some wax in his ears as well. Halcyon placed the other half of the wax in his left ear.

Fallow didn't wait for Dart to give instructions; he shouted to the gel monkey, a young junior seaman. "Fetch up blue and white jars of gel until I tell you to stop."

The seaman ran for the hold as a dozen other seamen did the exact same thing from different parts of the deck.

Fallow smiled at Dart. "I took the time to bring up gel for your blast-tube before Master Griffon started the exercise, by your leave, Midshipwizard Surehand."

"Sink me, Chief, anything you do for us is fine by me. That puts us seconds ahead of everyone else," Surehand replied.

Through clenched teeth, Ashe Fallow said, "Only if you get a move on, Midshipwizards!"

"Roll back the blast-tube! Open the firing port!" Halcyon shouted. They started rolling back the long tube of metal on its wheeled caisson.

The chief wasn't happy with their effort and his tone said so. "When you hear an order in this man's navy, shout it back to your officer. You need to make sure everyone knows what to do. Shout!" Fallow ordered.

"Roll back the blast-tube!" they all shouted as the ten-foot-long tube of brass easily rolled back. It gleamed in the dawn's sun. The caisson supported small wheels with a locking mechanism on all four wheels. LAST BREATH appeared in large burnt-on letters along the side of the caisson. Blast-tubes were named by the crews assigned to them at the beginning of their tour of duty. Four of the tube crew had large iron crowbars to move the tube right or left at the direction of the aimer. Blast-gel jars from the orlop deck went into racks at the center of the deck during battle. Seamen called monkeys started bringing up the jars and racking them. Thirty-pound round tube shells hung in racks with net coverings along the railings. The nets kept the heavy shot from rolling around during high seas. Their position on the rail also gave some protection when shots from the enemy pierced the hull of the dragonship.

"Open the blast port!" Halcyon ordered.

"Open the blast port!" they all shouted as Dart Surehand and Philip Getchel opened the blast port and pushed wooden slats through the port so that the violent action of the tube wouldn't slam the port shut during the firing routine. This blast-tube crew had experienced firing practice rounds before this and Dart positioned them on each side of the gun. Their assignments around the blast-tube determined their duties as the action started.

"Sponge in the rammer!" Halcyon yelled.

"Sponge in the rammer!" they all shouted as Surehand took the rammer and doused its spongy head in a large bucket of sea-water. Ryan Murdock filled another bucket so that two buckets were ready at all times. It didn't matter that the blast-tube was stone cold. The rules of blast-tube engagement detailed sponging the tube before every loading and sponge it they would.

Knowing that this practice session would happen, Halcyon had read the details of blast-tube firing until he was letter-perfect in them. He'd also asked the others in the wardroom, in previous days, to talk about their experiences.

"Load in the blue jar!" Blithe shouted.

"Load in the blue jar!" the rest of them shouted back as Mid-shipwizard Getchel loaded in a blue jar of blast gel and Surehand rammed it to the bottom of the tube. Dart and Philip gave him questioning glances at the choice of a blue jar instead of a white jar. They followed the order, but both thought a white jar was a better choice.

Made of hardened ceramic, the jars would not break if casually dropped onto the deck. The blue jars were the longest and held the most blasting gel. There was at least a gallon and a half of the enchanted mixture in the jar. The white jars, for medium-range shots, held a little less than a gallon of the magical brew, and the red jars held half a gallon. Each of these jars would explode to throw the thirty-pound ball at the enemy. The red jars were for throwing chain and case shot at close range. In a pinch, two of the red jars could serve for a midrange shot.

Halcyon had been told by his bunkmates that the tube could throw a ball at least a mile, and normally he would have loaded a white jar for the guessed-at range of the target. However, there was something his father had said about cold blast-tubes that made him pick the blue jar.

"Good choice," Fallow said as he stood at Halcyon's shoulder watching everything they did. "Everyone else loaded in white jars. Faster!" The urgency in Fallow's voice drove Halcyon on to a quicker effort.

"Load the ball, get a move on!" Blithe shouted to the rest.

"Load the ball!" they all shouted, and Ryan Murdock, the stockiest one of the thirteen-year-olds, loaded in the heavy ball taken from the netting of round shot by the blast-tube. The weight and bulk of the shot taxed his muscles as he picked up the shot and rolled it into the blast-tube. Dart rammed the ball to the back end of the tube.

"Ram in the batting!" Halcyon shouted.

"Ram in the batting!" his crew shouted back at him.

The watch bell started clanging, announcing the six bells of the morning watch. No one on deck wanted to think about what would happen if they didn't fire their tube by the time that sixth clang sounded. The menacing Master Andool Griffon stalked among them, glaring them all to faster action.

"Roll up the tube!" Halcyon shouted as many others shouted the exact same order along the decking.

"Roll up the tube!" they all shouted.

As Halcyon bent to help push, Fallow pulled him back. "Bend down, start aiming. Let your tube crew do the work they're supposed to do and you do your job of aiming. Every second counts."

The second clang sounded from the watch bell.

Halcyon bent over the barrel of the tube. In the distance, through the blast-tube port, he could see the enemy ship advancing. It was broadside to the *Sanguine* as if it was going to fire its own wall of steel shot. Halcyon's hands glowed green. He was going to lift the entire blast-tube, using air magic, to aim the shot.

Blast-tubes started firing all around him.

Fallow put his hand over Halcyon's eyes, breaking his concentration and the spell. "Don't use your magic for aiming. That's what the aiming wheel does. Raise your left hand and the tube crew pushes the tube to the left. Your raised right hand orders them to push it right. The aiming wheel raises the barrel up or down for your shot. You don't have enough magic in you to last an entire battle. Think, boy! Order the shot!"

The fourth clang sounded from the bell.

Halcyon looked down again, with Fallow's words ringing in his ears. He cranked the aiming wheel down, raising the barrel as high as it would go. He didn't have to crank much, as the barrel was elevated almost all the way. All the while, he sorted through the blast-tube stories of his relatives.

The *Sanguine* was at the bottom of the sea's roll. No one heard the fifth clang of the ship's bell. The din of blast-tubes firing was too loud.

Haywhen held the lanyard cord that would cause the firing device to drive a hot spike through the touchhole and into the jar of gel. The spike would break the jar, and the heat of the spike always set the explosive mixture off, firing the blast-tube.

Most of the blast-tube crews had to use a small hot pot to keep the spikes red-hot. The crews with midshipwizards could magically heat their spikes. That's what Haywhen had done. He wouldn't pull the lanyard until the order came from the aimer, no matter what the rest of them wanted to do.

Halcyon waited until the dragonship just started to roll up the next wave to give the order. The Maleen ship filled his vision and he thought of nothing else. "Fire!"

Tupper pulled the lanyard and the spring of the firing mechanism drove the red-hot spike into the touchhole and down into the blast-tube. The spike broke the jar and the red-hot metal connected with the blast gel.

KABOOM!

Halcyon would have stood there looking down the barrel as it fired. The chief grabbed him and swung him away from the tons of weight of the blast-tube as it rocketed backward.

"Probably not the wisest thing in the world to be standing behind a firing blast-tube," Fallow said.

Dart came up to Ashe and Halcyon. "Next time don't wait so long to fire the bloody thing. I don't want to have to face Master Griffon for being the last one to fire a tube."

"Well, Mr. Surehand, you are facing her now and your crew was the last one to fire their shot. Stand at attention." Master Griffon was at the blast-tube's side with her hands behind her back. She glared at all of them, but there was a half smile on her face. "I've asked Lieutenant Commander Giantson to work some special magic for this exercise. Please turn to the forecastle."

Halcyon looked up at the forecastle. Commander Giantson clearly had giant's blood in his ancestry, Halcyon thought. The wizard stood over seven feet tall with a massive head on his equally large body. The uniform of the day for him consisted of blue wizard's robes. As the lead spellcaster on the warship, he was the only one allowed to wear such robes, even though there were numerous wizards among the crew. He was casting a new spell as they all looked up to the forecastle.

An image of the enemy Maleen ship appeared on deck. It was a miniature version of the real thing and the crew gasped in surprise at the effect. As they watched, green round shot reached out toward the image. Some of the shot fell far short. A few of the blast-tube shots skipped across the water and struck the vessel at the waterline. Some of those bounced off and others hulled the ship. Only one shot, outlined in red, flew straight and true, striking a blast-tube port and causing another explosion to the blast-tube on the deck. This image replayed itself repeatedly.

Dart stepped up by Halcyon. "This is new. We've never seen the effects of our shots before. I can't wait to learn that spell." There was a touch of awe in his voice.

The illusionary image blinked out.

Master Griffon's voice carried to everyone on deck. "Well

done, Mr. Blithe." She turned to address all of the crews. "He used a blue jar in his blast-tube, because he knew that a white one would fire short, unlike the rest of you. People, cold blast-tubes throw their shot to shorter ranges. Think, because your enemy knows those tricks as well as we do."

That got Halcyon some harsh looks from other tube crews.

She continued to bellow at all the tube crews. "He elevated his tube for the maximum range, again because he knew his tube was cold."

Dart and Philip slapped each other on the back, filled with glee beside Halcyon; his success was their success. They liked being the only crew to succeed on deck. Their amusement ended with her next words.

"Mr. Blithe also stood like a grinning idiot behind the blast-tube to watch his shot. Only the action of Chief Petty Officer Fallow prevented the young fool from being crushed by the action of his tube." She turned from the rest of the crew and glared at the other five tube midshipwizards. "Do you think maybe one of his crewmates, each having fired these tubes in practices before, could have stepped in, instead of Mr. Fallow?"

Her words shouted up into Dart's face, as she stood toe-to-toe with Surehand. He looked down at her and she glared up at him.

He quietly said, "My fault, ma'am. It won't happen again."

She turned to continue addressing the blast-tube crews. "I won't ask Commander Giantson to replay results of the other shots. No one else hit their target. Cold blast-tubes, people, don't throw their shot as far. When I give the signal, we will commence the exercise again. This time you will fire two volleys as fast as you can at your targets. The blast-tube crew on this deck firing their tube last will all get their names entered in the captain's book for extra duty. Do I make myself clear?"

"Aye, aye," the entire deck crew shouted.

Griffon walked back over to Blithe and his crew. She reached up and twisted Blithe's face sideways with her hand. "Blithe, is that beeswax I see in your ear?"

"Yes, ma'am, it is." He'd noticed that she hadn't worn the rag around her head that most of the crew used to muffle the sounds of the shots.

She actually smiled up at Halcyon. "You take any other tricks you've learned from your proud family and teach them to these scallywags you have in your crew. You hear me, Mr. Blithe?"

"Aye, aye, ma'am." Halcyon kept himself from grinning as Master Andool Griffon walked off to ready the exercise.

Dart pushed Halcyon to the front of the gun. "Your aiming days are over for now, Hal. You take Ryan's place and throw the shots into the blast-tube as fast as you can. There's no sense having a great lout of a midshipwizard on the crew without using his broad back." He tossed his swabbing stick to Ryan. "No magic from any of you now. Sink me when I say we're not going to be the last ones to fire that second shot."

Illusionary ships appeared in the distance on the port and starboard sides of the dragonship.

Chief Fallow turned away from the midshipwizard blast-tube crew. He didn't want them to see the look of pride on his face. "Get a move on, you gel monkeys, these crews need your wares today," he barked.

Master Griffon shouted, "Begin!"

VII

✤ ✤ ✤

Blast-Pike Drill, Lesson Two

HIS MAJESTY'S ARTICLES OF WAR: ARTICLE VII

Every flag officer, captain, and commander in the fleet who, upon signal or order of fight, or sight of any ship or ships which it may be his duty to engage, or who, upon likelihood of engagement, shall not make the necessary preparations for fight, and shall not in his own person, and according to his place, encourage the inferior officers and men to fight courageously, shall suffer death, or such other punishment, as from the nature and degree of the offense a court-martial shall deem him to deserve; and if any person in the fleet shall treacherously or cowardly yield or cry for quarter, every person so offending, and being convicted thereof by the sentence of a court-martial, shall suffer death.

A few days later, Halcyon leaned on the forecastle bulwark looking down at the open center deck below. It was just seven bells of the morning watch and usually he should be in his bunk sleeping by now. Later in the day, his duty called for blast-pike practice, and he wanted to see the dragonship's marines go through their paces during their morning drill with that same weapon. He'd hoped watching them might give him pointers he could use in his own practice session.

Chief Fallow directed the blast-pike drilling of all the men on the ship. He was the Arcanian navy champion with the blast-pike. Hal also noticed Lieutenants Anderson and Jillian Durand down there throwing spells at marines while the troopers tried to block the magical attacks.

"Mr. Blithe, what is the twentieth navy Article of War," barked the captain, startling the young midshipwizard from his concentration of the action below.

Halcyon whirled and stood at attention. "Sir, the twentieth navy Article of War states, 'All spies, and all persons whatsoever, who shall come, or be found, in the nature of spies, to bring or deliver any seducing letters or messages from any enemy or rebel, or endeavor to corrupt any captain, officer, mariner, or other in the fleet, to betray his trust, being convicted of any such offense by the sentence of the court-martial, shall be punished with death, or such other punishment as the nature and degree of the offense shall deserve and the court-martial shall impose.' Sir."

"Letter-perfect, that was well spoken, Mr. Blithe," the captain said. "I notice you watching the marines practice with their blast-pikes. It isn't the most elegant of weapons. Certainly, it doesn't have the style and multifunctionality of the saber, but Arcania can be proud of how the blast-pike performs in battle. Are you nervous about your session this afternoon?" There was a stern look on the captain's face, but Halcyon thought he noticed a friendly gleam in the captain's eyes.

"Sir, I have never used the weapon before and want to do as well as possible. I thought watching them practice would help me understand the weapon better," Halcyon nervously answered his captain.

The captain leaned over the rail and looked down at the marines at work. "I remember my first practice session with the Arcanian blast-pike. It didn't go well. The weapon is serviceable, but sabers are better.

"Blast-pikes are a weapon unique to Arcanian navies. The rowan wood of the staff grows only in the high mountains at the center of our island nation. The enchanted metal for the blast-pike weapon head comes from clans of sprites on the east side of Arcania.

"Skilled use of the pike allows someone with no magical talent at all to block spell attacks made at them, as the wood and metal of the weapon absorb the spell if positioned properly.

"I have a bit of advice I would like to impart to you, Mr. Blithe. Our Senior Chief Petty Officer Fallow is remarkable in his use of the weapon. I've noticed he often tries to get in close under the blade of his opponent to try all sorts of expert maneuvers. When you practice with the weapon, choke up on the shaft so that the back half of the weapon is at your side and no more than half the weapon is in front of you. As I remember, you are the seventh son of a seventh son, aren't you?"

Still at attention, Halcyon had no idea why the captain asked him that question. "Why, yes, sir, I am. Is there a problem, sir?"

"No, no. I just think our good chief is in for an interesting surprise this afternoon." Captain Olden turned, chuckling to himself. Over his shoulder, he said, "Carry on, Midshipwizard, carry on."

Blithe found himself uncomfortable under the attention of the captain. He didn't know quite how to take what the captain said. He would certainly try to hold the weapon as the captain advised. He looked down at the rows of marines using the blast-pike; many of them held it just as the captain had suggested. He could hear Chief Fallow talking about fighting Maleen shapechangers.

"Nasty monsters, those Maleen shapechangers, I'm told. I

haven't faced one in combat yet. I've heard a lot of talk about dealing with them. The blast-pike is the perfect weapon for opening up those devils." Fallow was at the center of a large circle of marines. He held the pike lightly in his two hands.

"If you know you're fighting a shapechanger—" Chief Fallow stopped for a moment and leaned his body on the standing pike shaft. "Don't any of you lugs ask me how to tell if you are fighting a shapechanger. If you face an enemy that has more eyes than it should or has claws instead of hands, you're probably fighting a shapechanger. If you are ever in doubt just believe you're fighting a monster and maybe you'll live a few heartbeats longer.

"If you are fighting such a monster, arm and leg strikes won't hurt that type of foe a bit. Swing for the monster's neck or jab into the monster's body."

Fallow followed both of these instructions with demonstrations of the proper swing and the proper jab.

Halcyon thought he'd rather have a blast-pike in his hand if he faced a shapechanger, rather than a saber. Come to it, he'd like to be behind the barrel of a blast-tube if he was going to get his wish. His brothers and uncles had never once talked about fighting and killing one of those creatures in a battle.

Fallow ordered all of the marines to pair off and begin sparring with each other.

Then he noticed the marine that could only be Corporal Denna Darkwater. She was a large, well-muscled woman. At the moment when Blithe's eyes fell upon her, she used the butt end of her blast-pike to smash the chin of her fellow marine in the course of a mock battle. The man fell to the deck, knocked out by the blow. Darkwater didn't even look concerned. She picked up a small bucket by the railing and threw its water in the face of the unconscious marine. He didn't react at all to the water, but his chest was heaving up and down. He wasn't dead.

Noting the condition of her last adversary, she looked around for another sparring partner. Halcyon saw several marines move to other parts of the deck to avoid her gaze. Finally she found an equally large marine and they began a bout with the pikes.

He watched her through the entire practice. When it was all over, he went to his bunk and had a tough time getting any rest. Parts of his body were already starting to ache from the blows he knew he would receive. It didn't help that a frustrated Hackle barked at some of the other midshipwizards, but thanks to Tupper and Halcyon, all of the others knew their Articles letter-perfect. Even through Hackle's complaining, Halcyon was able to finally fall asleep with a smile of partial success on his lips.

Five bells clanged the afternoon watch and Senior Chief Petty Officer Ashe Fallow stood in front of the lieutenants, lieutenants junior grade, and midshipwizards. He was dressed in padded armor from head to foot. A heavy metal helm covered most of his head, but didn't hide the glare he was using on the officers in front of him. At that moment, rank didn't mean a thing. They were all supposed to dance to the chief's tune. He knew this, and his glaring expression told of his glee at the situation.

An eight-foot-tall Arcanian blast-pike spun lazily back and forth in both of his hands. He held it up for all of them to see.

"This is the finest weapon on the face of this earth. During practices, the razor-sharp metal of this pike head magically dulls itself so that it won't cut into your flesh. The metal does raise a nice bruise, however." He smiled almost evilly at all of them when he said this last. "Arcania is justly proud of its navy and the men who use these pikes. You all need to know how to use them. As Commander Wily is fond of saying, the Maleen love to close with their foes, board them, and attack hand-to-hand. This weapon takes away their troops' advantages in height and strength.

"Look at the spike; it's perfect for punching through armor." He twirled the pike as if it weighed nothing and lunged with the weapon. Fully six feet of it was in front of the chief. All those encircling him well imagined that spike cutting into the flesh of a foe.

"Observe the V-shaped blade, perfect for hooking a foe or chopping a neck." There was a log behind the chief, and he whirled, chopping the ten-inch-thick log in half, only to whirl again to face Halcyon with the weapon as if the chop took no effort at all.

"I have you all in a circle," Fallow said, looking around the group. "I want you to observe what others do as I spar with each of you. While I'm speaking imitate my moves; get set!"

The group was in the largest circle possible at the center of the open deck. Some of them were back as far as the port and starboard railings. There was about four feet between each officer.

Off-duty crew lined up along the forecastle, as the chance to see an officer bashed in any way presented an unusual entertainment no one wanted to miss. Many others looked down from the rigging among the sails.

Chief Ashe turned his body sideways and presented a thin silhouette. He also held the pike vertically in front of him. "Merand, lightning-bolt me!" First Class Midshipwizard Alvena Merand appeared startled by the order and the tone of voice; that didn't stop her from reaching out with one hand and throwing a powerful stroke of lightning right at the chief. The bolt crackled loudly from her hand, striking the pike in front of its wielder. The weapon clearly absorbed the potent magical energy, as the chief's body didn't even twitch when the magic hit his pike.

As Halcyon stood in the same pose as the chief, he could well imagine the usefulness of the weapon in a magical battle. That bolt he saw the midshipwizard hurl would have burned and knocked over an unprepared foe.

"Ah, she throws a mean bolt, our midshipwizard does. As you can see, it means nothing when she's faced with a foe who knows how to use a blast-pike," Fallow said.

Out of the stairwell from the middle deck strode Corporal Darkwater with her blast-pike in hand. All she had on for padding was thick leather armor on her arms and chest and a metal chest plate covering her front and back.

Dart nudged Halcyon. "You're in for rough seas, my lad, sink me if it isn't so. Keep your distance from her if you can, my bucko, that's a mean one she is."

Darkwater walked to the center of the circle and looked right at Blithe. There was an evil grin on her face. She was assessing him with her stare. He could see her looking him up and down, judging his strength. He tried to keep a bland face, but he'd never been appraised like a piece of beef before. His entire body tensed up from her gaze.

He tried doing the same to her.

Darkwater was tall, almost as tall as Halcyon. She twirled the heavy blast-pike just as the chief did, but she did it faster. Her eyes were almost black and her gaze never left Blithe's face. Her hands were heavily callused and her arms and legs were unusually thick. Her face was long, and even her neck was thickly muscled. Unlike that of most Arcanian women, her hair hung tight and short to her head. He noticed that her eyebrows were unusually thick.

Fallow shifted to a guard position with his pike, and everyone but Darkwater imitated him. "We have a tradition on this dragonship allowing our best marine to spar with the newer officers. It gives the marines a chance to practice some more and it allows officers to learn to deal with deadly opponents. Mr. Blithe, I believe you are the newest of our officers, front and center, if you please."

Sweat poured off of Blithe as he stepped into the center of the circle. His hands were wet around the shaft of his pike. It felt unusually heavy in his grip. He'd been warned by his mates just how bad Darkwater was going to be and seen evidence of it with his own eyes that morning.

He didn't have the good advice of his relatives to fall back on, as they hadn't talked about practicing with blast-pikes. He took a calming breath and tried to hold the pike as the captain suggested and he'd observed earlier. He knew she was going to get as close to him as possible, trying to fist him unexpectedly. He practiced in his mind what he would have to do to avoid that blow.

Five feet away, Darkwater started twirling her pike as if it weighed nothing. First, she would spin it with one hand, and then the other.

"Nothing fancy, Corporal. Just trade blows with our Mr. Blithe. He's a Lankshire man; expect him to give a good account of himself. Begin!" Ashe Fallow ordered.

With the word to start, Halcyon shed his nervousness. He lost sight of the ship and the people around him. His world focused down to Darkwater. Getting knocked unconscious was the worst that could happen to him, he thought to himself. That was nothing to be afraid of, especially in front of his shipmates, he kept telling himself.

He took a step forward with his pike at his side. It was what Darkwater was waiting for.

She rushed him and easily batted his pike head with her own weapon. With only one hand on her pike, she took great pleasure in striking at him with her free fist.

Expecting the blow, Halcyon turned to the side. The fist struck his thigh.

Totally off balance and surprised by his move, the corporal was caught off guard when Blithe thrust both his arms forward; his pike shaft smashed the corporal in the face, knocking her backward.

Blood gushed from the split lip and Darkwater angrily looked back at Halcyon. "Good one," she said, but she didn't sound happy.

Halcyon would have offered her his hand and apologized, but the corporal wasn't interested in his pity. She charged him again. Her look was murderous. She wasn't practicing anymore; she wanted to do real damage to him.

Blithe took a step back and held his pike just as the captain suggested. Quite by accident, the butt of his weapon struck the deck.

All Halcyon had in mind was to keep the pike head between his body and the corporal's. He also didn't want her to be able to bat aside his weapon as easily as she had before. He gripped the blast-pike as tight as he could to stop her from doing that again.

"Corporal, calm down!" the chief shouted, but she wasn't listening.

Screaming like a banshee, she rushed him and once again tried to bat aside his pike.

Blithe was holding his ground and his broad shoulders and arms were almost as large as Darkwater's. In his firm grip, his pike head didn't move an inch from her parrying attack.

She ran herself right up onto his point. The inertia of her rush lifted her up on his weapon. Her entire body rose over his head on the pike as her forward motion and weight did all the work. She came crashing down on the other side of Halcyon and hit the deck hard. She lay flat, barely moving. There was a grim smile on her face, even when she showed herself to be unconscious.

The watching crew shouted in glee and began cheering, "Huzzah!"

The pikes of the rest of the circle of watchers beat repeatedly on the deck in praise of his lucky action.

All Halcyon could do was look on in worry. He could tell she was breathing. At least his attack hadn't killed her. He didn't really know exactly what he had done; it all happened so fast.

"Bucket, Surehand," the chief ordered.

Dart picked up one of the several buckets of seawater around the circle. He dashed it in her face and all she did was groan. "Sink me if our good corporal doesn't seem to have gotten as good as she's given all these years. Chief, I don't think she's getting up for a while," Dart remarked.

"You idiots up on the forecastle come down here and carry Darkwater to sickbay. Get a move on." When the chief barked an order, men moved. Six of the largest seamen picked up Darkwater, showing great difficulty at the task, partly because she was heavy and partly because they were laughing so hard.

"Let's get back at it, shall we? Blithe, that was a well-considered set of moves. You obviously knew she was coming to take your head off. That sideways tactic showed cleverness. Come forward and we will try that . . ."

"Chief." Officer Wily walked into the circle with a blast-pike in his hand.

Everyone stood at attention.

"Sir!" Chief Fallow said as he came to attention.

"At ease, all," Wily said, smiling to the group. "I heard you mention my name at the beginning of the practice and saw our Mr. Blithe best the fierce Corporal Darkwater. I have a fancy to spar a bit with you if you don't mind."

Halcyon got out of the circle, not wanting to get in the middle of such a battle, wondering who would get the best out of the match.

Fallow kept a respectful tone, filled with concern. "Sir, you don't have any padding on. If you want to join the group we would be honored, but maybe you want to equip yourself."

Wily just smiled. He waved his hand in front of his chest and snapped his fingers. Instantly a red glow covered his entire body. The more experienced spellcasters in the group gasped in awe.

Blithe gave Midshipwizard Boatson a questioning look.

Boatson pointed at Wily, whispering, "That spell is called a

Drusan shield. It takes most spellcasters two hours to cast it on themselves. Our Mr. Wily is so talented at magic use, he could do the spell in seconds. You should be impressed."

"Chief, I'm ready to trade blows when you are?" Commander Wily seemed confident as he stood there with his blast-pike in one hand. At seven feet tall, he towered over the chief.

Halcyon thought he noticed an odd glint in the chief's eyes.

"Bouting rules or a free-for-all, sir?" said the chief as he started circling around the commander.

"Oh, let's make it a free-for-all. I know you're much better when all the rules are suspended. Let's have at it, Chief." The commander went from relaxed to dangerous as his pike came up to face the chief's.

Commander Wily kept up a dialogue as the pikes whirled at each other in a blur. "You all should consider yourselves lucky to be taught by Ashe, here. Chief Fallow is amazing with his pike. I've been watching him work you men for months now and he's impressed me every time I've observed him."

In those few words, Halcyon saw the pikes strike each other at least seven times and both men circled the other twice. It almost seemed to Halcyon like Fallow was irritated that the commander could talk calmly while they dueled. Fallow seemed to move faster and faster, as if he was trying to take advantage of the fact that the commander couldn't have his entire concentration on the duel if he was talking as well.

Wily continued to speak calmly, all the while defending himself from increasingly faster pike strikes. "In this duel between us, the first one to touch the other's body with the pike wins. Notice how the chief constantly lunges low at me in an effort to get me to lower my weapon shaft. That's not going to happen."

Blows rained down on the commander during his speech. It was impossible to tell how many Chief Fallow threw at him while Officer Wily continued to speak. Every Fallow attack failed, striking some portion of the commander's pike instead of his body. All the while, the chief kept a grin on his face, but the smile became more and more strained.

"I have noticed that our good chief here . . ."

His dialogue stopped as the chief used his pike as a pole with which to vault, raising his feet to the commander. When he slammed the pike to the deck, it became a lever to propel him at Wily's chest. The red glow of the commander's spell momentarily grew brighter. It was as if his feet struck a stone wall. The spell allowed the commander to be totally unaffected by the heavy blow instead of going backward, and, caught off balance, Chief Fallow fell awkwardly to the deck.

With that, the commander easily tapped Fallow on the chest with the pike, and the duel was over. He politely helped Fallow up.

"Good tactic that, it would have caught most off guard. I've never seen you use it. Thank you for your time." Wily bowed politely as those around him cheered his victory, slamming their pikes on the deck to honor him. He walked out of the circle not acknowledging the cheers of the watchers.

"Blithe, get back in the center of the circle," the chief ordered, clearly irritated. "The commander's encounter put us a bit behind schedule. As most of you know, wizards from Arcania can hurl their magic through a held blast-pike. That's why it's called a blast-pike."

The chief moved stiffly around the circle, glaring at those who watched. The grins at seeing the chief defeated were now stowed away, as no one wanted to face the chief when he was angry.

"Blithe here hasn't had the opportunity to use his magic through a blast-pike. I'm going to ask him to try in a few seconds. You will all remember your first attempts and refrain from laughing." The chief's glare looked them all in the eyes, and most shifted their positions uneasily.

"Mr. Blithe, your weapon is capable of . . ."

Suddenly six crewmen and a stretcher appeared on deck with the ship's surgeon. No one knew why, and Chief Fallow wasn't stopping for them.

". . . is capable of boosting your magical energy, but it's a difficult feat to master. You might be years in the training before you can even perform a mild blast from your pike. When you master it, you will find it takes less of your energy to use the pike with your magic than using your magic alone," Fallow said. "Having no magical ability myself, I have this on good authority from past officers with magical skills. I'm told the enchanted metal of the pike head and the rowan wood all work to help the spell-caster. Therefore, stand firm at the center of the circle and try throwing your spell energy through the pike at me. Don't be concerned if nothing happens. There is no honor to be lost in the effort. Begin."

Blithe was very hesitant to throw any kind of spell at the chief. On the other hand, Midshipwizard First Class Merand didn't hesitate when she threw her spell. The chief was standing there with his blast-pike covering the front of his body.

"Get a move on, Mr. Blithe. We haven't got all day," the chief ordered.

Nervous, Blithe breathed deeply, summoning up his inner magical resources, and threw all the energy he had through his hands and into the pike pointed at the chief.

In less than a second, Blithe's entire pike crackled with a blue energy and blue sparks flew off the head of the pike.

Chief Fallow's face had just a second to register surprise as a thick beam of blue sparks struck his pike and bashed it hard into his body. It seemed as if nothing of Blithe's energy was absorbed by the chief's pike. Thrown back at least ten feet, Fallow hit the deck with a bone-crunching thud.

Blithe dropped his pike and rushed over to the chief. There

was a big burn mark on the chief's padded chest and a dazed expression on his face. He was looking up at the sky.

"Chief, are you all right?" Blithe asked.

"Ack" was all the chief could say.

"Blithe, you are the seventh son of a seventh son, aren't you?" Senior Lieutenant Solvalson asked him as the others crowded around to look down at the fallen chief.

"Yes, I am. Is the chief going to be all right?"

Solvalson smiled back. "Oh, he will be all right, but maybe in the future when you are dealing with magical things, you should tell your instructors about your birthright. The pikes react differently to you than to others."

"Ack," the chief said again as the six crewmen carried him to sickbay.

The amused captain's voice came down from the quarterdeck. "I believe that will be all the blast-pike practice for the day. Carry on, men."

The lieutenants and junior lieutenants gave their weapons to the midshipwizards to rack in the armory. Awkwardly the younger officers carried bundles of the blast-pikes down the ship's stairs.

Dart was behind Halcyon as they made their way belowdecks. "Put down two of the ship's best today, Hal. That's quite the first practice you've had there."

Tupper, on the stairs below them, stopped for a second to look up at Hal. "If I were you I would just put myself in sickbay before the next practice because Fallow and Darkwater are going to put you there for sure the next time you meet them over blast-pikes."

All Hal could do was shake his head, knowing the next training session would be a bad one for him.

VIII

⚜ ⚜ ⚜

Man Overboard

As the midshipwizards assembled on the quarterdeck, Senior Chief Petty Officer Fallow approached Halcyon. "Mr. Blithe, a word alone if you please."

"Certainly, Chief, what do you need?" asked Blithe.

They moved apart from the rest of the group.

Fallow spoke in low tones. "I'm taking the helm in a moment. We're going to be doing some special maneuvers and I want to make sure they work themselves out flawlessly. I just wanted to say that I was on a frigate once, in the middle of a battle off the Sorbol coast. The frigate exploded under me and I found myself high in the air. Even surprised, I was able to take a big breath of air and hold it before I hit the water hard. Now, it may seem silly, an old sailor telling tales to a young officer like yourself, but you never know when such knowledge comes in handy, begging your pardon, Midshipwizard." With that, Fallow walked off to the quarterdeck and the helm.

"Not a bit, Chief," Halcyon said to Fallow's back, watching him walk away. Blithe raised his voice a bit louder to make sure the chief heard. "You can tell me anything you feel I should know at any time, with my thanks."

All of the midshipwizards were on the forecastle. Blithe noticed right away that topsails and topgallants appeared tied tight to the sticks. The ship could be cruising at only four knots at the most. Halcyon had started guessing speeds, as he had been spending time with the line and the timer in the last two days.

"Mr. Blithe, if you please, stop your woolgathering and pay attention," First Officer Wily ordered, standing tall and proud in front of the group. "We have much to go over in this training session today. As I talk, all of you take off your duty boots, now."

Everyone had the exact same questioning looks on their faces as they hunched down on the deck and shucked off their boots.

"Mr. Boatson," Wily asked, "what is the force of the wind at this moment?"

The midshipwizard had to stand up on one bare foot and one booted foot to look over the railing at the sea. "Force-four, sir. To my mind it's been that way for almost a week, sir."

"Correct, Mr. Boatson. Continue taking off your boots, if you please. How many of you consider yourselves swimmers?" Wily asked all of them. "Raise your hands for me, please."

All of the assembled crew of midshipwizards raised their hands.

"Excellent, some of you might be amazed at how many navy

men can't swim," Wily said, smiling at them. "Now, how many of you would call yourselves excellent swimmers?"

Only Blithe, Merand, and Swordson raised their hands in response to that question.

"Mr. Blithe, please stand up and come to the railing with me. While he does that, Mr. Haywhen, I'm told by a certain irritated junior lieutenant that you have become uncommonly good at reciting the Articles of War. What is the eighteenth article, if you please?" Wily asked.

"'All robbery committed by any person in the fleet shall be punished with death, or otherwise, as a court-martial, upon consideration of the circumstances, shall find meet,' sir." Tupper recited the article without faltering once.

"*Getting wet, you are.*" That thought flew into Blithe's head. Halcyon knew it was the sea dragon trying to talk to him. Halcyon shook his head, trying to clear his mind of the dragon's intrusion. Having been berated for not paying attention, he didn't want the officer to admonish him again. "*Later!*" he thought back at the sea dragon.

"Today, it's my duty to make sure all of you know what to do when a man goes overboard. There are several things you should keep in mind while in the water." Wily said this while pacing back and forth behind Blithe.

The young midshipwizard was the only one of the midshipwizards standing and it made him self-conscious.

Just then, the dragonship lurched and slowed down to a crawl as the dragon actually fought its sails and used its tail and flippers to slow down the ship even more. The midshipwizards were all startled. They'd never felt the dragon do such a thing and some of them had been serving on the *Sanguine* for years.

"A swimmer must try to stay calm." Wily had a strange grin on his face as Blithe turned his head to watch his first officer. Wily continued, "A swimmer must try to conserve their energy and not become exhausted fighting the sea. To better stay afloat, a swimmer should shuck their shirt and pants after taking off their boots. However, as I've always said, there is nothing like a fine example to teach a class. Mr. Surehand, at my signal please shout as loud as you can the words 'man overboard.'"

Wily then magically gestured, and with that wave of his hand Halcyon flew up off the deck and found himself hurled into the sea.

Halcyon hit the ocean hard. Even in his surprise, he'd managed to fill his lungs with air thanks to Chief Fallow's words of caution. He went a few feet below the water but bobbed right up like a cork. The numbing cold saltwater closed in around him.

Dart didn't wait for the officer to allow him to scream. He'd just seen his friend launched over the side. "Man overboard! Man overboard!" Dart leapt up to watch Hal strike the water.

Halcyon sputtered his eyes and face clear of seawater, and started stroking hard for the ship, even though he knew he could never catch up to it. Then the words of the officer hit him. He should be conserving his energy, maybe even taking off the now heavy shirt that was dragging on his arms.

Back at the ship, the rest of the class sat in shock at what just happened. "Mr. Argo, come to the railing and watch our Mr. Blithe as he tries to survive through this demonstration. It's vital that someone pay attention to where the swimmer fell off the boat until he is safe back on board. Note the swimmer's body in the water and feel free to constantly point in his direction to help others spot him." Wily spoke calmly as Argo rushed up to the railing.

The first officer smiled at the rest of the midshipwizards. "Alvena, Jacom, Dart, Elan, you help the crew man the dinghy. Let's see how fast you can launch it. Go!"

The four of them rushed to the forecastle where the crew was already working on the winches to take the dinghy over the side.

"As you can see when someone, our Mr. Surehand in this case, shouts 'man overboard,' the crew is trained to do certain things. The crew at the forecastle has a standing order to launch the dinghy," Wily remarked. "The helmsman will begin tacking the ship in a figure-eight maneuver that is guaranteed to get the ship back somewhere in the general area of where the crewman fell overboard."

In the water, Blithe rose and fell with the waves. He'd cast off his shirt, that made floating easier. At the crest of the waves, he would hurl the soaked mass into the air to help people spot him from the ship. Now his pants were starting to weigh him down. He was still in shock. He couldn't believe the first officer threw him overboard. Halcyon thought Wily liked him. If it wasn't for the warm sun beating down on his body, he didn't know how he would survive. He could feel his arms and legs going numb from the cold. It was still easy to keep his lungs full of air. He did shuck off his pants and was able to float even better. His mind filled with fear seeing the *Sanguine* turn away from his position.

The dragon started roaring loudly in obvious distress. Blithe thought that distress might be because of him.

Back at the ship, Wily continued the lesson. "So, we have a man in the water. He's at least a hundred yards away, what can we do?"

"Dive in after him," suggested Andorvan.

"Bad idea, that's sending more good men after one in danger. They might drown as well. Anyone else?" Wily asked.

"Throw out a lifeline," suggested James.

"Excellent thought, Mr. Grunseth," Wily said. "I would also suggest that the one who throws out that lifeline take the time to tie a loop at the rope's end. This gives the end more weight, allowing it to go farther in the toss." Officer Wily picked up part of a large coiled rope at the stern of the ship. He offered it to the midshipwizard. "Mr. Grunseth, if you please, since it was your idea. I myself would favor a bowline knot for the loop, but many others would use the reef knot. Next week remind me, all of you, and we'll review sailing knots. I promise not to tie anyone up." Wily smirked at his own jest. His watching officers-in-training were too nervous to laugh.

Grunseth quickly put a large loop in the rope. As he worked, the officer continued to talk.

"Those with no magic or ability to help the rope along should be tossing the rope underhand off the ship. That will take the line farther out to sea. There are some like Mr. Surehand, who I'm happy to see has managed to get the dinghy into the water in record time, who can use earth spells to throw the rope out even farther. Go ahead, Mr. Grunseth; toss the rope as far as you can."

The midshipwizard was able to toss the thick line out past the sea dragon's tail. The line began uncoiling farther and farther out to sea.

"All of you watch for Mr. Blithe. Mr. Argo, do you still see him?" Wily asked.

Jason had moved along the railing to keep Halcyon in sight. He was at the stern of the ship as the warship tacked along the top half of its maneuver. The sound of the dragon's distress was thundering in its volume. The creature clearly didn't like one of its crew over the side.

"Yes, sir. Halcyon's throwing up his shirt every once in a while. You can note his position easily from that." Argo never took his face away from the swimmer in the water.

"What a clever fellow our Mr. Blithe is. That's a good idea as long as he has the strength for it," Wily commented.

Captain Olden stood with his hands behind his back, scowling at Commander Wily and the midshipwizards from his quarterdeck. Naturally, Wily had consulted Olden about this lesson. The captain didn't like the thought of throwing one of his own overboard, but wanted to give Wily a free hand in the lesson as he agreed with some of the things it would teach the midshipwizards.

It had been the captain's idea to shorten sail that morning. Olden was amazed at the reaction of the sea dragon. The creature seemed quite beside itself as it roared new tones the captain had never heard before. Hours before, the captain conferred with Chief Fallow about the special maneuvers the ship would have to go through to try and pick up the overboard crewman. The captain chided himself for not thinking of launching the jolly boat into the water hours before the exercise began.

Blithe sputtered, catching a throatful of the sea. He was getting a bit tired and the cold was making him even more exhausted. He tried to think of a single spell that would help him at this moment. He knew only a few of them, but vowed that if he survived this exercise he would take the time to learn more water spells. There was a magical ring in his sea chest that would have allowed him to breathe under water; naturally, it was in his chest. He also vowed to learn some protective magics, never wanting to turn into a skipping stone for another wizard again. He hadn't liked being picked up by Wily's magic.

Wily presented a calm demeanor to the nervous midshipwizards. "Now, we've thrown out the lifeline. We've launched the dinghy in record time. Can anyone tell me why we do both?"

Midshipwizard Forrest raised his hand.

"Mr. Forrest, tell us," Wily ordered.

The young man gulped in nervousness as he faced his first officer. "The rope could fall off and the dinghy can still get the crewman. In addition, that rope might never reach the drowning man. We must use both the boat and the rope to increase the chance to save the sailor in the water," Mark answered.

"Exactly right, Mr. Forrest, good work," replied Officer Wily. "Notice that our Mr. Blithe has taken off his pants. I see he's thrown those up in the air for us to see. The cold of the sea is hard on a body. It makes one weak. Spellcasting for a wizard is made doubly difficult because of the numbing of the hands. It's times like those where spells cast just with words come in handy. Be sure to ask Lieutenant Commander Giantson to teach you some useful spells cast with just words.

"Now, there are a few other considerations we must keep in mind with a man overboard. He might be injured. In a battle, rigging can come down and cast a man overboard, often breaking an arm or leg. I've seen it happen in battles time and time again," Wily said. "Getting an injured man on board can be the most difficult part of the process. Anne Driden, how would you order a duty to get a wounded man back on board. Let's assume the dinghy is far away, pulling back to the ship. The drowning crewman has two broken arms and only the loop on the rope is keeping his head above water by the side of the ship. If we pull up that rope, the crewman could fall out of the loop. What do you do?"

Driden didn't hesitate for a minute. "I'd get a duty crew to tie lines to another strong crewman and he would go over the side. He's there to secure the wounded sailor in the water and we would pull them both up, sir."

"How many crewmen would you want in that pulling detail, Driden?" Wily asked.

"I'd want four men per body being pulled from the water, sir," Driden answered.

"That is a correct answer. I see the dinghy has reached our Mr. Blithe. Pull in the lifeline and coil it up. We should move to the forecastle to meet our shipmate and congratulate him on the success of his trial." There was just the oddest tone of disappointment in First Officer Wily's voice, or at least it sounded like that to some of the midshipwizards.

The dinghy managed to row its way to Halcyon. It was Dart's hand that reached out to pull his friend in. "Sink me, Hal, how do you get into these troubled waters?"

The sea dragon stopped bellowing when it saw Halcyon in the small vessel.

"Me! I was just standing there." Halcyon couldn't believe what his friend was saying. His shivering form struggled into the boat.

"At ease, Mr. Blithe," ordered Merand from her position at the tiller. She was staring hard at Halcyon. A grim look filled her face. "Dart, throw him a blanket. He needs to cover himself. Officers must appear decent in front of the crew. Mr. Blithe, Officer Wily used you as an example. That is his right as an officer of the ship. I don't appreciate what he did to you. After this lesson is over, you will dress yourself in a new work uniform and come to my wardroom. I would have a private word with you. You keep that blanket about you on deck. I don't want the crew seeing a good officer in less than his best. You will not regain that deck as a drowned rat. Understood?"

"Yes, ma'am." Suddenly Blithe felt miserable and he didn't even know why.

The tone of Merand's voice seemed so stern that the rest of the midshipwizards kept quiet as they rowed back to the ship.

When they reached the side of the ship, the dragon's head twisted to look at them all. *"Told you,"* the dragon thought at Halcyon.

He thought back, *"I know you did and thank you for the warning. Next time I'll listen."*

A rope ladder unfolded itself down the side of the ship and sea dragon. Before any of the other midshipwizards could go for it, Merand ordered, "We'll all ride the dinghy up the winches. We won't be using the rope ladder. When we make the deck, the rest of you get out first and, Dart, you stay in front of our Mr. Blithe until he reaches his wardroom. If Aberdeen Hackle is there you tell him he's needed on deck."

There were questioning looks from all the other midshipwizards, but none of them asked about the odd order. Alvena Merand was the first-class midshipwizard. To these other officers-in-training, her word was as good as the captain's. They would do as ordered.

The winch lines followed the ladder down to their position at the side of the heaving dragonship. Hands reached out to attach the guide wires to the cleats at the stern and bow of the dinghy. The dinghy slowly moved up the side of the dragon and then the side of the warship. Wily and the rest of the midshipwizards were at the railing to help them off the boat.

"Well done, Mr. Blithe. I truly appreciate you being available for my lesson. No ill effects, I trust?" Wily asked.

"None, sir." Inwardly Halcyon didn't appreciate the dunking. He knew he could do nothing about it. The officer had needed an example and this time he was it.

"That's the lesson for today. All of you fetch your boots. I imagine our good captain is going to want to set all the sails again. We should reach our duty station in three days if this wind keeps up. Carry on, all of you." The first officer moved toward the bow of the ship as the trumpet signals for full sail blared from the forecastle.

Tupper handed Halcyon his boots. "That should be the last time you volunteer information to an officer needing an example, right, Hal?" Tupper was smiling when he said it, but there was a tone of concern in his voice.

"The water was a bit cold, but quite refreshing really," Halcyon lied as he took his boots and kept the blanket tight around his body.

"Mr. Haywhen, you get yourself to your duty station and help with the sails. Mr. Blithe, you have your orders, carry them out." Merand glared at the two briefly and went belowdecks.

"I don't know what got her in a bundle, but we better get you dressed, Hal." Dart led the way below the forecastle down to the middle blast-tube deck and the midshipwizard wardroom. As they moved belowdecks Dart kept up the conversation. "I've had lessons on a man going overboard at least twice a year since I joined the navy. Sink me if I've ever seen a man thrown overboard in the middle of the high seas. Did you do something to make Mr. Wily mad, Hal?"

As they entered the wardroom, Lieutenant Junior Grade Hackle was on Halcyon like a leech.

"Where's your uniform, Blithe?" Hackle was twisting his hands in glee. "There will be marks in the book for being out of uniform."

Dart went to attention. "Mr. Hackle, Mr. Blithe was in an exercise with the first officer. He had to take his uniform off at the officer's order. I've been asked to tell you that you are needed on the quarterdeck, sir."

"Really?" There was a look of surprise on Hackle's face. "Well, why didn't you say so sooner, man?" He rushed out of the wardroom as if he were on fire.

"Sink me if that lieutenant isn't the worst officer in the entire navy. I swear he's a Maleen secret weapon. Hal, the gods only know what our Alvena Merand has in mind for you, but you better get your sorry butt over there double quick. I'll see you on deck when she's finished with you. Luck to you, sailor." Dart slapped his friend on the back and left.

Halcyon got dressed and moved through the lower blast-tube deck to the starboard side of the lower deck. There was a marine guard at the hatch. Blithe looked at the man, not knowing exactly what to do.

The marine made it easier for him. "You knock on the hatch and if she is of a mind, she says to come in. You keep knocking until you get an order from her."

Halcyon knocked on the wardroom hatch.

"Come in, Blithe."

The room appeared exactly like his wardroom, except it

smelled like flowers instead of the old-sock smell he'd become ac-
customed to in his quarters.

"Ma'am, Halcyon Blithe reporting as ordered, ma'am." Halcyon held his salute.

Midshipwizard Merand was pacing nervously when Halcyon
entered the room. She returned his salute. "Drop your pants and
stand at attention, Midshipwizard."

"Ma'am?" Halcyon couldn't believe what he just heard.

"Drop them now," she whispered the order out.

Turning beet red he did as instructed. Standing at attention,
he couldn't remember a worse day in his life.

"You have a problem, Mr. Blithe," she said, speaking quietly
and looking at his hips.

"Ma'am, I'm cold. I can't help how I am. What we are doing
right now is not proper." Halcyon couldn't remember being so
embarrassed.

"No, you idiot. Look at your thigh. You have the mark of the
demon on you," Alvena quietly said.

Halcyon looked down at the small demon head with horns on
his thigh. It had grown a bit larger than he remembered when he
looked at it months ago.

"The entire ship knows of your demon heritage. That's not a
problem, as hundreds of people throughout the navy have the
same heritage, especially among white-hairs. Your highly respected family wields great power in the admiralty. Their skills at
magic use are legendary in the cause for Arcania's freedom. How
can they not have told you about this special and feared mark and
what it means? Pull up your pants, man, and sit down." She sat as
well, kicking a chair out beside her for him to use.

"The mark wasn't on my thigh until I gained my magical
power," Halcyon said. "No one from my family has ever claimed
such a mark before. Naturally, since I'm an adult I don't appear
undressed around others at the castle. What does it mean?"

"How can you live in this modern time and not know about demon marks?" Alvena asked. "Everyone talks about them, especially when the month of demons occurs each year."

"My family hates its demon heritage," Halcyon said. "Seven generations ago a half-human, half-demon baby was born to the Blithes and the entire family has spent their lives trying to live it down. The family gives its sons and daughters extra instruction in fighting demons, but that's it. We have family magic items unusually effective in killing demons, but we never talk about what that demon blood does to us."

"I shouldn't be the one having to tell you this," Merand said. "Your father or your uncles should have done it if they found out about the mark. Sailors, especially sailors with no magical ability, are an extremely superstitious lot. In our navy, they have good reason, as our magic often attracts the attention of powerful enchanted creatures from the depths of the sea and the skies above. The older you get, the more that mark is going to look like a horned demon. What it means is that during times of stress there is a chance that you could turn into the type of demon that sired that half child so many generations ago. If any of the crew sees it, you're marked as a demon yourself. No one will want to serve with you. Normally, I'm supposed to report such marks. You would be given land duty useful to the navy, but you would never be allowed to officer a ship of the line."

"Why are you being so kind to me?" Halcyon asked. The thought of not being able to serve in the navy chilled Halcyon. He had denied himself his heritage for five years, thinking he would have to serve in the army. The proudest day of his life happened when his father told him he had come into his magical power. All he ever wanted was to serve in the Arcanian navy.

Alvena stood up and lifted her duty uniform. There was a large bandage tied around her slender waist. She lifted that to show the exact same mark Halcyon had on his thigh. It was a darker color and more of the demon's skull revealed itself on her mark.

"Don't let the crew see your mark. Tie a rag around your leg to keep it covered. You never know when some idiot of a superior officer will throw you in the water again." She was smiling when she said this to him. "It will be our secret until you turn into that fearful demon and we have to kill you. I'm told when the demons come into our bodies they have their own agenda and don't take kindly to others around them. Until then, when we dock get some tomes on demons. Know your enemy and they hold less fear for you. You have the makings of a good officer. I want to see you command your own ship. Someday I know I'm going to be doing the same. Carry on, Mr. Blithe."

He stood. "Aye, aye, ma'am." Saluting, he left her wardroom. There was a lot to think about. He shuddered, wondering about his fate, and the thought of turning into a demon filled him with a new fear.

IX

※ ※ ※

Feeding the Dragon

HIS MAJESTY'S ARTICLES OF WAR: ARTICLE IX

Dwarves, elves, gnomes, orcs, ogres, and any other humanoid race met in the line of duty or in battle shall be treated as a human and not an animal. If any officer, mariner, or soldier or other as aforesaid treats such individuals or acknowledged enemies as less than human on board His Majesty's ship, every such person so offending, and being convicted thereof by the sentence of the court-martial, shall be punished with death, or such other punishment as the nature and degree of the offense shall deserve and the court-martial shall impose.

The ship's hourglass hung on a wire off the mizzenmast. The lantern beside it lit the glass, showing the last grains of the hour sifting down to the bottom. Halcyon twisted the sand timer and promptly rang three clangs of the ship's bell to mark the heart of the late watch.

Lieutenant Pierce Solvalson commanded the night watch. He

was leaning on the port railing looking out to the sea. There wasn't a moon out, but the stars were providing plenty of light in the night sky.

For several nights now, Halcyon had worked with this lieutenant, who was only two years older than Blithe. Halcyon found him a friendly, talkative fellow. Right then there was a look of pain on the officer's face.

"Is there anything wrong, sir?" Halcyon asked.

"Mr. Blithe, you have no idea how lucky you are to begin your service on a dragonship of the line," the lieutenant said, continuing to look out to sea.

"I'm sure you are right, sir." Halcyon didn't know what else to say.

"You have no idea what I'm talking about, but I'm going to tell you," Pierce said as he turned to give an order to the waiting sailor. "Carstars, bring us up mugs of dunick, and hurry. We've got to feed the dragon in this hour and I want to be wide awake when that big dragon head slurps up its ration."

Dunick was a nasty brew made from blackened bread and oats with some herbs thrown in to cut the bitter taste. It was all the rage among the seamen and officers alike aboard the ship. Halcyon hated the vile mixture. He'd brought his own tea along and substituted his drink for the dunick whenever possible. However, he was going to have to drink with the lieutenant tonight.

"No, Mr. Blithe, you're lucky because you don't have to worry about splinters."

"Splinters, sir?" Halcyon stood by the lieutenant, clueless about where this conversation was heading.

"Splinters, midshipwizard, were almost the death of me when, not three years ago, I was a midshipman like yourself. I was serving on the frigate *Gold*. She was a captured Drusan fifth-rater and well put together," the lieutenant said with relish at the telling of his tale. "We were in a blockade off of the capital city of Easta.

The enemy decided they wanted to test our mettle and came sailing out, bold as you please, right at dawn. I'm guessing they
thought to catch us napping. Ten ships of the line, all filled with
Maleen troops, they were. They wanted to board us, but we
weren't having any of that."

Seaman Carstars came up from the galley with the steaming
mugs of dunick. Brewed constantly on the ship's stove, for the
night watch, the drink was credited with making the Arcanian
navy as powerful as it seemed to the enemy. Some said the longer
dunick brewed in the pot the better it was. Halcyon thought
burnt anything was vile, hot or cold.

Halcyon took a sip from his mug, hoping it would help the
headache he seemed to be plagued with lately.

"Carstars, gather the others and begin bringing the ten bales of
hay up to the forecastle. Don't forget the sack of sugar and the
bucket of tannin oil." Solvalson took a slug of his drink and continued with his story. "Come with me, Blithe, we'll go to the forecastle to supervise the feeding. Anyway, there I was, officer of a
thirty-pound blast-tube crew. We'd gotten off three shots as bold
as you please before the enemy got off one of theirs. That one
salvo from a second-rater was all it took. Look at this."

The lieutenant lifted his shirt to reveal a long row of jagged
scars all along his left side.

Halcyon had never seen so many scars on one man before.
Halcyon was shocked, standing there looking at the chest bathed
in the mainmast lanternlight. It was a mass of puckered ridges
etched along Solvalson's side.

The lieutenant put his shirt down and continued walking.
"Nasty, aren't they? Those are all from splinters. A thirty-pound
enemy ball hit between blast-tube ports and shattered our area. I
remember it like it happened seconds ago. The wood of the railing and blast-tube port exploded like a thousand arrows shot all at
once. My body hurled to the starboard railing, and everyone else

in my crew died in that blast. I woke up to see the surgeon taking out the last of twenty splinters. Some of them were longer than my arm. That's why you're lucky, Blithe."

"I don't understand. Enemy rounds can still crash into our ship," Blithe replied.

"Dragon hulls are flesh-and-blood. When a ball hits them, half the time they bounce even from close range. A sea dragon's hide is tough. When they do penetrate, the shots make a hole. It's only when they hit an oak support beam on the deck side that they cause splinters. Odds of that happening are low, making sailors serving on our dragonship of the line much happier about going into battle. No, Halcyon, from the lack of splinters alone you should consider yourself lucky to serve on this warship."

As they climbed the steps to the forecastle, Halcyon couldn't agree with the lieutenant more. Not for the first time that night, he rubbed his forehead. There was an aching pressure building there. Halcyon strongly suspected it was the cost of maintaining the weather spell for so long. He had headache powders in his sea chest, and he would take them when he had a free moment. Right now he wanted to help with the feeding process. He took the bucket of tannin oil from the sailor and dunked his hand into the thick stuff. He wanted to try mentally talking with the sea dragon again. With the touch of the oil, the familiar tingling of his body told him that the magical essence of the oil coursed through his veins. He started pouring the oil on the ten bales of hay.

"Seaman Carstars, don't use more than half that sugar bag. Spread it thinly over the oil trails Officer Blithe makes on the hay," Solvalson ordered.

"*Come eat,*" Halcyon mentally called to the dragon.

"*Smells good,*" the sea dragon answered back.

The huge dragon head delicately moved between the sail lines and dipped to pick up two bales at once. The head moved away from the deck and a high-pitched trilling came out of the dragon's nostrils.

"There we go; our old boy loves the taste of hay. It can't get it in the wilds," Carstars claimed.

"More sugar," came the thought from the dragon.

Halcyon could feel the sea dragon's pleasure. "Could I put on some more sugar, Lieutenant? It likes that."

"How in the world do you know that, Mr. Blithe?" the lieutenant asked.

"Well, I'm just guessing, of course, sir." Halcyon didn't want everyone to know he could hear the thoughts of the dragon. He could tell that many of the crew already thought he was odd enough just being a rope speaker. Additionally, the news that he had a demon mark, now covered with a bandage under his uniform, served to make Halcyon more secretive.

"Sure, why not? The dragon serves us well. Carstars, bring over a few more lanterns. I want you all to look at the dragon's head when it comes for two more bales. Mr. Blithe, go ahead and spread the rest of that bag of sugar on the hay," Solvalson ordered.

Halcyon spread the sugar evenly over the remaining bales as more lanterns brought increased light to the area.

The dragon's head dipped down for another helping. The light allowed the deck crew to see the long wattle under the dragon's chin. Its head frills were all dark green except for the first one. That spiky frill was paler than the rest of the frills all along its long neck. The light actually allowed the crew to see thick veins full of blood pulsing through the pale flesh.

"Notice the red veins on the top frill. You can see them on that one, but you can't see them on any of the other ridges along its neck."

"Are you feeling all right?" Halcyon mentally asked the dragon.

"I'd like to eat some meat soon. The fishing has been poor in this sea." The thought came back clear in the midshipwizard's mind.

"*These bales taste much better.*" The dragon's head moved back out of sight as it munched contentedly on the hay.

"Mr. Blithe, do you have any idea why that frill has turned pale?" the lieutenant questioned.

"Could it be because it isn't getting enough meat in its diet?" Blithe guessed.

"Well done, sir. Have you read Gray's *Anatomy of the Sea Dragon?*" Solvalson asked, showing some surprise at Halcyon's quick answer.

"I haven't yet, but I'd like to borrow a copy if the ship has one," the midshipwizard replied.

"After the watch, you can get the book from my quarters. You men hook up a winch off the mainmast. We'll haul up a pig for its dessert. It will gobble our pig and that frill will go back to its normal dark green color by tomorrow. Gray's *Anatomy* says a lack of meat slows the dragon down tremendously. We're going to join the blockade in a few days and we can't afford to sail into danger with a sick dragonship. Blithe, go down with Carstars and talk to the purser about the pig," Solvalson ordered.

"Aye, aye, Lieutenant."

The bow section of the upper blast-tube deck held stalls for steers, pigs, chickens, and goats. Fresh meat was preferred over salted beef and pork, and since a large supply of hay was necessary for feeding the dragon, the ship could carry more of other types of animals.

Lieutenant Josia Tinner was the ship's purser. His duty assignment gave him control of all the ship's stores and their use during the voyage. Up until that moment, Halcyon hadn't dealt with the man. Halcyon wasn't pleased at having to wake him up to get a pig. He knocked on the purser's hatch. Tinner rated his own billet, but it was next to the pens of animals. The smell was shocking, even with the pens cleaned twice a day.

"By the gods, who's knocking at my hatch?"

The man didn't sound asleep to Blithe. "It's Midshipwizard Blithe, sir. I need a word with you. Sorry to wake you."

The hatch flew open; there was a lantern in the man's hand. Tinner was fat, and even with the smell of the animals all about, a huge draft of rum struck Blithe in the face as the man opened the hatch.

"Whatta you trying to do here? Can't a man get some sleep after a hard day's duty?" The words came out slurred. The lieutenant had clearly been drinking hard in the last few hours.

"I'm terribly sorry to be waking you, sir. Lieutenant Solvalson wants a pig for the dragon's feeding."

"A pig! A pig needed at three bells of the night watch. That's just crazy. Get out of my hold!" The drunken lieutenant slammed the hatch shut in Blithe's face.

Blithe turned, holding up his lantern and seeing the pigs in question not ten feet away.

"I know what you are thinking, Midshipwizard. The halter's coming down any second and we could just take the pig while the purser sleeps in his cups. There would be hell to pay if we don't get his mark on the order. You could be fined for the pig and I could get a touch of the cat, if you get my meaning, Mr. Blithe," Carstars said.

The sailor was a twenty-year man. The patch on his left eye came from a battle ten years ago. The old salt wasn't about to take punishment duty for Halcyon's actions.

"I've been given an order and I will carry it out." Halcyon pounded on Tinner's hatch once more.

Tinner's voice bawled out over the sound of Halcyon's pounding. "By the gods, I'll have that middy's head on a stick!"

Not bothering with a lantern, Lieutenant Tinner threw open his hatch. This time he stood in shock, bathed in a red glow. A very angry Halcyon Blithe stood in front of the purser. All that drunken Tinner could see was the bright demon glow from

Blithe's eyes. Tinner's mouth became slack and he took several steps back into his berth. The angry red glow filled his room.

Halcyon, noting the power his eyes had on the drunk, strode into the man's berth. "I have orders to take a pig. Affix your mark on a loading ticket, Lieutenant Tinner." Halcyon didn't give the man time to think. Using the force of his anger, he pushed his face up to Tinner's. That did the trick. The man signed a form and handed it in fear to the midshipwizard.

The red glow faded from Blithe's eyes as he silently closed the hatch, leaving Tinner to recover.

"Those demon eyes come in handy sometimes, don't they, sir?" Carstars was smiling at the way Blithe handled the purser.

"Our purser wasn't at his best in the middle of the night. Go and cover the pig's eyes. The quicker we get it up and away the better, to my way of thinking," Halcyon ordered.

The hold cover came off and the crew on deck lowered a halter for the pig. With an empty sack of grain covering the big pig's head, the sleepy animal made little noise as it moved from one deck to another.

As Halcyon and Carstars came back on deck, the dragon scooped up the large pig in one quick bite.

"*Meat, tastes good.*" The dragon's thoughts were happy ones, but fading. The effects of the tannin oil were wearing off the midshipwizard.

"*Rest easy, dragon.*" Halcyon liked the feeding duty. The work made him feel closer to the dragon.

The dragon looked down at Halcyon and the rest of the crew. "*Weather magic, d . . .*"

Halcyon couldn't quite catch the last thought. The dragon gave an odd chirp and turned its head back away from the deck. It too knew that Halcyon couldn't hear its thoughts anymore.

"Blithe, I see you had no problem with our good purser, Mr. Tinner." Solvalson made it more of a question than a statement.

"He didn't like being woken up in the middle of the night," Halcyon replied. "It took a bit of talking to get the dragon's dinner. As you can see we accomplished your order."

"There's a bit more to the Tinner action than I'm sure you're telling me, if I know our Mr. Tinner." Solvalson shook his head, and Halcyon figured the lieutenant knew the purser would be drunk.

"Give me the lading ticket. If Mr. Tinner remembers things differently than you do in the morning, I will deal with him.

"The old dragon is properly fed for a few more days. You should have seen it in action at the battle of Sontal. I'd just been commissioned a lieutenant before that conflict. The action was fierce as two Maleen ships of the line, first-raters both, came upon us. Our broadside destroyed the port enemy. We must have hit their magazine. The other enemy warship was cleverer and we hadn't done much with our starboard broadside. That ship grappled us. Our dragon reached up and started plucking crossbowmen out of their rigging." The excitement in the lieutenant's voice was infectious as the crew around him hung on his every word.

"Our ship, sitting on the dragon's back, is higher in the water than normal enemy first-raters. They had a hard time getting to our deck. Normally, they use a huge plank called a corvus. It's got a spike on the end. They swing it over to an enemy ship and drop it down hard on the deck. The spike pierces the deck and holds the two ships together better than dozens of grappling lines. When they tried that with our higher ship, the corvus of theirs came down, but their deck was too low in the water. The end of the corvus never touched our deck. We just laughed at them as our double blast-tubes raked their decks, killing their troops.

"All the while the dragon was tearing away rigging and eating enemy crew by the dragon mouthful. Our blast-pikes worked hard that day, but the old dragon put the fear of the gods in the hearts of the Maleen. We made them surrender with hardly a loss to our side.

"Blithe, get back to the tiller. Our orders call for a starboard tack at four bells and I suspect we're near that time now. The rest of you men get on the mainmast lines for the tack," the lieutenant ordered.

Solvalson clearly enjoyed telling war stories, but duty called. The tacking maneuver took less than an hour and the rest of the night watch passed without any problems.

X

✣ ✣ ✣

Naval Battle Tactics, Lesson Three

HIS MAJESTY'S ARTICLES OF WAR: ARTICLE X

If any person in or belonging to the fleet shall make or endeavor to make any mutinous assembly upon any pretense whatsoever, every person offending herein, and being convicted thereof by the sentence of the court-martial, shall suffer death: and if any person in or belonging to the fleet shall utter any words of sedition or mutiny, he shall suffer death, or such other punishment as a court-martial shall deem him to deserve; and if any officer, mariner, or soldier on or belonging to the fleet shall behave himself with contempt to his superior officer, being in the execution of his office, he shall be punished according to the nature of his offense by the judgment of a court-martial.

Halcyon walked into the captain's cabin with the rest of the mid-shipwizards. A sense of wonder and almost dread filled his mind. The richly appointed cabin revealed many oak cabinets. A large oak desk and three stern chasers shared the back of the cabin.

Thirty-pounders presented themselves at the port side and the stern, but special tables allowed the tops of the tubes to support cabinets filled with tiny ship models.

"Gentlemen and ladies, please come all the way in and be welcome in my cabin," the captain said, waving the last of the midshipwizards into his private chamber.

The rest of the middies hustled into the cabin and Jason closed the hatch.

"While the steward fills glasses for all of you, I would like you to look at a luxury I give myself. I collect and make models of ships of the line," Captain Olden said, sweeping his hand around the room to show off the many glass cabinets filled with the tiny model ships.

"I've placed just a bit of water magic in each of these models and today we will use them for a lesson in tactics." As the captain talked he took out models from several different cabinets.

The midshipwizards circled around the large table at the center of the room. The table held a huge shallow pan filled with seawater. As the captain placed each model into the water, a green spark of enchantment lit up the hull of the ship and it stayed in place, floating on the surface of the water.

"At any point in time, if any of you have questions please ask them," the captain ordered. "The battle we'll display today is the famous battle of Ilumin Harbor fought almost twenty years ago. As you all should know from your academy training, schooners from Ilumin had reported a huge Maleen fleet approaching the capital on the fateful day."

As the captain spoke, he placed out perfect replicas of all the famous ships from that long ago battle.

Halcyon had a grandfather and great uncle in that battle and knew its history well.

"Was this the first time our navy faced dragonships of the line?" Mark Forrest asked the captain.

"Yes it was, Mr. Forrest, that's a good question," the captain replied. "I always put the dragonships out last as they are the most animated of the models I own." From a cabinet filled with dragonships of all ratings, he took out five dragonships and placed them in the Maleen line of battle.

"Legend has it that all five of these ships were first in the line of battle," the captain told the group. "But I've read accounts from the logs of both the Maleen ships and our own Arcanian vessels in that battle and the dragonships were spread to the front and middle of the line. As you know, that would cause them problems in the middle of the battle," the captain said, looking over the two lines of model ships floating in the tiny table-ocean. He was finished setting up the ships in the positions history reported them to be in at the beginning of the battle.

"Mr. Murdock, please review for the group the forces of the Maleen that you see before you," the captain asked of Ryan.

The midshipwizard coughed in nervousness. "Well, there were ten first-raters, among them the famous one-hundred-and-forty-blast-tube *Malua*, their fleet flagship. We would consider their first dragonships fifth-raters today, but twenty years ago they classified them as second-raters. Twenty more ships in the line were second-, third-, and fourth-raters. Ten frigates and ten brigantines were in a second Maleen line of battle behind the larger-rated ships. The Maleen plan of battle was to use their massive firepower to destroy the sailing capability of any warships coming out of port. Each of their ships had an unusually large number of Maleen marines. Then as now, they wanted to board the Arcanian ships and take them over that way."

"Very good, Mr. Murdock." The captain smiled at the midshipwizard and looked among the others, picking out Halcyon. "Mr. Blithe, please be so good as to detail the Arcanian side of this struggle."

Halcyon looked carefully at the mix of ships on both sides and knew the captain had gotten the order of battle perfect. He didn't need to look at the assembly of Arcanian models floating in their line to give the captain an answer. "The Arcanian royal fleet was in the harbor that day. Under the orders of Fleet Admiral Gray, they left the harbor in perfect battle order. Knowing the Maleen wanted to quickly approach and board them, the admiral gave orders to stay at maximum range and fire at will for as long as possible. In the days before, extra shot and blast gel had been loaded on all the Arcanian ships."

"Just the order of the battle line, Mr. Blithe, my little diorama will show us the way of the battle, if you please," the captain admonished Halcyon with a smile.

"Aye, aye, sir. The first-rater *Arcania*, the flagship of the fleet, led ten other first-raters out of the harbor, followed by ten second-raters. There were twenty frigates following them in the line of battle. The Arcanian fleet engaged the Maleen fleet at maximum range."

"Good answer, Mr. Blithe. Miss Merand, why was it unusual for the Arcanian frigates to be part of the main line of battle?" the captain asked.

"Normally, fifth-raters are ignored by the larger ships in favor of larger targets," she replied. "Frigates are usually used to tow away prize ships, or in the Maleen case, they approach and add the weight of their marines to an onboard melee. The ten to fifty-five blast-tubes from a frigate broadside are considered meager to the blasts of second- and third-raters."

"Excellent, midshipwizard," the captain praised her. "You are correct, our Admiral Gray knew he was outmatched, but placed his frigates in the line of battle knowing the nature of Arcanian ships. Now watch as the first exchange of blast-tube fire is acted out on our model here."

The captain waved his hand and the entire pan of seawater took on a green glow. From the north, the Maleen model ships strung themselves out into a long line and under battle sails moved briskly south. From the south, the shorter line of Arcanian ships stayed to the east of the enemy and sailed north, keeping a wide distance between themselves and the enemy.

The model ships were unbelievably real-looking. Their sails filled with wind. Their pennants and battle flags flapped in an illusionary breeze. The ships rolled up and down on the illusion-created roll of the ocean waves.

The Maleen dragonships were moving far faster than the other ships of the line. Those five living ships caught up to and blocked other ships as they passed them in the battle line.

Tiny puffs of smoke came out of the ships on both sides. The shots from the two lead Maleen dragonships splashed in the water in front of the lead Arcanian ship. The shots of the Arcanian ships struck the enemy dragonships. Puffs of smoke erupted from the models followed by holes in the hulls of the Maleen ships, while few of the Arcanian model ships showed damage from the Maleen broadsides.

The captain froze the battle when the lines had come midway through each other. All of the Arcanian ships appeared frozen with puffs of smoke belching from their port broadsides. The Maleen ships displayed erratic puffs from half of their starboard batteries. "Mr. Surehand, if you please, tell us what you have observed from this battle so far," the captain asked. He looked at his midshipwizards. Enthralled, the young officers were barely breathing as the battle unfolded before their eyes. Few had ever seen such use of magic.

"Well, sink me if I don't think the Arcanian ships are firing at least two times faster than the Maleen ships," Dart answered nervously. "I also think the Arcanian blast-tube shots are hitting the enemy more often than the Maleen shots are striking. The wall of iron shot fired by the flagship *Arcania* mauled those smaller dragonships. I noticed it's to the middle of the enemy line and almost untouched. Was it like that in the historical battle?"

"As you all know, the *Arcania* is the only first-rater of the Arcanian fleet that was sunk that day, but that happens much later in the day. I'll let the ships continue to battle against each other so we can see the now-famous actions of their dragonships. Mr. Argo." The captain was gesturing over the scene of battle, and the ships started moving and blasting out with their tubes. "Please tell us what happened to these dragons as we see the end of the battle lines come together."

"Like many of the ships of the Maleen line, the dragonships were crewed by inexperienced crew and captured crews from Toman and Drusan." Jason's speech slowed as he watched two of the dragonships ensnarling themselves, with the heads of the dragons snapping at each other and the friendly crews in the rigging of the other dragonships. "The five male dragonships got too close together and took a great deal of damage. They began fighting among themselves and fell hopelessly out of control. Soon they were blocking the fire of their other ships of the line. Signals from Admiral Gray ordered his fleet to ignore the dragonships and concentrate on any other ship coming into range."

While Halcyon watched, the dragonships moved about each other. He noticed that the Arcanian frigates purposely angled themselves quite near the dragonships. A sudden thought had him wonder what would happen if a frigate actually tried to ram the front of a dragonship. The dragonship would have only its bow chasers bearing on the frigate. It wouldn't sustain much damage, but the prow of the frigate would do mortal damage to the head and neck of a dragonship of any size if it managed to strike it. He didn't want to find out why it hadn't been done in all the battles he'd read about. There must be some good reason that he was too inexperienced to consider.

The naval battle continued slowly playing itself out on the surface of the water. By the time both fleets turned around and fired at each other once more, the dragonships were effectively out of the battle and captured by the last four frigates in the Arcanian line of battle.

Captain Olden appeared to enjoy the scene of the battle as much as his midshipwizards did. "History reports that there were two dragon speakers on those frigates and they were able to learn a great deal from those captured dragons. Very good, Mr. Argo, your knowledge of those dragonships is perfect," the captain said. "Now we'll watch the rest of the battle unfold."

Two more times the lines matched up and tore at each other. Each time the Arcanian ships fired faster than the Maleen ships and fired more accurately. In the last meeting, the flagship *Arcania* blew up in a huge burst of fire.

"That's the only thing I don't like about the battle." Captain Olden shook his head, smiling. "That's a difficult model to make and every time I go through that battle, I suffer the loss of that most excellent model. I should probably stop the battle before it explodes, but then we wouldn't be seeing the spectacular ending."

As the captain spoke, the ships of the Maleen turned away into the wind and unfurled their sails, running from the plucky Arcanian fleet still firing at them.

"Why didn't Admiral Gray give chase, Mr. Boatson?" the captain asked.

"It is the royal fleet's duty to protect Ilumin at all costs," Jacom answered quickly. "He couldn't be sure there weren't more enemy ships waiting for him to leave the area. One of the primary axioms of battle is to keep the defensive fleet between the enemy's target and the ships of the enemy."

"Quite right," the captain answered. "Well said. As you can see, the line of battle has served Arcania well. We fire faster and more accurately than the enemy does. We are usually outnumbered, but our experienced crews also help make up the difference between life and death. We place ships like the *Sanguine* at the back of the battle fleet, ordering dragonships to attack the rear of the enemy fleets. We rarely allow more than two dragonships in a fleet and always keep one to the front, usually the largest of the dragonships, and the other in the rear of the battle line."

As the captain spoke, the remaining enemy Maleen ships were far to the east. Frigates from the Arcanian line were cutting out and towing back ten Maleen ships of the line. None of the Arcanian ships were captured.

"I think that's enough of tactics today," the captain said, smiling to his young officers. "In the weeks and months to come we'll work out more tactics so that when all of you take command of your own ships and fleets, you'll know why older officers do the things we do. Dismissed."

XI

⚜ ⚜ ⚜

𝕽eading of the 𝕶ing's 𝕬rticles

"Move out, you slugabeds!" All the sleepy midshipwizards could feel Hackle's happy smile, even without seeing his nasty face. "You all know it's the fourth Harvestday of the month. Muster on deck for the reading of the Articles, that's the duty of the morning, get a move on!"

He's only happy when he's making us suffer, Halcyon thought as he placed his hat under his arm and walked out of the wardroom, ignoring Hackle's glare. He'd been up and ready for the muster long before Hackle's shout.

On the middle blast-tube deck, the marines were clearing away their hammocks and getting ready for the muster. They all made a point not to bump into Halcyon, even if he was a third of their age; he was an officer, after all.

As Blithe climbed up on deck, he tipped his hat to the forecastle in respect to the captain. He heard Midshipwizard Elan Swordson speaking to a cluster of midshipwizards.

"I tell you that demon spawn is going to cause us trouble. Mark my words, he's an unlucky midshipwizard. I don't care if he can rope-speak."

In his calmest voice, Halcyon asked, "Are you referring to me, sir?"

Elan spun around and they stood eye-to-eye. Elan was just a hair shorter than Halcyon, and almost as broad in the shoulders. He had a large paunch, where Blithe's waist was board-flat. There was just the faintest smell of wine on Elan's breath.

"Never you mind, young cockerel. Just keep out of the discussions of your betters. Get yourself to the mainmast with the rest of the children. The Articles are about to be read. That's an order, Middy." The sneering tone in Swordson's voice made it obvious what he thought of his fellow officer.

"Aye, aye, Midshipwizard Fourth Class Swordson." Blithe didn't want trouble with the slightly higher-ranked officer, but Swordson had been unusually argumentative of late. Halcyon walked to the mainmast and took a stance facing the forecastle like the rest of the crew. He noted the force-four winds and was pleased that his magic had made this voyage sunny and easy.

Unconsciously rubbing his temples—he'd been doing that a lot lately. He couldn't remember ever in his life having so many headaches.

"I saw Swordson giving you a dig," Tupper said, catching up to Halcyon. "You know you're going to have to do something about him."

"I've been thinking about my options with Mr. Swordson. I don't have a lot of choices if the man continues to talk about my family. I think I can ignore comments about myself, but the honor of my family is important to me," Halcyon answered back as the last of the men assembled for the Articles.

"Quiet in the ranks." Second Officer Griffon held the Articles for the reading. First Officer Wily and the captain stood next to her at the railing of the quarterdeck. Her voice washed clear and strong over the thousand men assembled on the deck below her. "By order of the Arcanian admiralty, the Articles of War shall be read every fourth Harvestday of the month to the entire crew. Reading these Articles prevents any sailor from saying they didn't know the rules by which we all serve our king and country. Article One . . ."

This was the first time he'd heard Officer Griffon read the Articles. He liked the quality of her voice. As she read the Articles, his mind drifted to his latest encounter. He tried to think of a way to stem the growing dislike Elan Swordson seemed to be developing for him. The demon-spawn remark was not a good thing to hear. Then, suddenly, he recalled a bit of advice his father had given him on his tenth birthday. In his mind, it was as if he were just hearing it now.

"Punch him in the face," his father said. "Sometimes you're going to encounter people, bullies mostly, that are just too stupid or bigoted to realize the error of their ways. Take them aside and beat the living tar out of them."

"But sir, what if they're bigger and stronger than me?" Halcyon remembered asking. That day a bully, the son of a soldier of the castle, had shouted at him. The bully was years older and much bigger than the young Halcyon.

"That doesn't matter at all, son. Some fights you're going to win and some you're going to lose. Defending your good name and reputation is important. Do it privately if you can and in the open if you can't. Nine times out of ten, in the odd chance when you fail, your foe will respect you for your effort. Mark my words, lad, you owe a duty to your superior officers, but in the orlop hold with the hatch shut between you and the crew, rank means nothing and honor can be established where it wasn't found before."

The midshipwizard shook his head, fondly remembering his father. The man was a warrior, but a gentleman as well. The Maleen took him away from Halcyon. That evil act called for some type of payment by the entire Maleen nation. Mr. Swordson would also have to change his manner, and Blythe's father's words of advice would help the son solve the problem he faced with the midshipwizard. He stood a little straighter and looked to find Swordson in the assembled group.

Halcyon concentrated again on what Officer Griffon was reading out loud.

"His Majesty's Articles of War, Article Twenty: 'All spies, and all persons whatsoever, who shall come, or be found, in the nature of spies, to bring or deliver any seducing letters or messages from any enemy or rebel, or endeavor to corrupt any captain, officer, mariner, or other in the fleet, to betray his trust, being convicted of any such offense by the sentence of the court-martial, shall be punished with death, or such other punishment as the nature and degree of the offense shall deserve and the court-martial shall impose.' . . ." She continued on, but Halcyon was again lost in his memories.

Halcyon remembered his brother Frank giving him a bare-knuckles lesson in the castle courtyard. Halcyon had been eleven and his brother fifteen. Halcyon tried unsuccessfully to punch past his larger brother's longer reach.

"Don't swing for the head all the time, Hal," his brother advised. "Everyone thinks they should aim for the face. Body blows are the thing to get the job done in a fistfight. The head is a smaller target and the hardest part of the body. When you're in a fight, go for the belly and chest. Your blows will land more often and you'll do more damage, mark my words."

His brother followed up by hitting him a good one in the gut.

Halcyon rubbed his belly, remembering how that blow knocked him to the ground. He didn't feel much like fighting any more that day. He remembered it with a grin. His brother now served as captain of a dragonship frigate fifth-rater off the eastern coast of Arcania. Halcyon hoped he was doing well.

Officer Griffon finished with the Articles and the captain took a step forward.

"Men, in two days' time we join our fleet in the blockade of Ordune. There'll be plenty of fighting and I imagine we'll take a prize or two."

The men gave a cheer at the thought of prize money.

The captain continued, "This morning we'll raise sails and I want record times from all of you. The crew that furls the sails the fastest gets an extra ration of grog tonight. The same goes for the port-side or starboard-side blast-tube crews who work the fastest. Officer Wily, beat to quarters."

The men cheered the captain again.

By now, Halcyon had the drill for furling and unfurling the sails down to a routine. All shifts of the crew practiced it every day. While the marines and some of the other crew moved to get the blast-tubes ready, the sail crews worked to configure the sails for what the wind and the battle situation called for. Today they would completely furl all of the sails. There were midshipwizards assigned to each mast with one for the port side and one for the starboard side of each mast.

"All right, you mainmast crews, we're going to be the first to-day to complete the duty." Blithe shouted this loud enough for the mizzen and foresail crews to hear.

Swordson, the crew leader of the foresail, looked back at Halcyon with a determined look on his face.

The drums beat the crew to battle stations and Halcyon started singing. He'd heard the rolling-home chantey several times, but this time he sang the chantey at a faster tempo.

Call all hands to man the capstan
See the cable run down clear
Heave away and with a will boys
For old Arcania we will steer
And we'll sing in joyful chorus
In watches of the night
And we'll sight the shores of Arcania
When the bright dawn brings the light

Rolling home, rolling home, rolling home across the sea
Rolling home to dear old Arcania
Rolling home, dear land to thee

His and Tupper's crews took up the tune and Halcyon's faster tempo. At first the mainmast crews were the only ones singing. The men hurried up the rigging and over the foot lines and the crews below pulled up the sails. The other two sail crews took up the chantey, but the mainmast crew held a big lead. The mainmast sails were the largest of the ship, but they had more men in their crews as a result.

Up aloft amid the rigging
Blows the loud exulting gale
Like a bird's wide outflung feathers
Spreads on high each swelling sail
And the wild waves cleft behind us
Seem to murmur as they flow
There are loving hearts that wait you
In the land to which you go

Rolling home, rolling home, rolling home across the sea
Rolling home to dear old Arcania
Rolling home, dear land to thee

Ropes slide faster; Halcyon touched the running rigging lines, giving them a plea to move at their best rate. He thought about pulling alongside the men, but his academy training told him that as an officer he wasn't to be doing the work of his crew.

He didn't know if his rope-speaking ability could make the lines move faster. He figured it couldn't hurt to ask the lines. All the while, the men pulled as fast as they could and sang the chantey. As the sails collapsed on themselves, the rigging crews tied them up in record time. A chance at another ration of grog was too good an occasion to miss, and everyone tried their best.

On the decks below, gel monkeys brought up jars even though they all knew the tubes wouldn't be fired that morning. Every beat to quarters required all the tasks of blast-tube firing even if it was just a drill.

Many thousand miles behind us
Many thousand miles before
Ancient oceans have to waft us
To the well-remembered shore
Cheer up Jack, bright smiles await you
From the fairest of the fair
And her loving eyes will great you
With kind welcomes everywhere

Rolling home, rolling home, rolling home across the sea
Rolling home to dear old Arcania
Rolling home, dear land to thee

With the last words of the chantey Halcyon and Tupper's crew were done. Tight to the sticks, the mainmast sails appeared perfectly furled. When they finished, the other two masts stood three-quarters furled. The crew on the mainmast gave a cheer.

Halcyon watched the mizzen crew finish its task. Swordson kept turning back to glare angrily at Halcyon, who stood with his arms folded across his chest staring evenly back.

The warship's chanter, a Master Chief Petty Officer Petree, came over from the mizzen crew to shake Halcyon's hand.

"Mr. Blithe, that was an excellent idea, you singing that chantey at a quicker tempo, that is. Using one the men all liked to sing, as well, was also a damn fine idea. Wish I had thought of it myself."

Halcyon turned red at the praise. "Why, thank you, Chief. I've been hearing your excellent singing for many days now and just used your good example for my sail crew."

Officer Wily walked over to add his compliments. "Well done, Mr. Blithe. Your sail crew won the contest by a good margin, thanks to you."

"You are too kind, sir. The men did all the work; I just gave them a small boost with my song."

"Did you use your rope-speaking ability to help things along?" Wily asked.

Halcyon stiffened at the remark, not really knowing if magical aid would be considered proper in the contest they'd just finished. "Sir, I'm still new to my meager abilities. I don't know if the rigging responded to my request or not."

"We will be going to full sails again in a moment. Continue to practice all of your skills, Mr. Blithe. The navy needs good officers like yourself."

"Thank you, sir." Blithe watched the first officer step back up to the forecastle as the trumpet signals ordered the crew to make full sails and the blast-tube crews heard the call to stand down from their weapons. The captain stood at the forecastle railing with a smile on his usually gruff face. Halcyon hoped the captain was pleased as well with his effort.

A hand grabbed Halcyon's shoulder and spun him around. "It was the demon's own luck that allowed you to win today, Blithe," Swordson bitterly complained as Wily went out of earshot.

Halcyon faced several smirking crew members as well as the angry Swordson. Some of his own crew were slow to the lines, wanting to hear what their midshipwizard would say.

"Mr. Swordson, after this duty, I think that you and I should inspect the blast-gel hold on the orlop deck. I know it's dangerous duty, but someone has to do it."

"Who made you a blast-tube master?" Swordson sneered back.

"If you think it's too dangerous, I'll understand," Blithe taunted.

With that, Swordson finally understood Blithe's real purpose in asking him down to the orlop. "No, I see exactly what you mean. I'll be there at the eleventh bell; you see that you're there as well."

They both went back to their duties and the rest of the morning work shift progressed as normal.

The eleven clangs ending the morning work shift sounded over the ship.

I'm feeling unusually calm, considering what I'm about to do, Halcyon thought as he headed belowdecks. As he was going down, Chief Fallow was coming up the stairs. The chief stopped on the stairs and looked up at Halcyon.

"You be careful of foul blows," Ashe whispered in Blithe's ear.

"Pardon me, Chief." Halcyon wasn't sure he heard Fallow correctly.

"If you didn't want the entire crew to know that you called out that young fool, you shouldn't have asked Swordson to inspect the blast-gel hold in front of your detail of men," Ashe said, still speaking in a hushed tone. "I said be careful of foul blows. I realize you're a Blithe and your sense of honor prevents you from striking a person in an evil way. Not everyone has the advantage of your family background and breeding. I've got seven gold on you walking out of the hold first, make us Lankshire men proud," Ashe growled at Halcyon.

Fallow moved passed the stunned Blithe. The midshipwizard had hoped to keep his encounter with Swordson quiet.

There was always a single marine guarding the blast-gel hatch. Today there were four men there and Corporal Darkwater was heading up the detail.

A stunned Halcyon stood in front of them.

"Fancy seeing you down here, Mr. Blithe," the smiling Darkwater said. "I've put on this extra watch to make sure no one disturbs your inspection duties. It wouldn't do to have blast gel exploding in the heat of a moment, now, would it, sir?"

"Quite right, Corporal. Has Mr. Swordson appeared?" Halcyon asked.

"No, he isn't here yet, I'll send him in when he arrives. If you pardon my saying so, Mr. Swordson has quick hands, but his gut is a target few should miss." Darkwater was giving him a grin, all the while appraising him up and down.

"Does everyone on the ship know he and I are inspecting the hold together?" The exasperation was clear in Halcyon's voice.

The marines all laughed at his words.

The corporal spoke for them all. "I suspect only the captain, Wily, and Giantson don't know by now. If they come into this knowledge, I'm sure your orders would have you reporting to them directly. Officers, as gentlemen, are not supposed to be doing what you're about to do. I've got two gold says you walk out of the hold first. There's a bucket of seawater behind the hatch. Be good enough to toss it on him just before you leave. I don't want to have to send a detail in there to pick him up and take him to sickbay. Luck to you, Midshipwizard."

He didn't reply. He just opened the hatch and walked into the hold. A good portion of the port side of the orlop deck was devoted to the storage of the blast-gel jars. Jars, sorted by their size, rested in large racks from floor to ceiling. As the jars were used up, the racks were taken down and stored along the side of the hold to provide more protection from enemy fire. Magical lights illuminated the area.

Halcyon could feel air passing through the racks as the special vents along the upper deck allowed cooling air into the hold. It wouldn't do to get the jars too warm.

Elan Swordson walked in and closed the hatch behind him. "Is that your cheering section outside the hatch?"

"I didn't tell the marines anything; this little inspection is between us. I didn't appreciate your words about my family this morning." Halcyon took off his uniform jacket and set his hat down on top of that. His actions made it clear what they were going to do.

"Well, this is a bit of unexpected pleasure. I am at your service, sir." Swordson started taking off his outer clothing as well.

"I would ask that nothing we say or do leave this hold, if you would, sir?" Halcyon took a fighting stance at the center of the hold. He faced Swordson.

"Nothing would give me more pleasure than beating you senseless. I suggest we both agree to not use magic or weapons. Is that agreeable to you?" Swordson asked.

"Agreed. And we'll break no bones or do anything to prevent us from serving on our next duty watch, if you'll agree to that?" Halcyon raised his fists and waited. He winced to see two slim daggers pulled out of Swordson's boot tops. He would have to get such daggers at the first port of call; they were a good idea.

"Agreed. Before I knock you senseless, I just want you to know that I don't give a damn about your family name. My family has been fighting demons for as many generations as yours has sailed the sea. I know the type of damage demon spawn can inflict. I don't think your demonic sort should serve on ships. When I become a captain I won't have your sort among the officers and crew." Elan started circling Halcyon. Blithe constantly turned on the balls of his feet and faced Elan.

Halcyon didn't let Elan's words sting him. More good advice from his father and his many uncles came to mind: "Whenever you're in a battle, do not get angry. When your foe makes you angry, you've lost. They try to make you go crazy in anger so that you lose control. You are going to lose enough battles as it is without giving them the tools to defeat you."

"I don't expect people to treat me differently because of my family history. I can't help the demon ancestor in my family's past. I'll prove myself a gentleman and gain whatever respect I can."

Elan closed in, jabbed with his left, and Halcyon easily blocked that blow. Swordson's right snapped out and smashed Blithe in the eye.

Halcyon took the blow and backpedaled, blinking back the pain. He moved back in toward Elan. He faked a right to his opponent's head and smashed his left fist in the man's gut.

Blows rained down from the fists of both men. Each was young and in good shape. For Halcyon's part, he concentrated on body blows. Elan constantly struck out at Halcyon's head.

Elan's guard went lower and lower as the battle progressed. His blows became weaker the more Halcyon connected with Swordson's big belly.

"You, sir . . ." Halcyon faked another blow to Elan's belly.

Elan, for his part, lowered his guard to block the blow he wrongly thought was coming.

". . . are no gentleman." Halcyon put all he had in his first punch at Elan's chin. He connected and the man flew back unconscious.

Halcyon stood over the unconscious body of Swordson. His breathing slowly returned to normal. Blithe sadly shook his head, not sure the fight had accomplished anything. His jaw and bruised eyes hurt like hell. Right then he didn't know what he'd do if Swordson continued to mock his family. He threw the bucket of water on Elan and the man sputtered in the water and sat up.

"Well, that didn't go as expected. You have a jaw of granite, Mr. Blithe." Elan rubbed his belly as he sat gasping against the port wall.

"I hope, sir, that we won't have to repeat this inspection." Halcyon still didn't know if it had been worth the effort.

Elan gave the other midshipwizard a grin, "No, I still haven't changed my mind, but I will keep a civil tongue in my head where it comes to Blithes. Allow me to recover a bit alone if you will."

"As you wish, Mr. Swordson." Halcyon walked out of the hold, but didn't feel like celebrating his victory. He had somehow hoped for a different type of ending.

The corporal was there with a tankard in hand. "It's a small potion from the surgeon for the winner. Drink it all down, even if it does smell like horse piss."

"Should we give it to Mr. Swordson?" Halcyon asked, as he smelled the nasty brew. "He's not in the best of conditions at the moment."

All the marines had big grins on their faces.

"No," Darkwater said. "We've got another mug for the loser. It smells even worse and has more of the curative powders mixed in the rum."

"How do you have this ready? Hold inspections don't usually end in bruisings," Halcyon asked.

"Oh, these types of inspections go on more than you would think. Hardly ever between officers, but oftentimes marines and sailors need to inspect the blast-gel jars. Well done to you, sir." The corporal was far happier about his victory than Halcyon was.

"If Mr. Swordson doesn't come out of the hold in a few minutes please be good enough to help him up," Halcyon requested of the marines. "I left him awake, but very wet, if you get my meaning."

"Oh, we understand. You can count on us to be discreet. After all, we are all gold pieces richer from your little inspection. Have a good day, Mr. Blithe," Darkwater said.

The woman grins too much, Halcyon thought as he went to his billet. He hoped Lieutenant Hackle wouldn't be screaming at the others just then.

XII

❧ ❧ ❧

Magical-Ways Drill, Lesson Four

HIS MAJESTY'S ARTICLES OF WAR: ARTICLE XII

If any person in the fleet shall find cause of complaint of the unwholesomeness of the victual, or upon other just ground, he shall quietly make the same known to his superior, or captain, or commander-in-chief, as the occasion may deserve, that such present remedy may be had as the matter may require; and the said superior, captain, or commander-in-chief shall, as far as he is able, cause the same to be presently remedied; and no person in the fleet, upon any such or other pretense, shall attempt to stir up any disturbance, upon pain of such punishment as a court-martial shall think fit to inflict, according to the degree of the offense.

"Yes, I know my cabin is very blue." Lieutenant Commander Wizard Daton Giantson smiled at the midshipwizards coming into his quarters. "We've discussed this before, but it bears repeating. I'm a water wizard and surrounding myself in the color blue increases my personal reserves of magic."

The class looked around at the larger versions of everything in the chamber. Large benches, a larger bed, larger sea chest—the room was filled with big furniture that dwarfed even the long tubes ready for firing along one side of the area.

"Your father's race, sir, giants I mean, they don't usually have magical abilities, do they?" Tupper asked as he sat on the floor of the cabin with the others. "I hope the question doesn't seem impertinent, sir?"

Giantson gave a deep laugh. At seven and a half feet, his cabin ceiling was the highest on the dragon warship. "No, young Haywhen, it's a natural question. I like talking about my parents. My father and mother met when he was not yet fully grown and she had just turned eighteen. They fell in love, as young couples do, and I was the result. As my father grew to his fifteen feet of height, they had to split up. They still correspond; he learned to write just to please her."

His blue robe held several strange designs on the sleeves and down the front. These same symbols appeared as wall hangings around the sides of the cabin. As he circled the area lighting blue candles, the designs on the walls and the ones on his robe glowed. A large golden pentagram marked the middle of the deck. The class sat all around it. When the commander stood at the head of the pentagram, it started glowing blue, lighting up the cabin and changing the yellow light of the candles to blue.

Giantson placed a blue candle at the middle of the pentagram and took up the last position on the floor with the other members of Halcyon's wardroom. It was their turn at magic lessons with the commander. "We'll take up again the nature of magic." Daton smiled and increased the light given off by the candles with a wave of his hand.

The room had a strange calming effect on everyone in it. Halcyon thought he could smell a strange spice in the air. "Commander Giantson, after the swimming demonstration I experienced the other day, could you teach us a floating spell?"

The rest of the group laughed uproariously at his question.

"Ah, yes, I only just became aware after the occurrence of Commander Wily's overboard lesson of the other day. All of you take out your notebooks if you will. The class can accommodate you, young Blithe. Young Driden, what would be the first component necessary in a floating spell? And tell us why, if you please."

Anne Driden was a pleasant-looking twelve-year-old. Halcyon hadn't seen her much, as she bunked in the female wardroom. "Every spell requires an opposite reaction of some type; I would think one would have to immerse oneself in water for every minute one wished to float above water. One could use a fly spell for the same effect if one had an airy nature."

"Exactly correct, young Driden," Daton said. "All of you have one of the earth, air, fire, or water natures as Arcanian wizards. Only Mr. Blithe has a dual nature of air and water. Such a dual nature stems from powerful parents with different natures. You, Miss Driden, would think of the fly spell because you are an air wizard. Young Argo, you are an earth wizard. Can you cast a floating spell?"

Always cheerfully smiling, quick with a joke or a friendly word, Jason Argo was a crew favorite. People liked working with him. He didn't have any problem answering the commander's question. "If I took the time to prepare the spell, I could cast it, but it would take most of my magical energy for a day. We earth wizards don't float very well for some reason. I can't imagine why." He scratched his head, looking befuddled, which got a laugh from everyone. They all knew that earth wizards sank like stones in the water.

"Yes, yes, quite true, young Argo. So we all know a nonwater wizard would use up most of his magical reserves casting a water spell. This is true of any wizard trying to cast a spell not of their nature. If I, as experienced as I am, try to cast an earth spell, it takes most of my magical reserve.

"Young Forrest, some spells have to be paid for far in advance, but spells like death spells can be paid for later. What happens if a wizard casting a healing spell doesn't do some destruction in the next forty-eight hours?"

At thirteen years old, Midshipwizard Mark Forrest was the biggest of his age group, almost as tall as Halcyon. Forrest was constantly lifting things, as he enjoyed the taxing of his strength. He prided himself on doing odd things with water and could juggle five spheres of water. "I'm told, as I've never done it myself, that a pressure builds in the mind and body of the caster. At first, it's barely noticeable. Hours or days later, depending on the power of the wizard, headaches begin. If, for some unknown reason, no payment occurs, the wizard goes mad and their body explodes inward from the pressure.

"Have you ever seen that happen, Commander?" Mark asked.

"Indeed I have. Prisoners taken in war don't have the chance to pay for spells they used before captured. Some of these prisoners die that way, not wanting to be captives. Let's get back to our floating spell. We know we have to immerse ourselves in water for as long as we would like to float. Paying for the magic happens before the spell occurs. I think you will all generally find that fire and air spells can happen with later payment, while water and earth spells must be paid for before the casting. There are exceptions to that general rule, but those are few."

The midshipwizards took notes on everything their commander said. Halcyon was starting to get just a bit worried about his weather spell, but he didn't want to ask the commander about it.

"So, young Haywhen, why do you think your friend young Blithe has a dual nature of air and water magics?"

Without hesitation, Tupper said, "Because he's the luckiest bleeding midshipwizard in this man's navy, that's why."

The class roared with laughter.

Commander Giantson just shook his head. He waited until they quieted down. "Luck aside, I was hoping you would mention the fact that our young Blithe here is the seventh son of a seventh son. That's a very magical occurrence, happening rarely. His nature has given him unusually large reserves of magical energy. It's certainly made him a rope speaker. The condition has allowed him to have air and water dual natures. I know we are embarrassing our young Blithe, but he will have to put up with it." The commander was giving Halcyon a reassuring stare. "Young Blithe, when did you come into your magic?"

"It was a little over eight months ago, on the day I turned sixteen. Why is it that I can do some magical spells even better than wizards who have been doing magic for years?" Halcyon asked.

"An excellent question, young Blithe," the commander said. "It has to do with our magical natures. I don't think young Surehand will mind if I speak of him out of his presence. He is of the royal family. They are all earth wizards of great power, nurtured to rule over the land. He has a terrible time with spells not of the earth. As this is our second class together, young Blithe, I've seen that you are more of an air wizard than a water wizard. You have unusually large reserves of magical energy allowing great use of air magic. When you are more experienced with spellcasting, the Arcanian admiralty will use your skills to make airships. Currently there are four other seventh sons of seventh sons working such magic. You will be surprised to know that all four of them are dual-natured air and water wizards."

The noon ship bell rang twelve times. Inside the cabin, several of the stomachs of the midshipwizards began gurgling in hunger.

Giantson laughed at his group of learning wizards. "You are all reacting to the bell. I don't want to get ahead of myself. First we will deal with the floating spell and then we will talk about why your stomachs are growling. Young Mactunner, do you imagine that you, as a water wizard, could do a floating spell without the use of material components?"

"Yes, Commander, I could do it just with the preparation and words. I could also just float myself without the use of magic." Andorvan Mactunner laughed at his joke. No one else got it for a few moments.

"Very funny, young Mactunner. He's admonishing us that we use magic far too much in our everyday lives." The commander got up and walked over to a large covered bowl. Taking off the cover, he revealed a large number of blast-tube shots. Each round ball of iron weighed just five pounds, and was used in the lighter blast-tubes on the forecastle and quarterdecks to blast away enemy in nearby enemy ships.

Daton continued, "For our next session I would like all of you to work on a simple floating spell that doesn't involve immersing yourselves in water for an hour and also doesn't use material components. Our young Blithe wants to be able to float in the water for hours on end without having the need to concentrate on the spell. Make sure your spells allow you to float for, say, eight hours. Now to the lesson at hand. All of you please stand by the bowl of blast-tube shot."

The commander walked over to the other side of the cabin and uncovered another bowl. This one had a pile of purple fruit in it. "For this lesson I need you all to be hungry. That hunger is going to make your magical task easier. These are zorvan fruit; they grow only in the mountains of my storm-giant relatives."

Daton took a bite of one of the fruits and the entire cabin filled with a mouthwatering fragrance. The smell alone was indescribably delicious. "You will find this fruit an incredible delight. It's usually very hard to get, but for this lesson, I've indulged myself. It's good to have relatives in high places." Smiling, he finished the fruit in front of his class. They were all drooling at the thought of eating one of these new taste treats.

"Young Blithe, you are our newest student. Please determine what you think you have to do to summon one of these fruits to your hand from across the room."

Halcyon answered without having to think much about the problem. "Every magical action requires some type of equal and opposite reaction. I can throw one of these iron balls in the direction of the fruit. If I concentrate on the fruit as I throw the shot, I think I can bring one to my hand. My hunger helps the spell as I have a need to eat."

"Excellent and totally correct, young Blithe. I want all of you to try this lesson. Don't worry about where your shot lands. I will prevent the navy's deck and furniture from denting. The sooner you all begin, the sooner you all eat." The commander stood against the wall with his big hands outstretched, ready to cast cantrips to catch the iron shot.

Tupper was the first to pick up one of the round balls and throw it toward the fruit. He kept his hand out, and as the shot passed over the top of the fruit one of the purple spheres appeared in his hand. He immediately munched down on the fruit with great relish.

Instantly the air filled with iron shot. Soon everyone but Midshipwizard Forrest ate a fruit they summoned to hand. After the tenth attempt, Daton shook his head at Forrest's efforts.

"Tsk, tsk, tsk, young Forrest. You had quite a bit to eat before you came to class today, didn't you?" Daton asked.

"Sorry, Commander. I heard the lesson was going to be through mealtime and I didn't want to go hungry so I ate. I don't seem to be able to summon the fruit to hand." The signs of his embarrassment were clear in the slumped shoulders and downcast face.

"Class, note the trouble our young Forrest is having. Your need for the magical effect tempers the shape and power of your magical spell. Our young Forrest isn't hungry at all. Thus, he doesn't need a fruit and can't summon the proper magic to bring it to hand, even though the spell is very simple. All you have to do, young Forrest, is discover another way to motivate yourself."

Suddenly, Mark's face lit up. He threw the shot and a fruit instantly appeared in his hand.

"Well done. What allowed you to find the way of the spell, young Forrest?" Daton asked.

"All I had to do was think about the ribbing I would take if I was the only one of the entire class that walked out of the cabin not able to summon a fruit to my hand. The magic came to me right away," said the smiling Forrest.

Laughing, Daton opened the hatch to his cabin. "Ridicule isn't the best of motivators, but it allowed you to succeed, which is a good thing. We will now all take one of the shots up to the forecastle and attempt the summoning of another fruit from there. Quickly move out, all of you."

"Do you want me to carry yours, Anne?" Halcyon asked, trying to be a gentleman and maybe catch Driden's favor.

"It's five pounds, Blithe," she said disdainfully. "My war targ weighs more than that. Just get a move on and get out of my way, you great lummox."

Halcyon knew she came from the mountain clans near the city of Gold. He chided himself for trying to treat her as he would a lady of his family's castle. Ship women didn't want their hands held.

The class positioned themselves at the stern railing.

Daton spoke to them with reassuring words. "Keep the image of the fruit in your mind. You know what it looks like, smells like, and feels like. Throw your shot as hard as you can at the mizzenmast. I will take care of where your shot lands. The shot you hold in your hand is far heavier than the fruit, so your spell should be easy to accomplish. Begin when you are ready."

Once again, the commander stood to the side, by the mizzen-mast. His hands were out and he would be using his magic to halt the progress of the blast-tube shot.

Halcyon felt good about performing this spell. He was a little worried about the floating spell, but he didn't let that bother him for the moment. He threw the five-pound shot overhand at the mizzenmast and a fruit appeared in his hand. Halcyon noticed that others had the same result. The fruit was delicious and he relished every bite, finishing it to its core. Even Forrest summoned his fruit and ate.

The commander used his magic to pile the shots by the mast. "Well done, all of you. I can't remember when I've had an entire group successfully summon from on deck. I want to try just one more thing. All of you are very familiar with the equipment found in your sea chests. Pick up one of the shots and summon something from your chests."

Each of the midshipwizards picked up a shot and threw it toward the stern. Halcyon imagined his telescope as he threw. Instead of finding it in his hand, a burning pain shot through his mind and he fell to the deck screaming out.

"Mr. Blithe, what did you do?" Daton asked, kneeling at Halcyon's side. The rest of the class clustered around the pair on the deck.

"I don't know. My head is on fire. I tried summoning my telescope. The second I threw the shot, I felt this terrible pain in my skull. It still hurts." Halcyon was sitting on the deck rubbing his head.

Commander Giantson snapped his fingers, and Halcyon's sea chest appeared on the forecastle. The large Blithe coat of arms glowed brightly on the lock of the chest. "It's warded, Mr. Blithe. Someone in your family must have told you how to open your chest and not be hurt by the magical protections laid in your family's coat of arms?"

"Yes, I just say a special word and the chest opens to my touch," Halcyon answered back.

"I'm sorry. Such chests are not usually protected." Daton snapped his fingers again and sent the sea chest back where it came from. "We will need to talk about wards in our next session. In my ignorance I've caused you harm. In the future when you try to summon things from your chest, say your opening word as you cast the spell. The wards on the chest will then allow you to summon your needed item. Let me heal you."

Daton's large hands turned bright blue and his fingers touched Halcyon's skull. All the pain of his summoning spells instantly went away. The smile on the commander's face dropped away.

"What is this spell I sense? It has been causing you discomfort for many days now." Daton stood up and began making magical passes, throwing handfuls of water out in front of him and around Halcyon.

A thick blue thread appeared, wrapped many times around Halcyon's body. The thread flowed up into the sky and disappeared in the far distance.

"What have you done, child?" Daton gasped.

The pain of the summoning spell gone, Halcyon stood up. He looked down at his body to see the thick threads of his own weather spell. He realized what the great pressure was that constantly squeezed his body. It was his own spell; he'd never seen the threads of it at work.

"I didn't know there would be a problem, sir. I just wanted good weather for my first duty. I figured I could release the spell when I made our first port of call. That way I could weather the storm in a safe harbor. I just wanted sunny days and a fair wind, sir." As Blithe spoke he knew his act was a grave mistake.

All of the other midshipwizards gasped at Halcyon's words. They now understood what the enchanted thread around Halcyon meant to them and the *Sanguine*. Each of them turned ashen at the thought of what was to come.

Suddenly the sea dragon screamed a warning as it realized what was about to happen.

"Young fool, you could have doomed us all. Tupper, go sound out the storm warning on the ship's bell. All the rest of you take your storm stations. Rig for heavy weather," Commander Giantson ordered the group. They dashed to do his bidding. "You come with me to the quarterdeck and don't do a thing to your spell, that's an order."

Tupper went for the ship's bell. There were few other reasons to clang the bell than to mark the hour. One of them happened with sea burials. The other was the warning of heavy weather. When the bell clanged repeatedly, the entire ship's crew rigged for heavy weather. The tones of the bell warned the entire ship of the coming danger. The clangs reverberated even down into the orlop deck.

With the clanging of the bell, Captain Olden came up on deck in full weather gear. He looked into the sunny sky and noted the force-four winds on the sea. He didn't observe a reason to sound the emergency bell. Then he noticed the blue thread flowing from his quarterdeck into the sky. What was that?

Climbing to his quarterdeck, the captain saw Midshipwizard Blithe and Lieutenant Commander Giantson at the mizzen. Olden's experienced magical eyes noted some type of weather spell around Blithe.

"Giantson, explain this," the captain commanded.

"I believe Midshipwizard Blithe placed a weather spell on himself as he arrived at the ship. For the last nine days he's been controlling the weather to bring us sunshine and fair winds." By now, Giantson was also in a rain slicker and storm hat. He'd summoned the clothes to him with a snap of his fingers.

Halcyon suspected he was in terrible trouble, but still wasn't sure why.

"Lieutenant Durand, trumpet the sails furled. Keep the forestaysail and the mainstaysail taut so that we can keep headway in the storm to come. Rig for force-twelve winds, raise the lifelines fore and aft," Olden shouted to the lieutenant.

Suddenly Halcyon knew what he had done. The destruction of the dragonship might happen because of his spell. "Sir, I can still hold the spell. Can't we reach safe harbor and then have me let the spell go?"

"Mr. Blithe, if we survive this storm you will be court-martialed for putting this ship in grave danger. No one knows how strong this storm is going to be. It's possible there will be no safe harbor available to any ship in the coming storm. I will not risk putting the Arcanian fleet in danger from your ill-advised action. Prepare to release your spell and pray to whatever god you believe in that we don't all die in the next twenty-four storm-tossed hours."

XIII

⚜ ⚜ ⚜

The Storm

HIS MAJESTY'S ARTICLES OF WAR: ARTICLE XIII

If any officer, mariner, soldier, or other person in the fleet shall strike any of his superior officers, or draw, or offer to draw, or lift up any weapon against him, being in the execution of his office in an unexpected manner, on any pretense whatsoever, every such person being convicted of any such offense, by the sentence of a court-martial, shall suffer death; and if any officer, mariner, soldier, or other person in the fleet shall presume to quarrel with any of his superior officers, being in the execution of his office, or shall disobey any lawful command of any of his superior officers; every such person being convicted of any such offense, by the sentence of a court-martial, shall suffer death, or such other punishment as shall, according to the nature and degree of his offense, be inflicted upon him by the sentence of a court-martial.

Standing on the quarterdeck, Halcyon couldn't remember a time when he felt more miserable. In trying to make things easier for himself on his first duty, he'd only made things worse. Only the words of his father kept him from crying like a baby. He thought about a day years ago, when he couldn't have been more than nine. He'd done something wrong; Halcyon couldn't remember what. He had an image in his mind of his father kneeling down, hugging him, and saying, "Son, never cry in front of your crew or family. Crying is a personal thing. I've cried to be sure, but such an act is between the gods and you. That sacrifice of salty tears unnerves a man and makes him less in the eyes of his crew and others around him. Part of being a man is showing strength in times of trouble. I know it's hard on you now, but try to be a man and shed your tears in private."

Halcyon always followed that advice, except for the one time when the family had a service at the marking of his father's death. They had no body, as he was lost at sea. The family placed an Arcanian flag and the crimson pennant of House Blithe in the tomb of his family to mark his death. He was the first of the seven brothers to pass away. All six uncles and the sons serving in the navy took shore leave on orders of the king to attend the service. Tears ran down everyone's face that day. That memory gave him strength now. He squared his shoulders back and held his head high. Halcyon wasn't about to show how bad he felt in front of his captain and crew.

Shaken out of his memory, he heard the shouted order of the captain.

"Chanter, sing out Strike the Bell," ordered the captain, in a calm voice clearly heard by the chief on the deck below.

The stunned man had never heard the captain request a chantey. The man's clear voice rang out. Immediately, the entire sail crew started singing with him.

Aft on the poopdeck
Walking about

There is the second mate
So sturdy and so stout
What he is thinking of
He only knows himself
Oh, we wish that he would hurry up
And strike, strike the bell.

Strike the bell, second mate
Let us go below
Look away to windward
You can see it's going to blow
Look at the glass
You can see that it is fell
We wish that you would hurry up
And strike, strike the bell.

Every Arcanian child knew the song the men took up. It was a work chantey sung only when a storm approached or rain fell hard from the skies. The crew didn't show its surprise at the singing of Strike the Bell. It didn't matter to them that it was sunny and clear. If the orders were to get into rain gear and strike the sails, then they would follow those commands no matter what the weather looked like. The ship bustled with energy as men took to the three masts, quickly furling the sails. Singing that song caused men to go below and put on their rain gear. That tune marked the worst weather possible, and even though it was a lighthearted ditty, it signaled dangerous times.

The captain relayed more orders to the lieutenant on watch while the sailors continued to sing.

Down on the main deck
Working at the pumps

There is the larboard watch
Ready for their bunks
Over to windward
They see a great swell
They're wishing that the second mate
Would strike, strike the bell.

Strike the bell, second mate
Let us go below
Look away to windward
You can see it's going to blow
Look at the glass
You can see that it is fell
We wish that you would hurry up
And strike, strike the bell.

The lieutenant ordered the crew to keep the forestaysail and the mainstaysail taut. Men were lashing down the thirty-pounders on all of the decks to prevent the heavy metal tubes from shifting in high seas. All the while, the sea dragon kept roaring the warning of danger. The crew constantly looked about for the harsh weather to come, but clear blue sky greeted them from horizon to horizon.

Belowdecks, the danger of fire in the violent seas forced the extinguishing of the cook fires. There would be a cold meal that night, if there was a meal at all. During high seas, few sailors felt like eating as they wondered if their ship would survive the blow.

Without moving an inch from their commanding positions on the quarterdeck, the captain, First Officer Wily, Second Officer Griffon, and the other officers serving in the day's duty all magically changed into rain gear with the snap of their fingers.

Blithe heard Griffon say, "I'm going forward to check on the lashing of the tubes, Captain. The ones on the forecastle are squared away."

"Carry on, Second Officer, carry on," replied the captain.

The men sang on.

Aft at the wheel
Poor Anderson stands
Grasping the spokes
In his cold, mittened hands
Looking at the compass
The course is clear as hell
He's wishing that the second mate
Would strike, strike the bell.

Strike the bell, second mate
Let us go below
Look away to windward
You can see it's going to blow
Look at the glass
You can see that it is fell
We wish that you would hurry up
And strike, strike the bell.

Lifelines were fastened to cleats running the length of all three upper decks on both the starboard and port sides. Coils of rigging ropes, their ends looped, were ready by the railings in case of a man overboard. Leather covers sealed all the ship's hatches on the exposed decks. The jolly boat and the longboat received extra lashings. The dinghy remained as normal, ready for launching in an instant. The men worked at a frantic pace, spurred on by the tempo of the foul-weather chantey.

Forward in the forecastle head
Keeping sharp lookout
There is Johnny standing
Ready for to shout
"Light's burning bright, sir
And everything is well."
He's wishing that the second mate
Would strike, strike the bell.

Strike the bell, second mate
Let us go below
Look away to windward
You can see it's going to blow
Look at the glass
You can see that it is fell
We wish that you would hurry up
And strike, strike the bell.

The crew on the mizzensails kept giving Halcyon odd looks. The wizard lieutenants could see a weather spell wrapped around the midshipwizard, but they hadn't heard yet what could happen from the effect of that magical incantation.

The stern glares of Captain Olden and Second Officer Griffon kept people from asking Blithe what he was doing standing by the ship's wheel instead of by his crew on the mainmast.

Daton snapped his fingers and Halcyon was dressed in a rain slicker. "You say you've maintained this spell for nine days?"

"Yes, sir," Halcyon replied.

"Remarkable. I could maybe hold such a spell for ten days before suffering physical harm. I see the strands of the incantation bind your chest and head. Didn't you feel them constricting you?" Daton asked.

Before he could answer, the captain spoke. "Mr. Giantson, the midshipwizard is not to be a subject of your curiosity. I don't care that he is a seventh son of a seventh son right now. Take your duty station and help my ship survive the coming storm."

"Sir, yes sir," Daton replied, and moved to his duty station at the other side of the wheel.

Aft the quarterdeck
The gallant captain stands
Looking to windward
With his glass in his hand
What he is thinking of
We know very well
He's thinking more of shortening sail
Than striking the bell.

Strike the bell, second mate
Let us go below
Look away to windward
You can see it's going to blow
Look at the glass
You can see that it is fell
We wish that you would hurry up
And strike, strike the bell

As with most chanteys, when the song played itself out and the chanter gave his finishing yodel, the ship appeared rigged and ready for the worst weather. Only a short crew stayed on each deck to handle damage from the storm. The rest were below. By now, word had spread about what Blithe had done. The curious looks of before were changed to angry glances.

Six men, three to a wheel, stood ready to steer the ship into the storm's waves.

First Officer Wily said, "We're ready for the storm, Captain."

Once again, stern Captain Olden faced Halcyon. "In your colossal ignorance, Mr. Blithe, you've put your ship and crew in deadly danger. If we survive this storm, a storm that you caused, you will face a court-martial. Release your hold on the weather and stand at your duty station. You will watch what your carelessness has done." The captain turned his back on Blithe.

"Aye, aye, sir" was all Blithe could answer. He released his hold on the sky. The dark blue thread wrapping around his body and flowing into the sunny sky vanished. Halcyon couldn't help sighing in relief as a great pressure lifted from his chest and skull.

Up until that moment, the choppy waves had a few white crests from the force-four winds Halcyon had purposely caused. With the releasing of the spell, the entire sea turned white with spume.

"By the gods, we're dead men," came a cry of dread from the forecastle. It was the worst of storms, with force-twelve winds that showed the white sea.

Griffon shouted, "Lieutenant, take down that man's name. We will have quiet in the ranks!"

The sky directly above the ship erupted in black clouds. The dark mass swirled round and round, growing in size until it blotted out the sun and the dragonship found itself cast in darkness. Black, lightning-laced storm clouds filled the sky from horizon to horizon. Lightning and a sheet of rain crashed into the sea and the ship.

"Storm lanterns lit," Wily shouted above the growing din, to all three decks. Large magical lanterns, brought up from below, now hung from the masts.

The sea dragon roared, but in seconds the wind drowned out even the loud roars of the beast.

Halcyon had never heard such a wind. It groaned in a mad circle around and then over the decks of the ship.

The sea was thick in white spume.

The wind tossed it everywhere.

The deafening howl of the air smashed against ears in maddening buffets.

From the choppy waves of minutes ago, the sea rose about the ship in walls of white, deadly water. Instead of the large ship of the line being master of the sea, it became a storm-tossed matchstick at the whim of every mountainous wave. The great size of the sea dragon became a detriment as it rose and fell among the titanic waves. The sea dragon's body bent cruelly from the wave action and the bruising force of tons of water smashing over its sides. Every time the dragonship moved between mammoth waves, the action of wind and water worked to bend the sea dragon, wreaking havoc along its body.

The captain had the ship turn in to the waves. Only this way could the ship have a chance of surviving in the storm. The two weather sails helped the ship, but the sea dragon itself also swam strongly, meeting each wave head-on, often rising to the top of the mountainous wall of water.

Over the roar of the wind, the ship's trumpet blared out orders to generate the talgon deck spell. The deck glowed the color of the moon as strategically placed wizards cast their magic to keep the water just off the deck, insuring the footing of the crew as they battled the storm. Magic couldn't stop the tons of water from smashing down time after time, but it could force the water to slide just inches off the deck, allowing the water to roll off the sides of the ship.

The talgon spell was the first one Halcyon had learned at the academy. The brutal power of the waves still crashed over the ship, but, with magically enhanced footing, the crew stood a better chance of surviving on the storm-tossed decks.

The miserable Halcyon stood on the deck clutching the life-line, watching walls of white water smash down on them, battering mind and body. As a midshipwizard, he lent his magical strength to the lieutenants who controlled the talgon spell.

"Don't belong here, don't belong here." The sea dragon's mental anguish blasted into Halcyon's mind.

At first, he didn't have the slightest idea what the dragon meant. Then he realized the dragon wanted to be under the water in its natural element. It hated being in the storm-tossed sea. Blithe's guilt grew as he realized that his action caused pain to the dragon as well as his crew. What a fool he was. *Gods, please don't take the* Sanguine, *take me but leave the ship and crew alone,* he prayed to the dark heavens above.

His only reply was more lightning and thunder from the angry sky.

After the first hour, numbness set in for everyone. Huge ship-tall walls of water continued to pound down hard over the decks. Every man was thinking the same thing repeatedly: *When will it end?*

Breathing became difficult as there was no relief from rain, spume, and waves beating and beating some more against the ship and crew.

Halcyon was across the deck when his crew took up the shout "Loose tube, loose tube!" One of the blast-tubes on the port side tore loose from its bindings and rammed itself across the deck into another blast-tube on the starboard side. The tons of metal could break masts and crew in its deadly slashes as its weight created a path of destruction wherever the storm tossed it.

Crewmen drew back, wanting at all costs to avoid being in the path of the hurtling weapon. Ignoring the danger, Halcyon lunged toward the deadly mass of metal. He mentally ordered the nearest coils of rope to grasp the blast-tube and hold it fast against the port railing. He didn't have a chance in the world of stopping the tube from its mad dash by himself, but his rope-speaking talent could do the work his body failed to do. Rope rose at his order, taking on a life of its own. The strands wrapped themselves around the onrushing tube. Attached to the railing, the ropes tugged with energy Halcyon gave them from his own inner reserves. The deadly motion of the tube stopped. In heart-beats the heavy artillery was fastened down and not going any-where as coils of rope wrapped themselves round and round the piece.

Lieutenant Solvalson shouted in Halcyon's ear over the roar of the storm, "Check the starboard blast-tube. The one this tube struck. You're a damned idiot, but that last bit was good work!"

Halcyon went over to the blast-tube. He found its carriage smashed from the loose tube crashing into it. He and the mast crew were easily able to tie it down tighter, even with the action of the storm battering them hard. The ropes around the blast-tube seemed to want to hold the weapon down as the crew and Halcyon worked to make sure the tube was secure. As they la-bored, some of the crew shouted at him, but Blithe couldn't hear a word they were saying over the roar of the wind.

In the third hour of the storm, half of the leather hatch cover ripped up and bent double on itself. Waves of water flooded down into the ship in the minute it took to refasten the cover. The hatch was tall and above the protective action of the deck spell. As the crew worked to restore the hatch, the lieutenant bent to-ward Blithe.

Solvalson shouted, "Get to the orlop deck, and check the dragon's heart and liver for sea damage. Hurry, man!"

Blithe moved as fast as he could, but he was bone-tired from the beating of the waves. Closing the quarterdeck hatch behind him was a relief as he went belowdecks. At least he could breathe easier out of the storm.

The heart of the dragon was one of the two uncovered organs

kept exposed on the back of the beast. It and the liver were the reasons the dragon wouldn't submerge itself. If any quantity of seawater covered those organs, the sea dragon would submerge itself under the water, destroying the ship and killing the crew. Halcyon was glad to see no water on the lower deck by the men manning the pumps. Their action was keeping the water away from the orlop deck. Special vents in each of the upper and middle blast-tube decks took any water that fell there to the starboard and port walls. The pumps would then take the water out of the ship and over the side.

Blithe raced to the heart chamber. Men clustered around the stairs of the orlop waiting for word on the storm. Halcyon ignored them. Moving to the center of the orlop deck, he found the heart-chamber hatch open.

The light of the chamber streamed out into the darkened hold. Magical lights constantly lit the heart chamber as a safety precaution. As he entered, Blithe thought it odd to find the hatch unlocked. There were two ways into the heart chamber and the keys to both hatches hung by their locks. Throwing open the hatch, he saw someone's back as the crew member left through the other hatch, but he could see only the officer's rain slicker and couldn't tell who it was.

"Hold up there, what are you doing down here?" Halcyon asked, but the other hatch closed before the person could answer.

The heart chamber was roomy, with ten feet around the huge beating heart. Halcyon hadn't been in this chamber very much. The blood-pumping organ of the dragon pulsed in the middle of the room. Thick, ropy red veins covered the organ and special steel clamps prevented the dragon's outer flesh from growing over the heart, as it normally would have in the wild.

Halcyon stood scanning the chamber, relieved to see no water on the deck.

The organ itself was ten feet tall. Magic from the ship's doctor caused the heart to enlarge to many times its normal size. When a sea dragon became a ship of the line, growth spells cast over the heart dramatically increased its size. As the creature grew older, the heart had to pump blood through the walls of the ship. Forcing the heart to a larger size allowed the dragon to maintain its health even with the increased flow through walls of flesh it didn't have to handle in its wild state.

As Halcyon watched the heart pump away, an odd odor that didn't belong in the chamber caused him to inspect the heart. Walking around the organ, he was shocked to see that someone had covered one side of the lower portion of the organ in blast gel.

The heart beat faster, as the dragon struggled to survive in the storm. The sea creature's organ grew hotter. Once it got hot enough—and Halcyon suspected that time would be soon—the gel would ignite, destroying the heart and killing the dragon.

Halcyon knelt by the heart. From his academy training with the gel, he knew he couldn't just scrape it off. Any forceful touch on the gel caused it to ignite.

The waves of heat from the heart muscle working hard told him the gel could explode at any time. If he didn't do something, and soon, the dragon and every man and woman aboard the ship would be dead.

Halcyon did the only thing he knew to prevent the gel from blowing up. He mentally said the opening word to his sea chest and summoned the crystal vial hidden in the chest. The vial appeared in his hand. The memory of the words of his dear mother explained the vial's use.

"Halcyon, keep this vial safe." She handed him the oddest vial he'd ever seen, green and glowing. It was a tiny thing in the palm of his hand—pixie work, he was sure. "These vials are gifts to our family from the pixies of the Tanar forest. Once, long ago, our ancestors did them a favor. The pixies have always rewarded us by giving each child a wishing potion. It's become a Blithe tradition, as new members join the navy, for a vial to appear for them, a gift of the grateful pixies. The magic of this vial is high magic, son, and very powerful. Think carefully on what your need is as you smash the vial. Whatever you wish for happens instantly, but you will pay a magic cost from your inner reserves of strength. Don't use it unless you have to and keep the wish simple. The magic in the vial works only once. At the academy, spend time reading about the nature of wishes. You can't alter what's already happened, but often you can fix recent past actions with an intelligent wish."

The ship rocked sideways in the storm, and if anything, the heart began to beat even faster.

Holding the tiny crystal in his hand, he thought about his options. Could he run to fetch Olden or Giantson before the heart exploded? No. Exhausted, could he use some type of air or water spell to rid the dragon's heart of this damage? No. He thought about Article III then, saying it out loud, going over the meaning of the words. "His Majesty's Articles of War, Article III states that the use of high magic is expressly forbidden on any of His Majesty's ships. 'If any officer, mariner, or soldier or other aforesaid uses high magic on board His Majesty's ship, every such person so offending, and being convicted thereof by the sentence of the court-martial, shall be punished with death, or such other punishment as the nature and degree of the offense shall deserve and the court-martial shall impose.'"

He knew that his weather spell and its damage to ship and crew was more than enough to get him hanged. He wasn't about to allow the *Sanguine* to die at the hands of a saboteur. Halcyon thought about the wish. He didn't even want to try to wish away the gel; that might cause it to explode. He also wanted to keep the wish as simple as possible.

Raising the vial above his head, he smashed it down on the back of the dragon. He focused on the blast gel, wishing for healing coolness and the ship to be safe. The crystal shattered, and a sparkling mist bent to Halcyon's will and wrapped itself around the lower portion of the heart. Some of the mist left the chamber. The emerald mist became thicker and thicker as the midshipwizard's reserve of magical energy flowed from his body and bent itself into the magic of the wishing potion.

Darkness filled the exhausted Halcyon. He fell to the deck unconscious, not knowing what his wish had done.

✣ ✣ ✣

XIV

Dreaming in the Eye of the Storm

HIS MAJESTY'S ARTICLES OF WAR: ARTICLE XIV

If any person in the fleet shall quarrel or fight with any other person in the fleet, or use reproachful or provoking speeches or gestures, tending to make any quarrel or disturbance, he shall, upon being convicted thereof, suffer such punishment as the offense shall deserve and a court-martial shall impose.

"He's not going to like waking up in the brig, I can tell you that for sure," Tupper said, standing over his sleeping bunkmate.

"It really doesn't matter what he likes or dislikes," replied Jock Woodson. "The scuttlebutt says he used high magic during the storm. Everyone knows if you break the Articles, you go in the brig."

"Shush, you'll wake him," Tupper whispered.

"The surgeon said he's in a deep sleep, that's common after using high magic. Blast-tubes going off in here couldn't wake him up," Woodson told his friend.

"Marine! Why is that brig hatch open?" barked Commander Wily, who'd come along the corridor and now stood outside Blithe's cell.

"Sir, two of the prisoner's friends are in there looking after him," replied the marine.

"Marine, this isn't a drinking hall, it's the brig! You two in there, come out here front and center, now!" ordered Wily.

The two midshipwizards rushed out of the brig cell and stood at attention in front of the very irritated first officer.

"What were you two doing in there?" Wily asked.

"Sir, we didn't mean any harm." Woodson quivered in front of the obviously angry first officer.

"We only wanted to see how our friend was doing," Tupper replied.

"Midshipwizard Blithe is in the brig for a purpose. This is not a social time for him," Wily stormed at the two youths. "You both get to your duty stations or berths, whichever is appropriate. I'll have no more friends in this brig. Carry on."

The two hastily left down the corridor of the orlop deck. Wily glared at the marine.

For his part, the trooper stood stiffly at attention.

"Marine, after this shift, you will place yourself on report. You will explain to your superior officer why you allowed friends of the prisoner into his cell." Wily entered the cell, speaking back to the marine. "I'm entering the cell now. You will close the hatch behind me and lock it. When I'm through here, you will open the hatch, let me out, and lock it again. Only superior officers are allowed in this cell. Is that clear to you, Marine?"

"Sir, yes sir!" the marine replied in his best military manner.

"Get back to your post," Wily ordered.

The marine closed the cell hatch and locked it. He then stood at attention by the hatch, not wanting to go down the corridor to the duty station and miss Wily calling out to open the cell.

For the next twenty minutes, the marine thought he heard Wily mumbling something in the prisoner's cell. If they were words of encouragement or orders to get up, the words were too faint for him to hear. At one point, he smelled burnt flesh, but there were all sorts of smells wafting through the orlop-deck corridors from the galley on the next deck. Cookie was probably burning the salt pork again.

Eventually, Wily came to the hatch and ordered it open.

The marine watched the first officer's back as he went away. The marine's only thoughts were of thanking the gods he hadn't been ordered to stand to the mast for a taste of the cat.

In the next three hours, other midshipwizards came to see their friend, but the marine refused to let them in to see the sleeping form of Mr. Blithe; orders were orders, after all.

Darkness.

Halcyon woke to blackness all around. As he looked up from his resting place, all he could see was a darkness blacker than anything he'd experienced before.

I remember the dungeons of my family castle and they weren't darker than what I'm experiencing now, he thought.

This is so odd. His thoughts were confused as he tried to move his arms and legs and found himself feeling nothing.

Am I dead, did making that wish kill me in the process? he wondered to himself as he tried to figure out what was happening. He thought he could feel himself looking right and left and even raising his head, but he couldn't tell what his body was resting on. He began to grow more nervous. It was as if he was floating in air without the ability to touch anything. He didn't ache anywhere, but not being able to feel his body was scaring him.

Nothing he tried allowed him to get in touch with where he found himself.

Then he heard voices. *At least my ears work*, he chided himself.

"I've been working on him for three days. He's dying, Ashe."

Halcyon tried to determine who was speaking. He knew that Chief Ashe Fallow must be there.

"Surgeon, he's a good lad. You're his only hope." There was concern in Ashe Fallow's voice.

"Even if I do save him," the ship's surgeon said, "he's going to hang after his court-martial. Chief, he used high magic on the ship. It was bad enough he caused that storm to blow up around us. Thank the gods it stopped. I suspect his use of magic in the heart chamber had something to do with that. I can't help thinking he's a dead man if he wakes up out of this coma."

"I'm telling you his hanging or not hanging isn't your concern. We have to save this boy and it's important to the survival of the ship. He put that ice there for a reason and we need to know the reason.

"Surgeon, I've known Blithes all my life." The chief's tone of voice wasn't very respectful, thought Halcyon. "I've served with some of his brothers and one of his uncles. Blithes are all cut from the same type of sailcloth. Each and every one of them is honest and brave. If he used high magic in that heart chamber there was a damn good reason. A reason we need to discover. This boy knows the king's Articles backwards and forwards. He'd rather cut off his own arm than purposely disobey one of the Articles. There must be something you haven't tried that might wake him up?" Ashe asked.

Halcyon wanted to sit up and tell them about the blast gel. He wanted them to know there was an enemy on the ship. His body just wouldn't cooperate.

"Well, I've tried all the normal things one does for a coma." The surgeon presented his theories logically. "Notice the mirror at his mouth. It fogs just a little even though one can't see his chest moving. This tells us he's breathing. His heart rate is very slow and barely heard. I've checked his head and found no bruising so I ruled out concussions. There are no punctures on his body or skin discoloration, so I don't think he was poisoned."

"I don't much care about what you can rule out. What have you done to wake him?" The chief sounded vexed.

Halcyon thought to himself that it wasn't a good idea to irritate the chief. Halcyon briefly wondered what the chief could do to the surgeon if he became angry with him. The midshipwizard couldn't think of anything, but would bet all his sea pay that the chief could think of at least ten things.

"Patience, Chief. A logical approach is the key to opening the lock of this medical mystery." The surgeon clearly wasn't cowed in the slightest by the chief. "The boy's body is weak and growing weaker. Something is causing that condition. I've used smelling salts on him with no effect. It's always dangerous to have unconscious patients swallow things, but I've given him several different types of stimulants, also to no effect."

"How did you know Halcyon used high magic in the heart chamber? Admittedly a giant chunk of ice around the heart is odd, but it's possible that was some type of water spell, isn't it?" the chief asked.

Ice, Halcyon thought. He used the most powerful magic in the world and all he got was ice around the dragon's heart. That was a bit disappointing.

Halcyon didn't know what he expected from his magical effort, but he wanted something spectacular. Instead, he put ice around the dragon's heart. At least, even if it was an accident, his potion also stopped the storm around the ship. He hadn't wished for that. *Damn this darkness.* He was starting to feel some of the frustration the chief was showing the surgeon. *This is turning into a nightmare and an uninspired one at that,* Halcyon thought.

"Ah, you show a good grasp of magic, even if you can't cast it, Chief." Now the surgeon's speech filled with exhilaration. "You have forgotten about the shards of green crystal found at our patient's feet when he was discovered in the heart chamber. I restored them with a simple spell. Look what the crystals turned into."

I wish I could see it, Halcyon thought. *Wait a minute, maybe I can use magic to wake myself.* He didn't have the slightest idea what to try. He hadn't learned illumination spells yet. He didn't have any spell components to work with. All he could sense was the darkness all around.

He tried imagining sunlight breaking up the darkness. For a moment, weak bright threads of yellow filled his vision and then vanished into the darkness. However, the yellow threads stopped a little in front of his field of vision and fizzled into nothing. Encouraged by the effort, figuring any change was something, he tried again. Attempt after attempt failed to change the darkness around him. Although he couldn't feel his body, he did start feeling tired. Soon he couldn't summon the mental strength even to try weak attempts at casting magic.

He continued to hear the two men talking somewhere in his range of hearing.

"What is that little thing?" the chief asked.

"I think it's of pixie make. If it is a pixie vial, then it's a wishing potion and very powerful magic. We have a full one of these at the university. There are amazing tales about the power of pixie potions.

"I'm sure the use of such a potion is enough to stop a raging storm and create ice all around the dragon's heart. This crystal, broken on the deck, is all the evidence needed to determine the use of high magic in the heart chamber. Did you hear that the lieutenant commander couldn't remove the ice? I saw him use some amazing spells. The captain wants that ice off immediately, but it's not going to happen. Naturally, I couldn't let them chip away at it. Nicking the dragon's heart is far too dangerous. Daton is quite put out by his failed attempts at melting the ice."

"Commanders get that way from time to time. So, did this pixie magic put the boy in this sleep?" asked the chief.

"Coma, he's in a coma. There's no way to tell if his condition is an effect of the magic he used or not. It's vaguely possible, but I doubt it. We have very little information on the use of wishing potions. In the seven different examples I'm aware of, the caster fell into a sleep of some type, but woke hours later none the worse for using the spell. There is some type of magical residue detectable about him, but I haven't been able to tell what it is. I've tried all the normal earth, air, water, and fire spells of detection and come up empty."

"What did Commander Giantson have to say when he inspected the boy for magic?" The chief was sounding more and more angry.

Halcyon was surprised. The surgeon was clearly doing his best. All the while Halcyon tried everything he could think of and wasn't getting anywhere. The midshipwizard was mildly curious to discover that every spell he tried manifested itself as threads in his vision. Now that he was thinking of it, his weather spell appeared as a thread wrapped around his body. He wondered if this darkness was a huge mass of wrapped black threads. He tried imagining his hands reaching out and pulling at the black strands. He couldn't feel anything, but he tried to pull harder, not having anything to lose from the effort.

"The commander wasn't happy, I can tell you that," the surgeon told the chief. "Anything affecting the life of the dragon is a concern. I saw Daton use several types of magical detections on the heart. We certainly can't chip away at that ice. It doesn't seem to be killing or harming the dragon. Quite the contrary. The ice has healing properties, but it gives off the normal cold that one would expect from ice."

"I don't care about the heart right now. I care about the patient in front of you. What did Lieutenant Commander Giantson say about Blithe?" The chief's voice rose several levels in volume.

If Halcyon had been able to, he would have shaken his head in warning to the surgeon. When the chief got going, few people dared to get in his way.

"Chief, I realize you're fond of this boy, but there's no reason to raise your voice to me. I've done everything I can. He's just not responding."

"Doctor, that's the point. If you can't figure out what's wrong with our Mr. Blithe, it's not a medical problem. What did Giantson say when he looked at the boy?"

"Well, he didn't look at him. What with the heart and its magic and the need to study that, the commander was busy. I didn't think there was a need to bring him in on this work." The surgeon now knew what the chief was thinking. "Oh my, you could be right, Chief. I will get Daton and bring him down right away."

"Marine!" the chief shouted.

Halcyon could hear a lock clicking loudly and a hatch swinging open.

"Marine, go to the midshipwizard wardroom and see if Mr. Haywhen and Mr. Forrest are available. Bring them down here."

"Chief, I'm not supposed to leave my post. I'm on guard duty," the marine said.

"Marine, you're guarding a prisoner in a coma. Get them down here; I'll stand your post. Move out!" Chief Fallow's voice didn't allow the marine to question his order.

Halcyon thought that few on the ship could tell Chief Fallow no. The marine certainly wasn't one of those few. Halcyon was having no luck moving the strands of blackness, but he actually thought he could feel the strands even if he couldn't see or feel his hands move.

"I won't be a moment, Chief," the surgeon said. "I'm sure Daton would love to help us if this is a magical puzzle."

"Mr. Blithe and I aren't going anywhere, Surgeon. He's not getting any stronger and I'm not getting any more patient." The chief's words were clear.

Funny, Halcyon thought to himself, *I don't feel weak.*

In just moments, Halcyon heard his friends.

"Chief, you sent for us." Both boys spoke breathlessly.

"Midshipwizards, we might have a problem. It's possible someone used magic on our Mr. Blithe here. The magic could be killing him and that means someone wants Mr. Blithe dead. We are going to get him awake and talking. I want midshipwizards to help guard him around the clock until his court-martial. It's going to be a very unofficial sort of guarding. Whenever anyone comes in this brig, I want you looking at them or running to tell me if they stop you from watching what they do. Can you do that for your shipmate?"

Good old Tupper spoke up first. "Of course we can, Chief. Why do you want us and not the marine guard doing the watching?"

"Good question, Mr. Haywhen. It's magic at the heart of this puzzle and marines aren't magical. I don't want a spell worked on the marine allowing whoever did this to get access to our Mr. Blithe while he's still in this state or while he's sleeping. Do you understand me?"

"Perfectly, Chief," Tupper spoke up. "We'll arrange everything among the mates. Only the midshipwizards will know. We'll get someone at this hatch around the clock."

"I'll take the first watch," Mark said. "Tupper, you go organize the others."

In a quiet voice, Chief Fallow said, "Remember that we want to keep this quiet. I don't want it getting about the ship that we are specially watching Halcyon."

"Aye, aye, Chief," they said.

Halcyon could hear them leaving the brig. *The brig*—that was a depressing thought. He bet his father, uncles, and all his brothers never spent a day of their lives in the brig. If he survived, this was going to be an interesting story to tell around the family dinner table. Then he realized that he used high magic on a king's ship. He wouldn't be surviving.

A few moments later, the surgeon and Commander Giantson were back.

"Chief, what are you doing here?" Daton Giantson asked.

"The surgeon and I were speaking of the boy here. There might be a magical reason why he's in this deadly sleep. We wanted you to look into it, sir. Mr. Blithe is frightful weak and we were hoping you could do something about that."

"Although Mr. Blithe is in a great deal of trouble, of course I can at least use my magics to strengthen his body. You and the good surgeon stand out of the brig for a moment while I work a strengthening spell," Daton ordered.

"I did try that," the surgeon said. "It had no effect."

"Surgeon, I have no doubt you did your capable best. Let me try a few things for a few moments." The commander sounded very sure of himself.

Halcyon took heart at his words as he heard the men leave.

Suddenly Halcyon's darkness lit up with tiny pinpricks of light. Halcyon was sure it was some of the commander's magic. Then the light faded away.

"Now, that's strange." Daton sounded very puzzled. "My spell didn't touch his body. All it did was wash over his form."

The darkness again lit up. This time a blue form appeared as if in the distance. Halcyon could easily recognize the outline of Commander Giantson.

"Commander, Commander, it's me, can you see me!" Halcyon shouted to the commander. At least he tried to shout, not being able to feel his tongue and mouth. The blue form didn't move closer. It seemed to be feeling its way in the darkness. The commander's shade had its hands out and it never got close to Halcyon. Then the image went away.

"More and more puzzling," Daton said. "Surgeon, do you have a willow wand among your medical things? I have one in my quarters, but . . ."

"Of course, here, sir," the surgeon replied.

"What's the need of that?" the chief asked.

"Willow wands are used to detect malevolence of all types. If a surgeon suspects evil intent used on a patient, he uses a willow wand to ferret it out. On a ship such as ours, I didn't try the wand. I never suspected foul play in this case," the surgeon replied.

"Quite right, Surgeon," Giantson said. "My strengthening spell was stopped by some force. It never reached Mr. Blithe's body. I also sent my spirit to the boy's mind and a blackness prevented me from getting through to him. That normally couldn't happen, which leads me to believe . . ."

Halcyon felt a sudden sharp pain in the palms of both of his hands.

"By the merciful gods," the surgeon gasped.

"What is it, what is it?" the chief demanded.

"Look at his palms. What appears as dirt on his palms is actually a brutal curse. The wand reveals a dark line of enchantment covering his lifelines on each hand. The curse is making him weaker and weaker. Someone came in here while he was unconscious after casting his high magic spell and laid a curse on him. It's very subtle. I don't think I've seen its like before." Giantson sounded surprised.

"How do we remove it?" the chief asked.

"That could be a problem. The spell will disrupt itself and vanish as soon as the boy dies. That's not going to do him any good. With most curses, ripping them away from the body also kills the victim. We have to break through the barrier of the spell and contact his mind. Once we do that, the curse lifts itself. However, I've tried my strongest mind-reaching spell and it didn't work. I'll have to consult my tomes; maybe there's something in them that will help."

"But he's dying now, you could be too late," Fallow said.

"True, but it's all I know to do," Daton replied.

Halcyon heard another person come into the room.

"The dragon is in a rage. What are you all doing down here to make it so angry?" Andool Griffon asked. She didn't sound very happy. "The captain and I keep hearing the same order, over and over again from the thoughts of the sea dragon. It's telling us to pour tannin oil over Blithe here. Daton, you don't think he's a dragon speaker as well as a rope speaker, do you?" Griffon asked.

"Where our Mr. Blithe is concerned I won't dismiss any possibility. The dragon is a very single-minded creature. It's also bright enough to know that the oil can enhance a dragon speaker's ability. Chief, that could be just the thing and a condition whoever cast this spell didn't think of when the spell worked its evil on young Halcyon here. Get some of the oil and we'll try it on him."

"Aye, aye, Commander." Fallow sounded elated at the news.

"Someone on this ship, one of the wizards of the crew, has tried to kill Mr. Blithe. I can't imagine why, can you, Surgeon?" Daton asked.

"I haven't a clue. We'll need to watch over the boy if we can remove the curse. He's going to have to face the court-martial if he wakes; I don't want some revenge-crazed madman hurling spells at Blithe in the brig," the surgeon said. "The captain will insist on Blithe's court-martial. I've never seen the man in such a rage."

"He thinks Blithe worked to destroy his ship. It's no surprise he's angry. I think this news of the attempted murder will interest him, however," Daton replied. "I also believe our Chief Fallow has taken care of guarding our young Blithe, if the appearance of

Mr. Forrest means anything." Now Daton was sounding highly amused.

Halcyon didn't like the news that the captain was so angry. He wasn't surprised at the information; he'd made a bonehead mistake. He didn't know what he would do in the face of his captain's wrath.

"Do you think it really was an enraged wizard wanting to extract some revenge for the deadly storm?" the doctor speculated.

"Possible but not likely," replied Commander Giantson. "I've worked with every spellcaster on this ship and none of them have displayed the power it takes for this strange curse. It's not Arcanian-style magic and all of our crew comes from our country. No, there is a deeper mystery here and we need to find out what it is. Besides, I can't remove that damned ice from the dragon's heart. I want to know exactly what Blithe wished for with that pixie potion. How ever did the boy come up with such powerful magic? We giants don't get along with pixies; I'd love to hear the story of how he came by it. Magical traces in the chamber allowed me to determine Blithe summoned it to hand during the storm. I'd be willing to wager in casting the spell he caused the storm to stop as well as the heart to be enwrapped in the healing ice."

"My studies have shown the dragon has been made much stronger by the use of Blithe's spell," the doctor revealed.

"Indeed, I could tell that too, but why the ice?" Daton questioned.

"Here's the oil," a breathless Fallow said.

"Excellent, Chief," Daton said. "Spread most of it over his chest. Leave some in the bottom of the bucket. We may want to anoint his head and feet as well. Let's just see what happens with this first dose, shall we?"

"The dragon's excited. It thinks it can talk to young Blithe here," Andool said.

"Halcyon, get to work, boy," Fallow said. "If you're going to live, you need to save yourself now."

Halcyon never felt the oil pouring on his chest. In a few moments he did feel the tingling of the tannin oil. For just a second he thought he even smelled the nasty root odor.

He tried moving his arms and legs again. Nothing happened.

Suddenly an image of the enormous dragon's head filled his mind and broke through the darkness. It was as if the creature was right there in the blackness with him. He could actually see the dragon in the air over wherever he was.

"*Human!*" the dragon thought at him.

Halcyon could sense a great deal of affection and concern in that thought.

In that instant he was in the mind of the dragon again. His vision encompassed the ship as the dragon saw it. Clear blue skies and a brisk force-five wind moved the ship along. The *Sanguine* was at full sail again. There was no sign of weather damage.

"*Where did you go?*" the dragon asked.

"*I haven't the slightest idea. Someone may have put a spell on me. At least that's what Commander Giantson thinks,*" Halcyon added. Halcyon could feel the strength and fitness of the dragon. It felt unusually healthy and strong.

"*Are you safe now?*" the dragon wondered.

"*Well, thanks to you I seem to be. If what the commander says is correct, you have just broken a curse by contacting me,*" a relieved Halcyon told the dragon.

"*Olden and Griffon are very angry with you. Why is that?*" the dragon asked.

"*It's hard to explain. I did some magic that I shouldn't have and caused that storm that hurt you. Then someone else tried hurting your heart and I used even more magic to try and fix that. I have to pay for my mistakes. We have important rules that I didn't follow.*" Halcyon dreaded the court-martial. He knew it would happen as soon as he woke up.

"*I'll talk to them. You tried to save me.*" The dragon showed its concern for Halcyon.

"*At this point I'll take all the help I can get, but I'm expecting the worst. Please try sending me back into my body,*" the midshipwizard asked the dragon. "*Hopefully the curse will be lifted by now.*"

Once again, Halcyon's mind filled with blackness and he felt nothing more.

XV

✿ ✿ ✿

Standing Before the Mast

HIS MAJESTY'S ARTICLES OF WAR: ARTICLE XV

There shall be no wasteful expense of any blasting shot, ammu-
nition, or other stores in the fleet, nor any embezzlement thereof,
but the stores and provisions shall be carefully preserved, upon
pain of such punishment to be inflicted upon the offenders, abet-
tors, buyers, and receivers (being persons subject to naval disci-
pline) as shall be by a court-martial found just in that behalf.

Click. Click.

Halcyon woke with a start. He threw his hands up only to find
his hands constrained by chains and thick metal bracelets.

"Easy, easy there. We're going to have some more rough seas
ahead." Ashe Fallow put a calming hand on Halcyon's shoulder.

"What are these?" Halcyon raised the manacles on his hands
and discovered the metal bracelets and chains attached to another set on his ankles. "Chief, are these necessary? I'm not really
able to jump ship in the middle of the ocean."

"You'll not be pleased to know you're wearing the manacles of Iben. I'm not pleased with the order to put these on you, myself. These manacles prevent spellcasters from working magic. Their use prevents you from escaping from the brig and flying off. I'm sorry I'm the one having to put them on," Chief Fallow said. "Don't be telling me you can't use magic. No one suspected you could put a ton of ice around the dragon's heart, either, but I just looked, and it's still there."

"I won't try to escape, Chief Fallow. I'm guilty. I'll take my court-martial and hang. Everyone can see I ignored Article Three, I know it and you know it, but I can stand like a man and take my sentence honorably." Halcyon spoke the words and his mouth went dry, as he fully understood what he just said.

"Boy, stand up and listen to me!" Ashe's order left no room for argument.

Even in the constricting chains, Halcyon stood and stiffened to attention.

"First, in the brig there is no rank. No one salutes you in here and you don't salute back. Second, you are a Lankshire man and you will hold on to life with your last breath. That is what I would do and that is what you will do. Is that clear?" Fallow shouted at Halcyon, inches away from his face.

"Yes, Chief," Halcyon boomed back.

"Guilty or not, there is always hope. Past hope there is always a way around everything, is that clear?" Ashe shouted.

"No, Chief." Halcyon relaxed his stance. "I did it, I see no way around . . ."

"Shut up! You aren't a midshipwizard in here, but they can't take away the fact that you are a Blithe and a Lankshire man." The look of anger on Ashe Fallow's face commanded all of Halcyon's attention. "If and when it happens, you will go to the hangman with your head held high. That's what your father would do, but until that happens don't just accept your fate. You are a Blithe with centuries of naval tradition to stiffen your spine, boy. Did you have a reason for using high magic?"

"Yes," Halcyon replied.

"I don't need to hear why you did what you did. As you sit waiting for them to call you, think about the actions causing you to end up in here. Make sure you tell them the reasons you used high magic before they say you're guilty. I'm guessing it will be good enough to keep that hangman's rope off your neck. Do you understand me?" the chief asked.

"Yes, Chief, I can do that." But Halcyon wasn't sure that he could say anything in his own defense.

"Let me tell you what's in store for you," Ashe said. "Tomorrow at twelve bells, you go before the mast. They take you out on deck before the assembled crew and the captain reads the charge against you. You just stand there and take it. After the reading, they escort you to the captain's wardroom and Captain Olden, First Officer Wily, and Second Officer Griffon judge you. They decide what you did, how you did it, and if you should hang for it. That's when you talk about your actions.

"Don't do anything stupid like saying you're guilty. When they ask you if you are guilty or not guilty say, 'I'm guilty with extenuating circumstances.' Repeat that back to me right now," ordered Fallow.

"I'm guilty with extenuating circumstances . . . but I'm just guilty, Chief." Halcyon felt terrible as he said those words. He'd deliberately broken an article in the king's navy.

"But me no buts, boy. Did your father raise any idiots?" Fallow asked.

"No." Halcyon knew his brothers were smart; he was no longer so sure about himself.

"Did your mother, bless her kind soul, put you in the navy to be hanged?" Ashe asked.

"Of course not," Halcyon replied.

"Repeat what I told you, this time without the stupid questions. . . . Do it!" Ashe yelled.

"I'm guilty with extenuating circumstances," Halcyon said.

"That's what you say and they'll have to listen to your story. You've got friends on this ship. You saved a bunch of them in that storm when the blast-tube broke loose. The storm was nothing; don't let it concern you. Most of us have survived much worse and I'm telling everyone you are the one who stopped that little blow with your magical wish. They aren't even charging you with that blunder because you can't face two death sentences at the same time.

"I will be at your back in that wardroom. No one is going to sentence you to death without your getting one chance to save yourself. Your mates have been standing guard over your body for the days you were asleep and helpless. Whoever cursed you won't get that chance again. You saved the ship. We now have marine guards everywhere all because of you. If that doesn't make you feel good, nothing will. Don't disappoint your mates, me, or your father, who I'm sure is watching right now, understood?" Fallow was leaving.

"Yes, I understand," Halcyon replied, appreciating Fallow's effort to stiffen his spine.

"One more thing, boy. I've spoken freely with you here, because I figured you needed a swift kick in the pants. Someone on this ship wants you dead. Whatever fate hands you in the next few days will happen. You trust in me and you trust in your wardroom mates. You don't trust anyone else on this ship until I catch and put a pike in the traitor's heart. Do you understand that, boy?" There was a deadly gleam in Fallow's eyes.

"Yes, Chief" was all Halcyon could say.

The brig hatch shut behind Fallow. Halcyon had never felt so alone in his life.

He sat back down on the cot. The weight of the silvery chains felt heavy on his body. For most of the last year, he'd greatly enjoyed the feeling of magic running through his veins. That energy put more spring in a person's step and allowed them to move about with strength and conviction. Denied that feeling by the magic of the chains, he ached to have his abilities back.

He found himself sitting on his bed looking down at the silver chains. A slow fire built up in his body. He didn't like the very feeling of the chains. Didn't he try to save the ship from destruction? His heart beat faster. He felt an indignation at his situation, a situation someone else on the ship forced on him.

Slamming the chains down on the bed, he thought if he ever got out of this, he would spend some time working on counter-magic to make chains like these not work on him. There must be a way; he wagered to himself that Daton might know how to be free of the effects of such chains. Maybe the maker, this Iben, might still be alive to reveal the chain's secrets. If he could pick the chain's lock, he could just shed himself of them.

His anger grew as he sat there staring at the brig's walls, thinking about the injustice of his being there when he had tried only to save the ship. The situation drove him to a madness he'd never known in himself. For a brief moment, the links of the chain glowed red from Halcyon's demon eyes.

Idiot, he thought. He wasn't going to have the time to become a locksmith in the brig. He would barely have time to eat his last meal.

"What's it like being cursed?" a voice asked. It was Tupper's voice. Halcyon looked up and the face of his friend appeared in the barred opening of the brig hatch.

"Tupper, it's good to see you. What are you doing here?" Halcyon rose, the anger leaving his body. He went to the hatch, happy to see his friend's face.

"It's my duty, unofficial duty, that is. We've all been down here a time or two, we midshipwizards. It's the chief's idea. Did you know about the curse while trapped in your own mind? What was it like?" Tupper showed his boyish enthusiasm in his broad smile.

"I couldn't move my body. I didn't know I was under an evil spell. I could hear the surgeon and Chief Fallow talking over my body, but I couldn't even move my eyes. All the while, I felt like I was in the darkest of pits. Why would anyone bother to curse me?" Halcyon shook his head, having no idea what attracted the attention of the saboteur to his bedside. "Aw, look at this, there's scars on both of my hands. I've got burn marks on my palms right along my lifelines. I've got several aunts who are going to be quite put out if they try to . . ." Then Halcyon realized he wouldn't be seeing those aunts again. His face went pale.

"The chief and the marines went over the list of names of crew who came to see you while you were unconscious," Tupper remarked. "Half the crew was in here before Officer Wily put a stop to the visits. There's no way to tell which one of them cursed you. The brig's a nasty place, but at least you don't have to deal with Lieutenant Junior Grade Hackle. He's all smiles at the thought. . . ."

"What were you saying about me, Mr. Haywhen?" Lieutenant Hackle's voice rang out in the corridor. The lieutenant was somewhere on the other side of the hatch.

"Sir, I was just talking to Mr. Blithe," Tupper said. The sound of his voice told Halcyon his friend had come to attention.

"None of that now, talking with the prisoner is highly irregular for a midshipwizard like you. I came to see the prisoner myself. Stand at ease, man, but get back from the hatch." Aberdeen Hackle's face appeared all smiles in the hatch opening. "So, I'm not surprised to see you being the first one of the wardroom midshipwizards to land in the brig, my boy." Hackle's glee-filled tone matched the huge grin on his face.

Halcyon sat back down on his bed. He composed his face and gave the lieutenant a stony glare.

"Marked for greatness, some were saying," Hackle taunted. "A Blithe through and through, so noble, others said. Just how many of the Blithes have found themselves in the brig, do you know, Hal?"

Suddenly the inside of his cell lit with a red glow. Halcyon knew it was from his angry eyes. He didn't care.

"Oh, got you angry, did I? Imagine that. Why, Halcyon, I didn't mean to do anything to upset you. It should be very interesting to see if your eyes still glow as you dance on the rope. I'm told it takes ten or twenty minutes for a strong man to die as he struggles for that last breath, swinging back and forth under the mizzenmast. Don't worry about getting word to your kin. I will, of course, be the one composing and sending the letter home telling of your actions on the ship. I'll put the best light on what you have done." Hackle left, laughing.

"Mr. Hackle, don't you have duties elsewhere at this time?" Commander Giantson's voice cut off Hackle's laughter.

"Sir, I was just checking on the prisoner. He's from my wardroom, as you know," Hackle replied.

"I do indeed know that. I looked for you in the midshipwizards' wardroom only moments ago. I believe that is your current duty station and that you are remiss in not being there. Mr. Hackle, carry on with your duties and get where you belong. I must work with the prisoner," Giantson said.

"Aye, aye, sir." Hackle's face left the window of the hatch.

Halcyon closed his eyes and calmed himself. He didn't want the commander seeing the effects of Hackle's taunting.

"Corporal, please open the hatch," the commander requested.

"Sir, I must ask why you wish the hatch open," the pleasant tones of Corporal Denna Darkwater could be heard past the hatch.

"Well, Corporal, I'm surprised you asked. I have something of the prisoner's that he needs to have and I would give it to him," the commander replied.

"I will open the hatch, but I have to inspect whatever you have for the prisoner, sir." The corporal didn't sound pleased at having to question Daton.

Halcyon was somehow very happy to know that Darkwater helped guard his life.

"Very well, Corporal. You can give these bracers to him. Young Halcyon, I thought you could use these. I got them from your sea chest. The ward your family put on the chest was quite interesting to overcome. Of pixie manufacture I think, what?" Giantson asked.

"Commander Giantson." Denna sounded most apologetic. "I have to know what these are. I've never seen their like before."

"Not a problem, Corporal," Daton said. "I believe them to be enchanted war bracers. They are a bit out of fashion in our modern times, but there are three spells placed on the bracers, I believe. The first magic hinders an enemy spellcaster from inflicting mind-control spells on the wearer of the bracers. The second spell causes curses to reflect back on the caster as they try to hurl them at the wearer. I believe that in young Blithe's current situation this is a uniquely fitting attribute of these bracers. The third spell provides strength and added courage to the wearer. I give you my absolute assurances that these bracers cannot help our young Halcyon escape. The bracers themselves hide no lock picks or weapons of any type. They are simple plates of metal bent by a smith's hand. One takes the bracer and bends it over the forearm. The two of them ward off blows to the lower arms. I venture to say these might stop even a strong pike strike from your own good right arm. Will that be enough information for you, young Denna?"

"Yes, sir, thank you, sir."

The hatch opened and the corporal handed Halcyon the family bracers.

A thrill of excitement filled Halcyon as he put on the items. He didn't care a bit that such armor was out of fashion in this modern age of blast-tubes and sails. Blithes had traditionally gone to war wearing bracers of this type for the last four centuries. Halcyon grew up hearing stories about how bracers like these saved the lives of his uncles and brothers and even his father. Locked away as he was, hope was something he didn't have, until a touch of his family fell into his hands and covered his arms.

Mindful of Fallow's words, he inspected his bracers, making sure that nothing had changed on the metal and leather. Physically they were just the way he left them in his sea chest. He'd have to trust that there were no magics placed on them by an enemy.

Daton Giantson stood in the hatchway of the brig. "Normally, those in the brig aren't allowed to have personal items. However, prisoners don't usually acquire curses in this man's navy while confined in the brig. Your fate at the hands of the court-martial officers will become tempered by the fact that you were attacked while you slept. I'm going to make sure that comes out at your court-martial.

"Someone on the ship is a danger to all of us and that person isn't you," Daton said. "We've put extra security throughout the ship. It should be much more difficult to harm the dragon or its crew, thanks in part to what we found out about you and your curse. I will be there at your court-martial tomorrow. Some of my observations should carry weight in the final decision concerning you.

"I hope you'll excuse the fact that I went through your things. Naturally, with you being a prisoner of the brig, I took the order to search your billet. I was the only one on board who could get past the wards on your sea chest. I hope to talk to you about them when we have more time and find ourselves in happier circumstances. Luck to you, young Halcyon."

Halcyon gushed with appreciation. "Thank you, sir, anything you can do on my behalf is greatly appreciated."

"Not a bit of it. Besides," Daton said, "I want to talk to you about that unique spell you placed on the dragon's heart. Do you know the ice still covers the heart and hasn't melted a bit in three days?"

"No, sir, I didn't know that. I really didn't know there was ice on the dragon's heart, until I heard it talked about from the brig." Just the thought of where Halcyon was weighed down his very soul. He sat again on his bed.

"Try to get some rest, you'll need it for tomorrow." With that the commander left.

Tupper once again looked into the brig, but he could see his friend shaking his head and looking sad. Tupper wanted to make Halcyon feel better, but there wasn't a thing he could think of to say. Looking down at him in the confining walls of the brig made Tupper want to cry for his friend.

Haywhen backed up and leaned against the corridor wall. He looked over to see the stern face of Denna Darkwater as she stood in a resting stance by the side of the hatch. *It's going to be difficult to curse Halcyon again with her at the hatch*, he thought.

Halcyon must have dozed off, but he heard the loud orders of an officer speaking to Tupper on the other side of the hatch.

"Mr. Haywhen, don't you have duties elsewhere on the ship?"

Halcyon couldn't quite make out who spoke.

"No, Commander, I'm stationing myself here to watch my friend," Tupper replied.

Dire Wily's voice was now clear. "Really, a fine young midshipwizard like yourself voluntarily hiding away in the bowels of the ship. I find that amazing, sir."

"Yes, sir," replied Tupper.

"I've come to see the prisoner. Corporal, please open the hatch," Wily requested.

"Yes, sir, the hatch will be left open at all times, if you please, sir," Darkwater told the commander.

"That's a tad unusual, but our Mr. Blithe is worth the extra effort," the commander said as the hatch opened. Dire Wily filled the hatchway. "Mr. Blithe, you look like hell."

Halcyon didn't know if he should rise and salute or remain sitting on his cot. He got up. "Sir, I'm sorry, sir. I really do feel fine. Commander Giantson was kind enough to give me the Blithe family bracers from my sea chest. He came just a few moments ago and it's made all the difference in the world. Are you here to talk to me about the court-martial tomorrow?"

Once he saw the bracers, the commander stepped back into the corridor, leaving the hatch open.

"Three days without food can tire a man out. As soon as I heard you were up and talking, I ordered the galley to make you a meal. When it comes, eat it all, now. You're going to have a very hard day tomorrow."

"That's what people keep telling me," Halcyon said, trying to keep up a bold face.

"Commander, begging your pardon," the guard said. "We had to send that tray from the galley back. Our own marine cook will be making the prisoner's meals until sentencing."

"Damn the impudence! I see no reason for that action. You marines can go too far in your martial efforts. Get that tray back here now. That's an order, Marine." Wily shouted the command, looming over Deena.

Halcyon watched the very large Denna Darkwater stand toe-to-toe with the much larger Commander Wily. She didn't back down an inch in front of his anger.

"No, sir, I won't be leaving my post. Only marine trays of food go into the brig on my watch. My orders are clear. They come from my marine major. You may of course talk to him if you don't agree with his commands. Until he relieves me, we will be doing this the marine way." There was steel in her voice and an implied threat that didn't go unnoticed by anyone in the hall or sitting on the cot in the brig.

"As you wish, Corporal, though that seems a tad overcautious." There was the faint hint of anger and frustration in the commander's speech, but he was clearly backing down from his previous order. He turned back to Halcyon. "Make no mistake about it. The charge against you is deadly serious. We must keep within the strict rulings of the Articles no matter how much we might like you or your family." Wily seemed to be apologizing for what he had to do tomorrow. "Daton tells me you freely admit violating Article Three of the naval code of conduct. That gives us no choice. The captain will read the charge to the assembled crew and you are then marched into the wardroom. You will plead yourself guilty as charged and be sentenced. We won't let you suffer. Your death will be swift and sure. I'll talk with your surviving relatives and let them know you did your best. Until then, I will tell you that I admire your courage. Few would be able to admit to violating one of the Articles with a sentence of death over their heads. I say well done, sir."

"Commander, thank you for the visit. I'm sure you, the captain, and the second officer will do what is proper," Halcyon said.

"Quite right, carry on, Corporal, Mr. Haywhen, Mr. Blithe." Commander Wily left, and the corporal closed and locked the brig hatch once more.

Halcyon, seeing the hatch close, chided himself about the foolishness of thinking about picking the lock. He imagined himself stealthily picking the lock with a bit of metal and then trying to face down Denna Darkwater with his bare hands. The picture was so funny he laughed out loud.

Darkwater watched the commander leave the corridor and go

up out of the orlop deck. "That commander is an odd duck," Darkwater said. She looked in to see the laughing Blithe sitting on his cot. That was a good sign, she thought.

"Why do you say that?" asked Tupper.

"He's a good officer, but tomorrow he could easily order Blithe hanged. Just a few days ago, he spent the better part of an hour in the brig muttering nice things about the midshipwizard over his unconscious body. It just seems odd to me, that's all," Darkwater said. "How can a man show one face to Blithe and act in a caring way and then coldheartedly order his death the next day?

"I've killed my share of enemies. I've done it without anger, as quickly as I could. I guess that's the difference between a ranker and an officer. Officers seem trained to be detached, even soulless. I like young Blithe in there. No one could get me to do the duty of hanging him from the yardarm. Yet one of the officers, and I bet it will be Hackle, will be ordered in a day to put a noose around his neck and push him off the spar. It's just not right; give me death at the enemy's hands any day."

"I can hear you out there, Denna, you better be careful or someone will claim you have almost a feminine way about you," Halcyon said, trying for a laugh, and he got one from both the corporal and Haywhen.

XVI

✼ ✼ ✼

The Dagger Points Toward You

HIS MAJESTY'S ARTICLES OF WAR: ARTICLE XVI

No person in or belonging to the fleet shall sleep upon his watch, or negligently perform the duty imposed on him, or forsake his station, upon pain of death or such other punishment as a court-martial shall think fit to impose, and as the circumstances of the case shall require.

Halcyon lay on his cot. He hadn't been able to sleep all night, with the death sentence hanging over his head. In the long night, he'd thought about every single word of Article III, and there was no escape from the fact that he'd used high magic. In the night he'd asked for writing things and written a brief note to his family apologizing for the disgrace he was bringing to the family name.

It was ten bells of the morning watch when he heard people talking just outside his brig hatch; he ignored them.

"Food for the prisoner," someone said in the corridor.

"Forget it, I don't want any," Halcyon nervously shouted to the guard.

"You'll eat it and like it," Ashe Fallow said as he opened the hatch. "I knew you'd probably have that attitude. You're going to need all your wits about you this morning. You'll be helped by food in your belly."

"I can see there's no arguing with you on this," Halcyon said with a wry smile as he sat up.

"I brought a taste of the captain's wine for you as well. I figured if the man is going to hang you, the least we could do is drink his wine," the chief quipped as he poured a tankard for Halcyon and himself.

"You didn't?" Halcyon couldn't believe what he just heard. The marine guard at the hatch smiled at hearing the chief's words. He looked down at the tankard he'd been drinking in stunned surprise.

The chief unlocked the manacles and let them fall to the deck.

"I did and damn anyone to hell that tries to kill a Lankshire man I say." The chief toasted Halcyon with a raised leather tankard. He looked back at the marine with a knowing smile. If the marine told the captain on them, he would have to explain that he drank the wine as well. The marine shook his head, smiled, and went back to his post.

Halcyon drank the captain's wine, suddenly feeling very wicked. He wolfed down the oatmeal, finding an appetite he didn't know he had.

Mark Forrest brought Halcyon's best uniform into the brig a few minutes later. He brought Halcyon's brush kit as well. "Commander Giantson opened your sea chest and let me bring you fresh clothes. We're all pulling for you, Hal." Mark came to attention and saluted. "Luck to you, Midshipwizard."

Halcyon didn't salute back, but Chief Fallow did. "Well said, Mr. Forrest. Carry on, sir, and we will see you on deck."

Mark left.

"Mr. Grunseth, you can also go up on deck. I'll take the watch duty on our Mr. Blithe from now on," the chief said.

"Aye, aye, Chief." From outside the hatch, James gave Halcyon a friendly salute and left as well.

"Your wardroom mates are good men. I was proud of them watching over you and still maintaining their normal duty shifts. It's good to have friends in this man's navy and you've done well to have those midshipwizards like you," praised the chief.

"They helped a lot as I sat here. Do you really think someone would have tried to curse me again?" Halcyon asked.

"I don't know and I don't care. All I know is with those midshipwizards watching over you, nothing happened. We need to get a move on, Mr. Blithe."

Halcyon dropped his brig clothes and put on his fresh things. Suddenly his hands started shaking and he couldn't manage the buttons on his coat. The enormity of what he was about to face filled his eyes with tears.

Ashe could see what was happening and moved to help Halcyon fix his coat.

"Mr. Blithe, I've served with your brothers and one of your uncles. We being Lankshire men, I feel the need to tell you what they would have all said if one of them had been standing here in front of you. Stand tall, Halcyon. Don't let anyone see what you are feeling."

The chief grabbed both of Halcyon's lapels and pulled him face-to-face. With an angry intensity he said, "You did your best. You tell them what happened and you trust in duty and your own sense of honor."

Some of the fear left Halcyon. "Thank you, Mr. Fallow. Shall we go now?"

Ashe could see the grim determination in the boy's eyes and he liked what he saw there now. "An excellent idea, Mr. Blithe.

Leave your bracers here in the brig and we'll go and give them our own version of hell." Ashe put the enchanted manacles back on Halcyon's wrists and ankles. "After you, sir."

There was a little bit of steel in his spine as Halcyon walked down the long corridor of the orlop deck and up the stairs. As he came onto the open deck, he relished the taste of fresh salt air. He tipped his hat to the waiting officers on the quarterdeck. The sky was cloudless above him and the sun's warmth gave him even more strength to face what was ahead.

He walked in his chains to the mainmast. There was an empty circle there, and two marines waited to flank him. He stood facing the three officers above him on the quarterdeck. The rest of the crew assembled around him on the open deck. His wardroom mates were all there, smiling and giving him what support they could without saying anything.

Hackle was there too. The junior lieutenant's white skin shone in stark contrast to everyone else's tanned flesh. He also had a big grin on his face. Hackle was clearly enjoying Halcyon's situation.

Andol Griffon signaled the stern double blast-tube, and it was fired.

KABOOM!

Captain Olden spoke loud enough for the crew on the forecastle to hear his words. "Mr. Blithe stands before the mast accused of a grave act. Mr. Wily, read the Article Mr. Blithe is accused of breaking."

Commander Wily opened up the book of Articles and read aloud, "His Majesty's Articles of War, Article Three: 'The use of high magic is expressly forbidden on any of His Majesty's ships. If any officer, mariner, or soldier or other aforesaid uses high magic on board His Majesty's ship, every such person so offending, and being convicted thereof by the sentence of the court-martial, shall be punished with death, or such other punishment as the nature and degree of the offense shall deserve and the court-martial shall impose.'" Commander Wily closed the book.

The captain spoke up again. "First Officer Lieutenant Commander Wily, Second Officer Master Andool Griffon, and myself will now stand as judges in this case. In all cases of court-martial in the king's navy, the three senior officers of the ship stand as judges for the crime. The accused may state his case and bring any witnesses he feels are useful for his testimony. Marines, bring the prisoner to my wardroom. Crew, carry on with your duties. That is all."

Halcyon walked into the captain's wardroom with the marines in front of him and Chief Fallow behind. In the few weeks he'd been aboard, he'd wished for an invitation to the captain's wardroom. All the midshipwizards hoped for that. He was suddenly very sorry that a court-martial was the way he would be introduced to the area.

The captain's wardroom was long, with a huge table in the middle. At one end of the room was another table, with a bell and stack of papers. Three chairs stood behind that table. Halcyon stood in front of a chair facing the smaller table. The three officers, the captain's clerk, Commander Giantson, his two marine guards, and Chief Fallow were the only ones in the large room. The captain's clerk sat at a small table to the side, ready to record every word said during the trial. Everyone was standing.

The captain took a large dagger with a gold hilt and rang the bell on the table three times. "This court-martial will come to order. Let the record show that the prisoner has heard the Article. How does the prisoner plead?"

Halcyon tried to get the words out, but he was too nervous. He coughed hard to get some moisture in his mouth. "I'm guilty with extenuating circumstances, sir."

The captain and Commander Wily looked up, surprised.

"Chief Fallow, take off the prisoner's manacles. Lieutenant Commander Giantson, cast a truth spell on Mr. Blithe. When the spell activates, Mr. Blithe, you will tell this board of court-martial, in your own words, what extenuating circumstances could possibly cause you to violate one of the most important articles in the king's navy," the captain said.

Halcyon had been preparing this speech all night. With the manacles off, Giantson cast a spell, causing Halcyon's body to take on a silver glow. He could feel the magic pressing in on his mind as well. There was a light pressure touching every part of his body, but he felt it on his head most of all.

"If Mr. Blithe tells any falsehood, the silver glow will turn red," Daton advised. "I need to state for the record that the spell only reacts to what Mr. Blithe believes in his mind. He could state things as he believes them and they could still be false and the spell won't react."

"Your spell will be satisfactory for this court," the captain said.

Halcyon was extremely nervous, what with Giantson's spell surrounding him. He didn't want to say anything wrong for fear of the spell branding him a liar. He started telling his story, growing less and less nervous as he detailed what happened that day. "I'm terribly sorry my magic caused the storm to strike the *Sanguine*. I want you to know I never meant for that to happen. During the storm, the waves and wind blew up the hatch cover so the sea flowed into the hold. Lieutenant Solvalson and I managed to reseal the cover. The lieutenant then ordered me down into the orlop deck to make sure seawater didn't get into the heart or liver chambers.

"I rushed down to the heart chamber. As I entered, some other officer left out the other side of the chamber. I could tell he was an officer from the rain slicker he wore, but his back was to me and I couldn't tell who he was.

"There was an odd smell in the chamber and I inspected the

heart, noticing there was no seawater entering the area, and that the hatch seals were still intact . . . however, I found the lower portion of the heart covered in blast gel."

"You what?" the captain shouted. "Commander Giantson, in your working with the heart did you notice the ice was covering blast gel?"

Giantson was at the side table. He stood up. "No, sir, but the ice is very thick on one side of the heart. Although I haven't been able to remove the ice with my magics, I'm sure I could cast a spell that would allow us to look at the heart underneath the cov-ering of ice."

"We'll do that, but first, Mr. Blithe, finish your testimony," the captain ordered.

"When I saw the blast gel I acted," Halcyon reported as best he could remember. "I didn't think I could summon another officer before the gel exploded. The heart was beating faster and faster because of the storm. I feared that at any minute the gel would explode.

"My mother had given me the pixie wishing potion, caution-ing me to use it only in dire emergency. I thought this was just such an emergency. I didn't have the skills needed to use my air or water magic on the heart. I've only been a spellcaster for eight months and know I have a lot to learn. I felt that if I didn't act in a heartbeat the gel would explode and the sea dragon would die. I remember the exact wish I made. I wished for the ship to be safe and the heart to be given a cooling healing. I remember that I didn't want to risk wishing off the gel for fear that it would ignite in the process. I'd hoped the ice would keep the gel still and cool at the same time.

"When I broke the crystal, a green mist rose up around the heart and some of the mist left the chamber. The potion pulled what magical energy I had out of me and I went unconscious. I woke up in the brig."

The three officers ignored Halcyon and started talking excitedly among themselves.

"We have a saboteur on board. When I heard Mr. Blithe was cursed I thought it was an angry wizard bent on revenge. Now I see there is a real danger among the crew," the amazed captain said.

"We don't know there's blast gel on the heart. The boy could have imagined that," Wily pointed out.

"Any amount of blast gel going off on that heart would have destroyed it. We really need to see if there is gel under that ice," Griffon said.

The captain stood up. "Marine, bring Lieutenant Solvalson here. Also, summon Major Aberdeen to the heart chamber. This court will adjourn to the heart chamber to see for ourselves if the prisoner's statements are true. Commander Giantson, you will accompany us and use your magic to clear away the fog of the ice."

The officers left and Halcyon breathed a sigh of relief for the first time since he walked in.

"Make no mistake," Chief Fallow said, "you've given them plenty to think about. Your story might just save your life. Look over there at their table. See that big dagger by the bell?"

"Yes, what's it for?" Halcyon asked.

"These fine officers are going to come back in here and ask you a few more questions." Bitter sarcasm filled Fallow's hushed voice. He spoke so that the clerk couldn't hear him. "Then maybe they'll ask Solvalson and Commander Giantson a few questions as well. They'll go off to the captain's cabin and decide if they feel you're guilty or not guilty. That dagger's the important thing to your fate. The captain will ring the bell three times with that dagger and place it down on the table. If Olden places the dagger hilt toward you, the sentence isn't going to be hanging. If he places it blade toward you, they're going to hang you, boy. Either way you'll get one chance to make a statement before you hear their sentence. Whatever you say, tempered by which way that blade is pointing, I'll personally make sure your last words get back to your family. Luck to you, boy." The chief's hand gripped Halcyon's arm, lending him strength and courage.

"Thank you, Ashe," Halcyon said.

The minutes dragged on to an hour. Lieutenant Solvalson came into the room and sat down in the back. He smiled at Halcyon in a supportive manner.

Finally the officers came back into the wardroom. With them came Major Aberdeen, the commander of the marine detail on the ship.

The captain spoke again. "Let the record show that we did indeed find blast gel coating the lower portion of the heart. The record will also show that the ship's wizard still can't do anything to remove the ice around the heart.

"When I heard that Mr. Blithe was cursed I strongly suspected an angry spellcaster among the crew. This latest testimony and the proof of the blast gel forces me to realize Mr. Blithe stumbled onto a deliberate act of sabotage. Mr. Solvalson, front and center," the captain ordered.

"Sir, yes sir," Solvalson said.

"Lieutenant," Griffon asked, "about how long was it after you ordered Mr. Blithe down into the ship that you saw the storm stop?"

"That's hard to judge, ma'am. It wasn't longer than half an hour. With the waves and the wind beating down on the ship, I couldn't tell you exactly. It might have been fifteen minutes or so," the nervous lieutenant said.

Griffon weighed Solvalson's words carefully. "Fine, Lieutenant, that's a close enough approximation. You may go now. I also want the record to show that if Mr. Blithe had tried to remove the blast gel on the heart by scraping it off, the gel would have ignited. Also, the quickly beating dragon's heart does indeed generate more than enough heat to set off the gel if the movement of the heart muscle doesn't cause the explosion."

Wily spoke up. "Major Aberdeen, isn't the blast-gel hold guarded at all times?"

The major stood up. He was a big man. Graying hair at the temples showed that he was a bit past his prime, but he moved easily for a large man. "The hold is guarded by a marine day and night," he said.

Wily continued, "Did anyone, including Mr. Blithe here, go into the blast-gel hold on the day of the storm?"

"No, sir. My guard would have told me if that happened. When I saw the gel on the heart, I asked my men and they told me no one took jars of the gel that day."

"Major," Griffon asked, "if you wanted to steal a jar of the gel without anyone knowing it, how would you do it?"

The big officer thought for a second. "Well, if I wanted to do a foolish thing like that, I would get a jar during one of the blast-tube practice times. It would be easy to hide a jar then, what with all the monkeys coming and going from the hold. No one counts how many jars get taken out and used with the leftovers being put back again."

The captain was red with anger now. "Someone among my crew tried to destroy my ship. Intolerable, I tell you, intolerable! By the gods, I swear the culprit will be found before they can strike against my ship again."

With a visible effort of will, the captain calmed down, but his face was still flushed red. "Mr. Blithe, is your testimony that you used the wish potion because you thought your ship and its crew were in deadly danger?"

At first Halcyon didn't know what the captain was getting at. Halcyon had just testified to exactly what the captain was saying. He wondered if he hadn't made himself clear enough.

"Mr. Blithe, I just asked you a question," the captain said.

"Sir, yes sir. I thought the heart was going to explode and I did what I thought best, knowing it violated Article Three, sir," Halcyon was aghast at what he was saying.

Wily interrupted. "Master Griffon, surely there are many ways to safely remove that gel from the heart?"

"No, there aren't," Griffon said. "Currently I'm thinking it would take the facilities of a port, and even then, I'd wager, no matter what the engineers did, the gel would explode."

Wily, clearly not believing what the master blast-tube officer was saying, went to Giantson with a question. "There must be many ways to magically remove gel. Blithe could have come to you to save the ship, could he not?"

"The ice is the best of all solutions, but my ice spell couldn't last and I'm sure I couldn't have gotten down into that hold before the heart exploded. The ice also stops the gel from contact by any outside forces. Clearly, the high magic is keeping the dragon unusually strong. I suspect if Halcyon concentrates on the ice when we reach a port, the high magic will remove the gel as the ice vanishes."

"Do you have anything else to say, Mr. Blithe?" Wily asked.

"No, sir."

"We have the information we need. We will confer in my cabin and come back with a sentence." The captain rose and the three of them left the wardroom.

Halcyon sat in his chair sadly shaking his head. His heart beat heavily in his chest as he wondered if he would live or die.

It wasn't many minutes before the three officers came out of the captain's cabin. They took up the chairs again, and the captain rang the bell three times. "The prisoner will rise and receive the sentence of the court-martial." The captain placed the hilt of the dagger toward Halcyon.

He thrilled at the sight. He was going to live!

"Before the sentence is passed, does the prisoner have any last words?" the captain asked.

With a new energy, Halcyon snapped to attention. "Sir, I only acted to save the ship in time of danger. I realize that my weather spell placed this good ship in peril and for that I'm truly sorry."

The captain looked Halcyon in the eyes. "Mr. Blithe, this court finds you guilty of violating Article Three of the naval Articles of War. As the captain of this ship, I'm permitted a great deal of leeway in your sentence. Through your testimony, I have determined that your actions were fitting considering the circumstances. I am hereby pardoning you for the article violation. Navy protocol requires me to present you with five hundred bars of gold in payment for the wish spell you used on the heart. For damages to ship and crew as a result of the storm your action caused, I'm fining you five hundred bars of gold. This court is adjourned."

Fallow and even Solvalson slapped Halcyon on the back in congratulation.

The captain coughed and the men quieted down.

"Mr. Blithe," the captain said, "I would have a word with you in my quarters."

"Aye, aye, sir," Halcyon replied.

As the captain went into his cabin, Halcyon followed.

"Close the hatch behind you," the captain ordered.

"Sir" was all Halcyon said as he did what he was told. The captain's cabin was large, with blast-tube ports on three sides. The guns didn't interfere with the space as the cabin had plenty of room for the captain's things. Halcyon was amazed to see the captain offer him a glass of wine.

"I wasn't pleased to discover that you used high magic on my ship. Don't let it happen again," the captain said as he took a sip of his wine and waited for Halcyon to taste his.

"No, sir, I truly won't, sir," Halcyon nervously said.

Olden took another sip of the wine, this time savoring the smell as he swirled the liquid in his glass. "We won't even go into the stupidity of you using that weather spell. Commander Giantson is an excellent teacher in the arts magical. Follow his lead and you can't go wrong."

It was impossible for Halcyon to relax in front of his captain. Each of the captain's words hit him like a hammer blow. "Sir, yes sir." Only a great effort of will kept Blithe from snapping to attention with every one of the captain's statements.

"The reason the navy has rules against the use of high magic is simple. Such spells are wildly unpredictable. You could have turned the *Sanguine* into a goose as easily as putting that ice around our old dragon's heart. For that reason, I feel the need to change your duty station for the length of this tour."

Halcyon didn't know the course the captain was heading in, but he doubted he would like it.

"Your new battle station will be the heart chamber of the ship. I want you to stand guard inside the chamber and under no circumstances are you to leave that guard post while we are in battle. Have I made myself perfectly clear in my order?" the captain asked.

"I am to guard the dragon's heart at all cost to my life. I understand perfectly, sir." Halcyon's disappointment must have revealed itself in his tone.

"I realize that for a young fire-eater like yourself, and a Blithe at that, you might think such a post lacks the glory of a blast-tube officer or even a boarding-party officer. I'm telling you I have a problem on my ship. There is a hidden enemy here. That enemy will strike again at the dragon's heart. I want a good man protecting that heart. Are you such an officer, Mr. Blithe?" the captain asked.

"Sir, I will not let you down. As long as I breathe, no one is going to harm that heart." Halcyon's tone was certain and determined.

"Good answer, sir. Finish your wine and report to your wardroom. I only have two bottles of that Alm wine left and it's certainly too good to leave any in the glass." The captain's tone was almost jolly.

Halcyon feared that the captain had only one bottle of that wine left, but he wasn't going to say anything. He closed the hatch softly behind him, leaving the captain to his own thoughts.

XVII

✤ ✤ ✤

𝔈𝔫𝔢𝔪𝔶 𝔖𝔥𝔦𝔭𝔰 𝔖𝔦𝔤𝔥𝔱𝔢𝔡

HIS MAJESTY'S ARTICLES OF WAR: ARTICLE XVII

*All murders committed by any person in the fleet shall be pun-
ished with death by the sentence of a court-martial.*

Eleven bells rang out the start of the late-night watch. Halcyon
was there early, as was his habit. "Lieutenant Durand, Midshipwizard Blithe reporting for duty, ma'am."

"Get your name in the ship's log, Mr. Blithe," Jillian Durand
said. "Then I want you to take a glass and climb to the topgallant.
It's good to have you back in action. I have all sorts of scutwork I
need you to do. First, I want you to look nor'west along our
course. That little storm of yours blew us farther east than we
planned. I'm thinking I've seen the glow from a ship's stern most
of the evening. I put on some more sail just to see if we could see
something interesting in the distance. Get a move on, Midshipwizard, and find that ship for me."

"Aye, aye, ma'am," Halcyon said, also glad to be back in action. He opened the storage locker below the course cabinet and took out one of the ship's telescopes. It came in a leather case, which he attached to his belt. It wouldn't do to break a piece of the king's equipment. After all, the captain might want to fine him a hundred bars of gold to replace it.

Smiling at his own jest, Halcyon used the ratlines to move up past the mainsail, maintopsail, and the main topgallant.

Force-two winds at best, he thought as the ship's sails billowed and shook in the very light gusting breeze, but never filled to their full capacity. *It's not likely we can catch much tonight if the wind doesn't pick up*, he thought.

He reached the crow's nest on the mainmast. Hooking a safety line to his belt, he sat down on the platform and allowed his feet to hang on either side of the rigging. With the harness on, he wasn't going to fall even if the ship tacked suddenly. Halcyon enjoyed the clean, crisp night air. It was a dark night, with no moon, and the stars appeared dim in the night sky.

Only the lantern by the great wheel allowed him to see the deck below in the darkness.

For just a second he thought of raising a small wind to push the ship along faster, and then realized the foolishness of the idea. "There's no way in the world I'm ever going to cast a wind spell again," he chided himself. "Let's just see if we can find this phantom ship of Miss Durand's."

Halcyon was in no hurry to climb down, and there was no time limit put on his searching the horizon.

Taking the glass out of its leather case, he wrapped the attached cord around his wrist as he brought the glass up to his eye. The academy had taught him not to close the other eye when he used the glass so focusing with it was easier.

"There's nothing to the north," he said to himself after minutes of searching. He turned to the northwest.

" 'Ware the crow's nest," came a voice from below.

Halcyon looked down, but could only make out a dark shape on the ratlines. The shape turned into Seaman Hunter.

"Welcome, Seaman Hunter. What brings you up to this rare perch?" Halcyon asked good-naturedly.

"Durand's idea. Two sets of eyes have twice the chance of sightin' the enemy," Hunter told him.

"Welcome aboard the good ship *Crow's Nest*," joked Halcyon.

"Huh?" the sailor said, clearly not getting the little joke.

"You look nor'west; I'll scan the west for a bit. Let's see if we can find Durand's ship," Halcyon ordered.

Minutes turned to an hour as both men scanned the night and the horizon.

"See anything, Hunter?" the midshipwizard asked.

"I think I've spotted her, but she's right on the horizon," Hunter observed. "The only reason you can see her at all is that I'm bettin' she's a first-rater and has more than her fair share of runnin' lights. Look when the *Sanguine* is at the top of the next crestin' wave. She's just at the horizon and we can only see her stern lights when she and the *Sanguine* are both at the top of a wave's crest."

It took several minutes for the waves and the ships to be just right again.

"There she is, thirty-five miles out at least. Just at the horizon. Well done, Hunter," Halcyon said enthusiastically.

"She must be with other ships. That's why she has those runnin' lights on," Hunter remarked.

"I'll go tell the lieutenant, you keep watch until relieved. Call out if the ship changes direction or more ships appear on the horizon," Halcyon said excitedly.

The midshipwizard almost flew down the ratlines. The thought of facing an enemy ship excited him, making his heart beat faster.

Hitting the deck, he ran to the wheel and Lieutenant Durand on the quarterdeck.

He came to attention in front of Durand. "Ma'am, there's a ship on the horizon, just as you thought. Seaman Hunter and I believe it could be a first-rater by its running lights. There could be . . ."

"Blithe, calm down," Durand interrupted. "Since it took you more than two hours to find it, you can take more than two seconds to report it. Begin again; give me all the details as you know them."

Halcyon came to parade rest with his feet firmly planted wide on the deck and his hands behind his back. He took several deep breaths. "Ma'am, Seaman Hunter and I scanned the horizon for almost two hours. Approximately five points off of north and to the west along our current course, we spotted the running lights of a ship. We speculated that it was a first-rater by the configuration of the lights and the fact that a merchantman wouldn't advertise its presence at night to the enemy.

"We don't seem to be catching up to it, as we can only see the lights on the horizon when our dragonship and their ship are both at the top of the sea's roll. I have ordered Seaman Hunter to call out if the course of that ship changes or more ships appear on the horizon.

"Should I sound battle stations, ma'am?" Halcyon asked.

In the light of the lantern, Halcyon could see the woman make a face of disgust.

"Of course not," she replied. "Waking the captain and Major Aberdeen with battle stations at this time isn't how lieutenants like myself get promoted in this king's navy. We're in a stern chase, Mr. Blithe, and the wind's not helping at this moment. It could be two days before we're in firing distance and that's if the ship in front of us wants to dance to our tune. We'll hold our course and look at the situation tomorrow afternoon. You get a reprieve from me; Lieutenant Commander Giantson requires your presence in the heart chamber. Get down there and see what he needs."

"Aye, aye, ma'am," Halcyon said. Suddenly, he wasn't so excited about the coming battle. He'd momentarily forgotten that his battle station was to be in the heart chamber. There'd be no blast-tube shooting for him.

It took only a few minutes to go from deck to deck into the depths of the ship. There were now more marine guards posted in key positions in the ship. The heart and liver chambers had two marines at each hatch. The ones at the heart chamber came to attention when Blithe appeared.

"At ease, men. Is Commander Giantson in there?" Halcyon asked.

"Yes he is. He told us to let you in as soon as you came down," one of the marines said. He opened the hatch for the midshipwizard.

Halcyon walked into the heart chamber and once again marveled at the huge dragon organ beating at the center of the chamber. This time he smelled something different in the area. Sniffing the air, he couldn't quite make it out.

"It's a summer meadow," Giantson said as he came around the heart and noticed Halcyon.

"What, sir?" Halcyon asked.

"That odor you smell is the fragrance of a summer meadow." Giantson was looking at the heart, minutely inspecting the ice edge. "I myself know little about pixie magic. It's a mystery to most magical scholars. Pixies and giants don't get along at all, which makes me with my giant heritage especially curious about them. The magic you've set loose in this chamber has the odor of the pixies that made it.

"In any event, I've brought you down here to see if you can have any effect on this ice you created. Attend me if you will, young Halcyon."

"Certainly, sir, I'll do whatever I can," Halcyon said, coming next to the side of the wizard.

"This ice is filled with magic," Daton observed. "Normally, ice would harm the tissue of the heart after prolonged exposure. That was my first concern when I saw this ice wasn't melting. Naturally, because of the blast gel we can't bring fire in here, but notice this."

The wizard placed his large hand on the surface of the ice.

"My hand's warmth would normally melt ice and it isn't doing a thing. I've also carefully chipped at the ice and it doesn't come away at all. Try your hand on that same spot."

The ice was several feet thick where the wizard pointed. The top half of the heart was free of the ice. Halcyon reached out as instructed and placed his hand on the ice. He felt the cold, instantly, but it was a pleasant tingling on his palm.

The white ice turned clear under his touch and his hand did indeed melt the ice.

"There, I thought so," Daton said, pleased with his speculation. "Let's have a look at your palm."

Halcyon showed his open palm to the commander. He was surprised to see the black scar of his cursing gone from the lifeline on his palm. "How did that happen?" he asked.

"The high magic is tied somehow to the wisher. I'm sure you will be able to make this entire ice sheath all go away with a little time and effort. It's a healing magic so it healed the scar on your palm. I know it will heal the other one if you want."

"Why can't we just leave the ice on the heart if it helps our dragon?" Halcyon wanted to know.

"The blast gel is of course the problem," Daton said as he moved over to the section of the heart covered in the blast gel. He waved his hand in a magical spell and the white ice turned clear on that side of the heart. The large patch of green blast gel was clearly visible under the many inches of ice. "It's between the heart and the ice. Blast gel is nasty stuff and very poisonous. That's why I suspect the ice has such great healing properties. It's restoring, second by second, the damage to the heart that the gel is doing.

"I also suspect a strong blow to the ice will still set off the gel under the ice," Commander Giantson said. "When we get to port, we'll bring in a fire wizard and you and the wizard will work on this ice and the gel. I've every reason to believe if you died suddenly, the ice would vanish, and the gel would explode. Try hard not to die. That's an order, young Halcyon."

"I'll do my best, sir," Halcyon said in all seriousness. He looked at his left hand and the scar on his palm. "I'm going to keep this one. It's a good reminder of what happened to me."

They spent the rest of the watch taking measurements of the heart and the ice. Halcyon had several technical questions about defensive spells he'd been meaning to ask. Daton asked Halcyon about his experience with pixies.

The midshipwizard wardroom was relatively quiet with only the creaking of the ship and the snores of a few of the sleepers to break the silence. Suddenly, the hatch flew open.

"Get up! Move your bones, for battle stations!" Hackle screamed out to the sleeping boys in the wardroom.

At the words "battle stations," all of them rushed out of their beds.

"Drums, where's the sound of drums?" Grunseth asked.

"Commander Wily wants you on the quarterdeck in full battle gear. We're a day away from a fight, but he wants to know you're all ready. So get a move on. Wily doesn't want to wait for slugabeds like you all," Hackle said with too much relish at waking the tired boys.

Throwing open his sea chest, Halcyon reached in for the equipment he'd need. All of his things were brand-new. Other, older brothers had gotten magical equipment from former

Blithes. He didn't care; he cherished every one of the things he'd received, because they came to him at the order of his father. As Halcyon put on the enchanted bracers, the luck ring, the water ring, and the belt of strength, he could remember his father giving him every one of them.

His father's words came to mind. "Halcyon, we Blithes send our sons and daughters off to war generation after generation. I know you'll do the family proud. We give each of our new recruits the best equipment we can afford. Bring it all back and give it to your son when you retire. I love you, my son, and I'm proud of you."

Halcyon's father was gone now, but his spirit still lived on in Halcyon. The midshipwizard strapped on his saber and ignored Hackle's badgering. Walking out of the wardroom, Halcyon was as ready as he could be for whatever battle would bring him.

Coming up on deck, he tipped his battle helm to the quarterdeck. Looking past the prow, he would make out his enemy ship still more than twenty miles in the distance. However, the *Sanguine* was catching up.

"*Good work,*" he thought to the dragon. The dragon's head turned and looked back at him in response. He waved up at it and then climbed those quarterdeck steps. Dart and Elan were there at attention already beside Commander Wily. Dart winked at Halcyon as he came up.

"Reporting for inspection, sir," Halcyon said as he saluted Wily.

"Stand with the others, Mr. Blithe" was all Wily said to him.

Eventually all of the midshipwizards came onto the quarterdeck.

"Mr. Forrest, you are the last to report again," Commander Wily barked. "What is the nineteenth Article of War?"

"Sir: 'Every officer or other person in the fleet who shall knowingly make or sign a false muster or muster book, or who shall command, counsel, or procure the making or signing thereof, or who shall aid or abet any other person in the making or signing thereof, shall, upon proof of any such offense being made before a court-martial, be cashiered, and rendered incapable of further employment in His Majesty's naval service.'" Mark quoted the article without hesitation.

"Mr. Forrest, you will be the first or second crew member to muster for the next three watches or I will know the reason why. Do you understand me, sir?" Wily's tone of voice was grimmer than his smiling face would indicate.

"Sir, yes sir," Forrest said, standing at attention.

"At ease, everyone," Wily ordered.

The group came to parade rest on the rocking deck.

"Midshipwizard Merand, I have to compliment you on this batch of midshipwizards. I've never known a group of young officers that knew their Articles so well," Wily said.

Alvena just stood with the rest, a big smile on her face.

"I've called you all here to talk of the upcoming battle. Some of you have seen action before, but most haven't. I was young once and know how your heart races and your bones ache to come to grips with the enemy. He's out there right now. I want you all to take a look at him." Wily pointed to the northwest, and all eyes turned to the ship in the distance.

Halcyon noticed the captain standing by the great wheel. The captain's eyes turned as well. He was clearly listening to what Wily was saying.

Wily continued, "That's a first-rater we will be facing. The standard Maleen battle tactic is to close with the enemy and board. That ship has at least one hundred blast-tubes. They have a huge boarding plank called a corvus. It comes over our deck and crashes down with a spike at its end. That maneuver will be difficult for them, as this dragonship is taller than they are.

"Mr. Haywhen, front and center, draw your weapon and come on guard," barked Wily.

Tupper drew his saber. The weapon glowed from some type of

magic. Halcyon hadn't seen that glow before. This wasn't a practice weapon; its edge was magically razor-sharp, and its point could kill.

Wily started circling Tupper. He gestured with his hand and the red glow of the Drusan shield came alive around the commander's body.

Halcyon had talked to Commander Giantson about the Drusan magical shield and learned a great deal about its properties. He also now knew that Commander Wily had to be an unusually capable spellcaster to make that shield happen with just a simple gesture. Halcyon noted a look of concern on the captain's face.

Wily drew his own saber. The weapon was longer and thicker than Tupper's. "Arcanians come to battle wearing helms. None of our enemies wear such equipment, much to their regret."

Tupper refused to stand still as Dire Wily circled him. He stayed on guard, his body tense, just as if he faced a real enemy. Halcyon thought Tupper was itching to lunge at the commander.

"The marines of the enemy are slightly larger than I am, and all of them wear a chest plate that few of you could punch through with your weapons. Mr. Haywhen, when you are ready please lunge for my chest. Let me worry about any damage you might inflict. When you are ready, sir," Wily said casually. The commander was almost twice as tall as little twelve-year-old Tupper. Today his arms bulged with thick muscles, and Halcyon wondered if maybe the commander hadn't cast some type of strengthening spell.

The commander went a full circle around Tupper. "I . . ."

Tupper had been waiting for the commander to start his next sentence before he struck. He feinted left and lunged straight into the chest of the commander.

Wily tried to beat away Tupper's blade, but was completely fooled by the left action, and Tupper's tip struck deeply into the chest of the officer. Only the bright red flair of the shield stopped the blade from taking the commander's heart.

Tupper stood back, a look of shock on his face. If not for the magic of Wily, he would have killed his commander.

"Well done!" Captain Olden shouted.

Wily stood there surprised as well.

"Urh, yes, Mr. Haywhen, fall back in line. You obviously have the ability to pierce a Maleen's chest. Mr. Spangler, front and center. Draw your weapon, man, and be prepared to use it," ordered Wily.

The thirteen-year-old Spangler was a little larger than Tupper, but still looked small next to Dire Wily.

Wily again circled the boy and talked to the rest of them. "Young Spangler here hasn't fastened his battle helm, notice his strap is dangling at his neck."

Robert reached to fasten the strap.

In a blur of motion, Wily closed chest-to-chest. Using his off hand, he struck off Robert's helm; then he smashed him in the face with a head butt. The boy dropped his weapon and went down on one knee in pain.

"It's no good having a helm if the first enemy you encounter can knock it off. Also, my first rule of battle is, no one expects a head butt. Remember that and it could save your life someday." Wily bent down to help Robert up. The boy's nose was bleeding. "It hurts now, I know, but I venture to say you'll never forget to fasten your helm again. Back in line, boy."

Wily paced back and forth in front of all of the midshipwizards. He looked each one of them over. "Mr. Blithe, front and center. Draw your weapon, boy, and don't let me get close, I warn you now."

Halcyon, his heart beating faster than it ever had before, drew his weapon and pointed it unwaveringly at the chest of Commander Wily.

The commander began circling Halcyon and suddenly stopped. His blade pointed over at Surehand and Boatson. "Gentlemen, please move to the stern part of our little circle, I see the enemy ship is changing position."

Everyone's eyes shifted to see the enemy ship—everyone's eyes but Halcyon's. His weapon and his eyes remained focused on the chest of Mr. Wily. Halcyon thought he noticed an irritated expression briefly cross the smiling face of the commander.

Suddenly Dire lifted his off hand into the air and made a fist. "Torna, teseact!" he shouted. A dark mass covered his fist and he threw that mass at Halcyon.

For the boy's part he tried ducking the spell, but couldn't. He felt his bracers gently squeeze his arms. The darkness turned to dust and fell all around him.

Failing the spell, Wily came in attacking. Half lunging, slashing when that failed, he managed to cut into the sleeve of Halcyon's jacket.

"There, notice those very special bracers Mr. Blithe is wearing," Wily said. "The magic I used should have captured our Halcyon's mind, but failed because of those bracers. Such equipment is not standard in our navy. Those bracers are of pixie work, I wager, aren't they, Mr. Blithe?"

"Yes, they . . ." Halcyon stopped talking, interrupted by Wily's lunge at him. He barely parried it and stopped talking.

"Hold a moment," Captain Olden ordered as he moved between the two officers. The captain had his saber drawn. "Our Mr. Wily is a skilled swordsman. He's stronger than you are, Mr. Blithe, and he has far more experience. You must fight him absence-of-blade. Don't let his blade strike yours so that his stronger wrist and arm can batter at your defenses. On guard, Mr. Wily."

The look on Dire Wily's face told Halcyon he didn't really want to do what the captain asked, but the captain's weapon didn't give him any choice. Their blades passed back and forth for many minutes. Every time Commander Wily tried to slash at the captain's weapon, it moved aside, as did the captain. The amazing tactic of not allowing the enemy weapon to strike the captain's sword revealed itself to all of the midshipwizards. They were all swordsmen enough to realize how to perform the tactic they saw revealed in the captain's action.

"Halt," the captain ordered. Both men stopped and lowered their weapons. Wily was breathing hard, but the captain seemed totally fresh. "Mr. Wily is giving you all an important lesson here, but I just wanted to break in to give you a possible new tool to use in your fencing bag of tricks. When we all fence together again, I'll work you all on the absence-of-blade technique. Carry on."

"Yes, quite. Thank you, Captain. Mr. Blithe, if you please, come on guard again." Wily gave the order, but he was looking past Halcyon toward the enemy ship. There was a questioning look on his face.

Halcyon refused to be distracted. His blade point and his eyes never left Wily's chest.

Failing to distract him, Wily threw a lightning bolt at Halcyon.

The midshipwizard's luck ring flashed briefly and he did manage to duck the attack. The bolt went through the space recently vacated by Dart and Jacom.

"What a surprising array of things you have, Mr. Blithe. The luck ring I now see you wearing is also an unusual piece of equipment. I hope none of your enchanted things ever fail you, forcing you to have to count on just yourself. Return to the line," Wily ordered briskly.

Halcyon sheathed his saber, happy to be out of the spotlight. Now he glanced at the enemy ship in the distance, and it did seem closer. He also looked back at the captain, noting a friendly grin in response. It quite warmed Halcyon's heart to see the encouraging glance from the captain.

"We stand on the deck of the *Sanguine* as ready as we can be for the upcoming battle." Wily's words were bold. "The enemy we face is strong and ruthless. It will take all of our skill and abilities to survive and win the day, and maybe even then it won't be enough. You men and women are the backbone of this ship. You must display heart and courage in front of the rest of the crew. When the heat and terrible destruction of battle crashes all around you, be strong when others are running in fear. When twice your numbers of enemy troops come boiling over the railing at you and yours, work to save the lives of the crew and the *Sanguine*. Take your battle stations until the next ship's bell. Carry on," Wily ordered.

Halcyon shook his head at Wily's speech. Half of his speech needed saying and was good to know. The other half, Halcyon thought, only sent chills down one's spine.

"Sir, Dori didn't mean to," one of the crew said, shaking Halcyon out of his thought.

"What did you say, sailor?" Halcyon asked.

"Begging your pardon, sir, Deadly Dori, that's the blast-tube here. The one that pulled loose in the storm, it didn't mean to break loose." The sailor was nervous; he kept twisting his sailor cap in his hands. There were five other men all looking expectantly up at Blithe.

"I should hope not. Next time we have a storm, make sure it's tied tight." Halcyon was smiling at the men, but there was a tinge of guilt in the statement, as it was the storm he caused that made the blast-tube tear loose.

"It won't tear loose again, and old Dori will make us all proud in the coming battle, mark my words, sir. We just wanted to say thank you for saving it and us. We were on deck that day and would have been killed for sure in the storm if you hadn't acted the way you did."

"Think nothing of that. I appreciate your words. The damn

storm shouldn't have happened in the first place. If Dori there does well in the coming battle, I'll stand you all to a drink at the first inn we come to. Continue on, men, continue on." Halcyon walked away, feeling good at having done something right as a result of that foolish storm.

XVIII

✿ ✿ ✿

On Being an Officer and a Gentleman

HIS MAJESTY'S ARTICLES OF WAR: ARTICLE XVIII

All robbery committed by any person in the fleet shall be punished with death, or otherwise, as a court-martial, upon consideration of the circumstances, shall find meet.

"What did you say?" Halcyon couldn't believe what Midshipwizard First Class Alvena Merand was telling him.

"I said, the captain has requested the presence of both of us at his table tonight for supper." Her tone showed her own nervousness.

"I still don't understand. Why in the world, before a major battle, would he ask for you and me at his table? Captains never ask midshipmen, wizards or not, to come to supper, do they?" Halcyon started pacing back and forth in the wardroom.

"That of course isn't the worst thing that's going to happen to you. Halcyon, you have to sing a supper song," Alvena said in all seriousness.

"I have to what?" Halcyon felt himself go pale.

"The lowest-ranking member of the captain's table must lead the rest in a song at meal's end. It's the custom of the captain's. I wanted to warn you so you wouldn't go all cotton-mouthed in front of the others. I know it's going to be hard; you'll just have to stiffen your spine. I'll be by tonight at almost seven bells. See that you're dressed and ready in your best. Do you have any questions, Midshipwizard?" Alvena asked.

Halcyon stood at attention. "Not a one, ma'am. Thank you, ma'am."

She walked out of the wardroom, and all the other boys rallied round their friend.

"By the gods, what did you do to merit that?" both Grunseth and Murdock asked at the same time as everyone spoke at once.

"Is it a good thing or a bad thing to be invited to dine with the captain?" Ryan Murdock asked.

"You have to bring two bottles of wine, it's tradition for the first meal with the captain," Tupper said.

"I don't have any wine. Who brings wine on a dragonship?" Halcyon said, dismay filling his mind and body.

"I've got two bottles, I'll give them to you to take," Tupper said.

"I'll work on your boots, they're a mess," Mark offered.

"Yes, we'll all pitch in for the honor of the wardroom. You're representing us, after all," Jock said.

Anne Driden burst into the wardroom. "Two more ships, to the north. There are three enemies now!"

Those who had them grabbed telescopes while the others ran up on deck.

The thought of the looming supper with the officers of the ship dropped from Blithe's mind as he ran up to the forecastle with the rest of his mates.

Other midshipwizards and lieutenants were there as well. Halcyon raised his telescope to look at the two new ships.

In the distance, at least twenty miles away, both ships appeared as twins of one another.

"They're fifth-raters, both from the Drusan navy. You can tell by their prows. They're flying Maleen colors. I'm betting they're filled with Maleen marines, sink me if they aren't," Dart remarked.

"They're coming downwind of us, they could be here in three hours," Andorvan nervously said.

"That's not going to happen." Elan Swordson sounded irritated. "Look at the first-rater, it's still running from us. I don't think two smaller warships are going to do the work their first-rater should be doing."

Standing behind the midshipwizards, ignoring the ships in the distance, and quite enjoying the conversation among the youth of the ship, Andool Griffon was secretly pleased at their displayed eagerness for the coming battle. They hadn't seen her come up on the forecastle deck.

"Mr. Surehand." She called him to attention. "If you were the captain of the first-rater, running before us right now, what would your orders be?"

"What, a great dragonship like the *Sanguine*, coming up my stern and me with only three ships to fight her? Sink me, Commander; I'd tell them all to run in three different directions like chickens!" Dart laughed at his jest, as did the others.

Andool only gave him a slight smile. "You are probably correct in your thinking, but I don't believe the Maleen admiralty would agree with your choice. As you reached port and news of your behavior became known, they'd probably hang you. While our Mr. Surehand is hanging, Mr. Boatson, what would you do?" she asked.

Jacom Boatson was a thin young man, middling good with a saber and very good with the technical details of sailing a ship. He was always looking over a pair of glasses at those about him. He talked unusually slowly. "I believe the Maleen standard battle tactic is to board as soon as possible. Toward that end, I would have my small squadron run away from the *Sanguine* until after dark. Then toward dawn I would come down on the ship and board with all three warships and take the *Sanguine* as soon as possible." He spoke so matter-of-factly that many of the other midshipwizards paled at the thought of losing so quickly and easily.

"Mr. Boatson, you are correct in thinking that is what they will probably do. However, I asked what you would do if you were in command. I was hoping for a little Arcanian wisdom, and found it sadly lacking this day in you. One more time, then." She looked at the assembled young men and women. Many of them turned to view the three ships, clearly hoping to escape the questioning of the second officer. "Mr. Blithe, what would you do if you were their commander?"

Without taking a second, he answered, "At dawn I would start a bombardment of the *Sanguine* on the port and starboard sides while the smallest of the three ships rammed the *Sanguine* head-on, thus killing the dragon and the ship at the same time."

"You'd what?" a stunned Griffon asked.

"My father always told me to look for weakness in any ship I served with," Halcyon replied. "Father felt knowing the ship's weaknesses could help any crew defend the ship better. The sea dragon is our greatest strength and our greatest weakness. A ship coming to ram the front of the *Sanguine* is difficult to stop, as our prow blast-tubes are few. If the enemy ship collided with the *Sanguine*'s head or neck, the dragon dies and so do we."

"Well done, Mr. Blithe. Your observation is a correct one. I'm glad to say they haven't thought of the tactic on the enemy side as yet. There'll be a battle of some type tomorrow, in the morning I should think. Get some rest, all of you, tonight," Griffon said as she left the forecastle.

"Sink me again, Hal, where did you get such an idea? Ram the ship, that's just crazy," Dart chided.

"I don't think it's so insane," Tupper chimed in. "It could work."

"Dragonships can turn fast, it would be a hard maneuver to carry out," Grunseth commented.

"Not that hard if the dragonship captain wasn't expecting it," Mark said. "It could be a good thing to remember when we fight other Maleen dragonships. I don't plan on being on this first-rater forever. One day I'm going to captain a frigate of my own."

"On that day, I look forward to seeing the seven fiery hells all iced up, Mark, because when they are solidly iced is the only time you're going to be captain of a ship," Anne teased.

Dart came up to Halcyon and got in the way of the midship-wizard looking at the enemy in the distance. "Hal, I heard about the captain's invitation. Well done, your fate is assured if the captain's on your side. Do you have a fresh handkerchief?" Dart asked.

"Handkerchief? I packed weapons, clothing, and lots of other things, but no one ever told me I'd need nose cloths, sink me," Halcyon quipped, smiling back at Dart.

"I've got loads of them. We'll get you on the proper course to looking good for this supper. You should see our Alvena if you think you're nervous. I bet she's redone her hair three times since she heard the news that she'd be dining with the captain. You know she only got invited because the captain wanted to dine with you?" Dart asked.

"No, that can't be true?" Halcyon couldn't believe what he was hearing.

"As the rain comes down and the king smiles at his treasure room, it's a sure fact," Dart said with his hand on his heart. "I've been to a few fancy suppers in my day. Let's you and I go to my wardroom and compare notes on things so you don't look a fool. Have you decided on which song you're going to sing?"

Halcyon groaned at the very thought and walked away from

the rail thinking the enemies they would face tomorrow would be as nothing compared with the meal with the captain that night.

Later, in the afternoon, Halcyon was glad to see Lieutenant Hackle leave the wardroom as the other midshipwizards helped him get ready for the captain's supper. It was clear that the lieutenant didn't dine much with the captain. It was also clear that he couldn't do much to interfere, as it was the captain and Halcyon could very well say something about Hackle that would get the junior lieutenant in trouble.

Before seven bells, a very smart-looking Merand walked into the wardroom. The female dress uniform consisted of a gray jacket with blue piping along the sleeves and collar. The male counterpart was a blue jacket with gray stripes along the sleeves and collar.

Everyone came to attention when she entered the room.

"At ease," she said. She held a small basket with two bottles of wine. It matched the basket Halcyon had on the table. "Well done, we will have a great evening after four bottles of wine are sipped by everyone. Are you ready to go, Mr. Blithe?"

"Ma'am, yes ma'am," Halcyon replied. They stepped out of the wardroom and moved to the stern.

When they walked into the captain's wardroom, Halcyon couldn't help but have the exact same feeling of dread he had at his court-martial. The room appeared vastly changed from that time. There were at least thirty silver place settings. The captain's steward, Kendal, greeted them both at the hatch.

"You've both brought wine, well done. It's so good to see young officers these days honoring the old traditions," Kendal said. "I'll make sure the captain knows you brought them. Your places are marked at the head of the table alongside Captain Olden. Enjoy the meal; we're having the last of the corned beef tonight. The officers usually stand waiting at their chairs until the captain enters the area. The captain gives a toast to the king and you all sit down. When everyone has finished the blood pudding, I'll serve your bottles and you will be singing, Mr. Blithe. The captain enjoys a good song after his meal. Carry on, you two, carry on."

In moments the wardroom was ablaze with color. The marine officers walked in wearing their red coats. All the men were clearly fighters—big-boned, with rippling muscles, many with battle scars. Major Aberdeen wasn't the biggest of the lot by far.

A blushing Marine Corporal Denna Darkwater was dressed all in green with red stripes down her sleeves and collar. She didn't look the trained killer in her dress uniform, Halcyon thought. The war braid down her back was full of tiny skull beads showing off her skill in combat. Halcyon knew that tradition dictated there be a bead for every enemy officer killed by the owner of the braid. There were more than twenty beads in her hair. She looked up, noticed his friendly stare, and glared at him for a moment.

The lieutenants of the ship came in, and Jillian Durand stood out in her gray uniform, much the same as Alvena did.

Giantson and Wily walked through the captain's hatch laughing about something. After them came an arguing captain and Second Officer Griffon. They were clearly in a heated discussion. As the captain came to his place at the head of the table, he stopped arguing and smiled at the assembled crew.

"Ladies and gentlemen, please raise the glasses in front of you." The captain waited for everyone to take up a full wineglass. "Our first toast of the evening is always to His Arcanian Majesty, long may he reign."

"To the king!" The officers drank the toast.

The captain continued, "Please, all of you, sit, sit. I'm ordering you to drink and be merry, because tomorrow might find some of us very grave men and women, what?"

Only half the table got the joke, but Halcyon laughed the

loudest of the group, perfectly understanding what the captain meant.

The captain started walking round the table. Picking up a large bottle and smiling, he helped refill some of the glasses. "I'm noticing a nasty trend, Major Aberdeen."

"What trend is that, sir?" the major asked.

"I'm serving a rather excellent Ilumin red tonight at the table," the captain observed. "All of my lieutenants have sipped of it rather modestly. Even my two midshipwizards—welcome to my table, you two—have only sipped their wines. However, look at your marines. Most of them have finished their first glass. At this rate we'd better capture all three enemy ships tomorrow just to plunder their stores of wine for you marines."

Once again, the wardroom rocked with mirth.

"Well said, Captain," Major Aberdeen commented. "Get us near enough and we marines will do our part. After all, we'll more than do our part tonight with your wine, of course."

The captain circled the table, emptying two more bottles of wine as he reached Halcyon's seat. "Ladies and gentlemen, I would introduce Midshipwizards Alvena Merand and Halcyon Blithe. Mr. Blithe comes from that famous line of Blithes so bravely serving the king and navy for many generations. Some of you have worked with our Mr. Blithe. Corporal Darkwater, I believe he put you on your ass the first time you two met."

The corporal turned beet red at the mention of that practice session. Her major spoke up for her.

"I'm sure she is ready for a rematch at the pleasure of your young midshipwizard, but at the moment there's Steward Kendal's corned beef to seriously consider," the major quipped.

The captain sat down at his place. "And consider it we will. Steward, serve the beef if you please." The captain waved in the main course, and the table broke up into many different conversations. The sounds of eating and conversation filled the wardroom for many minutes.

Halcyon wasn't at all sure he could eat, he was that nervous. At his right Alvena sat quietly with the captain on her other side. On his left, Andool Griffon chatted with the major across from her at the table. They were having a spirited conversation about the beef.

"It's good Arcanian beef that has made our country strong, ma'am," Major Aberdeen maintained.

"Not our mighty navy, not the crews of its ships, not even the just rule of the monarchy?" Andool shot back at the major in a teasing manner.

He sputtered a bit at her words, and then forked a large chunk of the corned beef up for inspection. "All those things you mentioned are important, of course. Nevertheless, beef gives a warrior vigor. It adds to girth and powers muscles, allowing amazing feats martial, if you will."

The major forked in the beef with Halcyon noting that the chunk was clearly larger than one normal man could handle in an hour. The major was out of the conversation for some time to come.

"Miss Merand," the captain said, "I would like your youthful opinion on an argument my second and I were having as we came in."

"Yes, sir." Alvena put down her fork—she'd barely touched her food—and waited for the captain.

"Our Griffon here has a new blast-tube shell she wants to try out," the captain explained. "It's pointed at one end and much longer than the normal round shot used in our service. She made me bring two hundred of the bloody things on board the ship. Now she expects me to use them tomorrow in the battle against three of the enemy. What do you think of such foolishness? Now,

I know she is your superior officer, but I want your honest opinion." The captain's tone was earnest and others at the table waited for the midshipwizard's answer.

"I'm not familiar with such shells myself. Why does the second officer want to use the new type of shot?" Alvena asked.

"She claims the range of them is two miles instead of the one mile of our old shot," the captain said, putting a great deal of emphasis on the word "claims."

"Midshipwizard Merand," Andool interrupted. "For the sake of this argument let's assume that indeed these shells can be hurled almost two miles instead of the one of the old-style round shot. Now what is your opinion?"

"You are telling me I have the chance to kill Maleen two miles away instead of one. I want a ship full of these shells, Captain." Merand's answer was excitedly bloodthirsty.

"Hear, hear, well said," Major Aberdeen and several of his lieutenants said.

"Hear that, Andool? I see the marines on my ship aren't the only fire-eaters we have in the crew. I'm clearly outvoted here. A captain outvoted; now, that's a funny thought." Olden grinned and many smiled along with him. "We'll use all two hundred of those shells in the first few salvos tomorrow at dawn. I have no doubt the enemy will have closed with us by then. If the shells work as you've promised, we'll have put two broadsides in their first-rater before they know they are in the battle."

"I agree with your first judgment, Captain. I have no faith in these new long shots. They'll strike the water a mile short and then we'll be able to get on with the real battle," Wily spoke up. "Mr. Blithe, I asked the captain to bring you to table because of your amazing thought on the forecastle this afternoon."

Gulping, Halcyon looked to Mr. Wily. "What thought is that, sir? We were all just looking at the three ships."

"Did you really suggest to Andool that the best way to kill a dragonship was to ram its skull?" There was a bit of wonder in Wily's voice.

"It seems like the best idea to me. The sea dragon keeps its head under the water during blast-tube exchanges," Halcyon replied matter-of-factly.

"Well, Mr. Blithe, I have to say in over twenty years of battling using sea dragon warships, not one has been destroyed by ramming. I don't think any captain has tried the tactic," the first officer said.

"That doesn't make it invalid, does it?" Halcyon said, looking to the captain.

"Indeed not, Mr. Blithe," the captain replied. "I think the idea is such a good one that fifth- and fourth-raters will be getting new assignments in both navies in the near future. You've rammed into a capital idea, and damn me for not thinking of it first."

"Rammed, what?" Major Aberdeen was the first one to get the jest. His laughter was infectious.

The steward came to fill Halcyon's glass a third time. Halcyon refused and asked for water. "I have to have a clear head this evening, I have the late watch."

The captain observed Blithe refusing the third glass and smiled in appreciation.

Jillian Durand was arguing with one of the lieutenant majors of the marines, a Mr. Bladeson. "I say the ship's skin has grown thicker since the storm and the ship moves faster as well."

"I have to disagree, but I'm sure Commander Giantson knows the answer. We should ask him. Commander, has the dragonship changed its skin or speed with the magic Mr. Blithe used on it?" the lieutenant major asked.

"Miss Durand is exactly right. The dragon's skin has thickened an inch since Mr. Blithe's wish, and the sea dragon is much more vigorous. The good captain here is going to be unhappy when the ice vanishes from the heart. I suspect the dragon's performance will be back to normal then," Giantson replied.

"Mr. Blithe, you must tell us," Dire Wily asked, "where did you get such a rare thing as a pixie wishing potion?"

Halcyon sputtered while taking a drink of water. Everyone was looking at him now as all conversations stopped for his answer. At that same second, he realized they had all been eating the blood pudding and he would soon have to sing. He hoped a good story would allow someone else to have to sing.

"Well, those wishing potions appear at the bedside of the oldest female Blithe whenever one of the family is going to go to sea for the first time," Halcyon answered. "She is supposed to present the wishing potion to the leaving family member. It's been a tradition helping the Blithes to prosper since the earliest times of the family.

"The ancestral story goes that many generations of Blithes ago we were a very prosperous family of sea merchants. In those days, women weren't allowed to fight in the armies and navies of Arcania. Amenda Blithe was a young girl then and resented the fact that women couldn't go to war."

Andool spoke up: "As well she should."

"Yes," Halcyon responded to her. "I'm sure for lots of reasons we men are glad to serve alongside Arcanian women. However, these were ancient times and the men of Arcania didn't know any better. Anyway . . ." Halcyon was warming to his story and the chance to tell it to his fellow shipmates. "She had a hard leather ball she was quite proud of. She called it her tanthum. Amenda's use of that name, what with her at the age of seven, quite shocked her mother and father."

"When you say tanthum, Mr. Blithe," interrupted Major Aberdeen, "are you talking about the process of taking an enemy's head, coating it in several coats of plaster, and using it as a missile against the family of the dead enemy?"

"Yes, it was an outrageous claim for a little girl in her day. It quite shocked her parents, but they loved her and the story goes that she became unusually good at striking targets with the leather ball. She would go about the castle and the courtyard hurling her ball at this or that target with bone-crushing results. After a while she never missed what she was aiming at."

The rest of the table men and women were smiling and shaking their heads at the bloodthirsty nature of the little Blithe as Halcyon told his story. The stewards had taken away the dessert dishes and uncorked the four bottles of wine brought by the young officers. The steward rang a small bell to stop Halcyon in his storytelling.

"This wine has been brought by the two midshipwizards. Mr. Blithe has brought an unusually fine Ilumin white wine, and Miss Merand has brought golden wine from the city of the same name."

"Hear, hear!" Everyone beat the table with their hands in praise of the wine they were about to drink.

"Carry on, Mr. Blithe, with your excellent story," Commander Wily ordered.

"So, one day as the family story goes, little Amenda was playing on the beach with her two bodyguards. In those days, as today, young griffons would fly down from the mountains to eat of the fish on the shore. This day a griffon swooped down and landed near Amenda and her guards. It was rooting in some driftwood and a beautiful pixie revealed itself and called to Amenda and her guards for help. The pixie sported the rainbow-colored wings of royalty. At the time, none of the Blithe watchers knew how important the little pixie was.

"Amenda was all for helping, but her guards refused to let her charge into battle. The small griffon was about to snap up the pixie when Amenda threw her hardball right into the open beak of the griffon.

"The hard leather ball caught in the beak of the creature, allowing the pixie to escape. The next morning Amenda found a wishing potion by her bed. From that day forward all of the Blithes have been given one wishing potion each for the kindness little Amenda showed that day."

"Well, no wonder the Blithes have done so well. Any family could prosper with wishing potions helping them generation after generation," Wily remarked.

"Commander, I agree with you," Halcyon said, ignoring the depreciating statement of Wily's. "It's a family tradition to only use those wishes in the service of others, but the pixie's generous gifts have benefited many down through time. I was only too happy to use mine to save the ship."

"Quite right, Mr. Blithe," the captain said. "Now, my fine young officer, I would have you lead us in song. Some of us have a long night of planning ahead, so begin, sir."

Halcyon stood up, trying to look much calmer than he felt. He toasted those around him with the water glass in his hand. Marshaling his courage, he sang.

The Sanguine is a ship me lads,
For the port of Ordune it's bound
At the quay it's all garnished
With bonnie lassies all around
Captain Olden gives the order
To sail the ocean wide
Where the sun it never sets me lads
Nor darkness dims the sky.

All of the men and women knew this song and joined in with the chorus.

And it's cheer up, me lads
Let your hearts never fail
For the bonnie ship the Sanguine
Goes a spoiling for a fight?

Along the quay at Ilumin
The lassies stand around
With their shawls all pulled about them
And the salt tears runnin' down

Oh don't you weep, my bonnie lass,
Though you be left behind
For the rose will grow on Talken's ice
Before we change our mind

And it's cheer up, me lads
Let your hearts never fail
For the bonnie ship the Sanguine
Goes a spoiling for a fight?

Here's a health to all the king's ships
Likewise the crews serving them as well
Here's a health to the king himself
And the Sanguine a ship of fame
We wear the trousers of the brown
And the jackets of the blue
When we return to Ilumin
We'll have sweethearts one or two.

And it's cheer up, me lads
Let your hearts never fail
For the bonnie ship the Sanguine
Goes a spoiling for a fight?

It'll be bright both day and night
When the Sanguine's *lads come home*
With a dragonship full of bounty
And money to our names
We'll make the cradles for to rock
And the blankets for to wear
And every lass in Ilumin
Sings a lullyby for us to hear

And it's cheer up, me lads
Let your hearts never fail
For the bonnie ship the Sanguine
Goes a spoiling for a fight?

The assembled crew sang the song again, and the captain stood when the tune was finished. Raising his glass once more, he said, "We had good food and better conversation. This is the good life of the navy and what we were all born to do. Tomorrow we'll defeat the bastards assembling before us, I've no doubt of that. I will also find the bastard who tried to sabotage my ship and my retribution will be swift and hard. To the *Sanguine*, long may it sail!" he toasted.

"To the *Sanguine*!"

Halcyon and Alvena left the wardroom filled with the energy of youth. Halcyon didn't like the fact that his battle station was at the heart of the ship, but he would do his duty. There was no thought of sleeping in the few hours before he would go on watch. He went up on deck to find the winds gusty and the darkness hiding the enemy in the distance.

XIX

✤ ✤ ✤

𝔅attle 𝔖tations

HIS MAJESTY'S ARTICLES OF WAR: ARTICLE XIX

Every officer or other person in the fleet who shall knowingly make or sign a false muster or muster book, or who shall command, counsel, or procure the making or signing thereof, or who shall aid or abet any other person in the making or signing thereof, shall, upon proof of any such offense being made before a court-martial, be cashiered, and rendered incapable of further employment in His Majesty's naval service.

False dawn crept slowly up in the east. The dark held little of the sun's light, but there was enough to outline the three enemy warships. Halcyon raised his telescope for the hundredth time, and with this attempt could finally see the decks and rigging of the three Maleen ships as more than just vague outlines in the darkness. *They're not five miles away at the most,* he thought.

Dart climbed up into the rigging of the mainmast with Halcyon. The two of them watched the enemy.

"They've already got their hammocks slung in the rigging," observed Dart. "The hammocks catch falling timbers and rigging cordage as shots rip them apart. They're ready for blast-tube combat."

Halcyon erupted in a perfect imitation of Second Officer Andool Griffon. "'The Arcanian navy, our navy, fires its shots at the bottom of the sea's roll. We want to kill our foes at the water level, not toy with their rags and sticks. Our shots are meant to kill the enemy firing at us. If I catch anyone firing their tube on the top of the sea's roll, I will personally flog them myself, if they live through that battle.'"

"Hal, you should be in a minstrel show, sink me if it isn't so." Dart's voice filled with amusement at his friend's imitation. "That's word for word what she said."

"I know. Even if I'm forced by my orders to be out of the action, I want to remember what it's like to crew a blast-tube." Halcyon was glum and couldn't help his mood.

"I think I know how you feel," Dart said sympathetically. "But the danger from the saboteur is just as real as those enemy blast-tubes not five miles away. We all do our parts as best we can. You did cause that healing ice to be stuck to the heart, saving all of our lives. Fate and the captain have their reasons for having you protect that heart again. Besides, if you kill the saboteur, you could get a medal."

"There'll be damn few medals passed out this morning," the captain said as he climbed up to the two midshipwizards in the rigging. "Don't salute; I don't need my crew tumbling to the deck just before a battle. What are the three little warbirds doing?" The captain turned his own telescope toward the enemy squadron.

Through Halcyon's glass, the midshipwizard saw the three warships heading on a nor'easterly course. The first-rater was apart from the other two. Halcyon thought it was clear the enemy hoped to catch the *Sanguine* between the ships for boarding. Even with his limited knowledge of naval battles, he knew from his brothers and uncles that most normal sea battles consisted of long lines of ships firing at each other trying to cripple the enemy doing the same thing back at them.

"The Maleen certainly are predictable. I don't think they've ever had an original thought in their dreary lives," the captain observed. "It won't be long now before we see the enemy squadron shortening sail and turning to fight. Mr. Surehand, how would you command the good ship *Sanguine* in this coming battle?"

A nervous Surehand answered, "I'd trust to our blast-tube crews. If Master Griffon is correct, we'll have placed two broadsides into the first-rater before they come within a mile of us. I'd hammer four more into her, ignoring the other two ships. If we damage the big one enough the other two will run."

Halcyon nodded his agreement with Dart's thinking.

"Mr. Surehand." The captain's tone was jovial. "I believe you to be correct. I don't have the faith in those new shells that Griffon has, but I still think we can slam several deadly broadsides into the first-rater before they come close. I've had those new shells stationed by all the blast-tubes. We'll shed ourselves of the foolish things in two broadsides, in any event.

"They'll want to board us and capture the dragon. I pity them that effort. We'll keep their first-rater between us and their other ships for as long as possible. It was foolish of them to think a dragonship with its greater ability to turn in to the wind might find itself between them in a death trap of their devising.

"Ah, I see that they're turning," the captain said while starting to climb down the ratlines. For a second he stopped and looked up at Halcyon. "By the way, Mr. Blithe, that was an amazing imitation of our Miss Griffon that you just performed. If she ever hears it, she'll kick your ass off this ship, in port or on the open sea, it won't matter to her. In addition, I won't be as gentle as our

Miss Griffon if you ever try to imitate me in my hearing. Just a thought you might consider, carry on."

"Yes, sir," they both said.

The two young men watched the enemy turn toward the *Sanguine*. It wouldn't be an hour before they were in blast-tube range.

"Well, that's for it, Hal. We're going to see a little action," Dart said as they climbed down the ratlines. "Luck to you, my friend, keep your guard up and your wits about you."

They both hit the deck at the same time. Gel monkeys were already spreading sand on the deck to help with the footing.

"Guard and wits, I'll remember if you remember, Dart." Halcyon shook his friend's hand.

"Sound battle stations," the captain ordered from the quarterdeck.

First Officer Wily came to the railing of the quarterdeck and shouted down to the deck below, "Mr. Solvalson, give my compliments to Second Officer Griffon and Lieutenant Commander Giantson. Tell them it's time. Sound battle stations, if you please."

Lieutenant Solvalson shouted to the marine drummer boys, "Battle stations, sound battle stations!" He rushed off to get the two officers.

The two drummer boys stood each to an entrance to the decks below. They started a loud steady beating of their drums. As the beat sounded belowdecks, the crew and marines hurtled to their posts for the upcoming battle. Halcyon entered his belowdecks wardroom. The wardroom was empty of his mates. Most of them had been up on deck for hours, ready for the battle. He threw open his sea chest and put on the equipment of war. His magical rings and bracers were on in a heartbeat.

He felt his throat drying up at the very thought of battle. His guts were in a knot as well.

His battle helm strapped quickly and easily to his head and his sword went to his hip. He was as ready as he'd ever be for the coming battle. He thought he would be more nervous, but he wasn't shaking at all.

"Of course I'm not shaking," he said to himself. "I have to sit the entire battle out in the heart chamber, guarding something not needing guards. I'm sure to become a famous naval officer listed in all the Arcanian posts at this rate." His own sarcasm wasn't lost on him as he briefly watched the marines tear down the walls of the wardroom and stow the wall panels away. "I can see the first sentence of the post right now: 'Newest navy Blithe successfully guards a room.'"

In less than a minute, the long deck appeared cleared for battle. All the lower cabin walls went down on the deck when combat became a certainty. Free of the walls, the blast-tubes could be better serviced in the larger, more open deck area.

Halcyon quickened his pace and ran down to the orlop deck to the heart chamber. Two marines guarded the chamber hatch. He saluted them and entered the area. For a few heartbeats, he stood in the chamber hatch enjoying the meadow smell of the chamber. The rest of the ship held many stenches, from farm animals to unwashed men. Since the magic of the wish spell, this chamber was extremely pleasant. For some odd reason the chamber's new-found smell reminded him of home, even though the family castle never smelled like a meadow.

The wizard Giantson had brought in extra lanterns for his examination of the heart. Halcyon lit all of them, and all the shadows of the chamber dissolved in light.

The sea dragon's heart beat a little faster as the creature reacted to the battle-station drums. Normally the huge organ slowly pumped blood throughout the dragon's body. Today the heart beat quite a bit faster as the dragon reacted to the drums. Halcyon had no doubt the creature could see the three ships in the distance and knew what was in store. The sea dragon had been in many battles in its nineteen years of service.

Part of the lessons for all midshipwizards was a study of their ship's past duty assignments. Halcyon knew the *Sanguine* to be a proud ship with many past battle honors. He'd felt that pride in the sea dragon's mind, the few times he'd been able to communicate with the creature.

Halcyon marveled again at the ice his wishing spell had created. Putting out his hand, he touched the quickly beating heart and the ice at the same time. Suddenly he was looking through the eyes of the dragon again. This wasn't like the encounters using the tannin oil; there was no communication with the creature's mind.

"Sanguine, can you hear me?" Halcyon mentally tried speaking with the sea dragon. There was no response. He speculated that some connection with the ice magic and the heart was allowing him to see what the dragon was seeing.

The dragon roared a battle challenge. Halcyon could hear it even from his closed chamber deep in the orlop deck. The midshipwizard felt the ship tacking to starboard.

As the captain ordered the tack to starboard, the *Sanguine's* bow chasers fired, and the four splashes showed the rest of the ship's blast-tube crews just how far the new shells could reach. The four water plumes landed just in front of the enemy first-rater.

That must have given them a surprise. Halcyon smiled to himself.

At little over two miles away, the enemy couldn't do near as well. In fact, their bow chasers fired early; clearly the crews of those tubes thought they could do as well as the *Sanguine's* crews. The shot fell well short of the maneuvering *Sanguine*.

The port tubes fired as they bore on the first-rater, as it advanced within two miles.

Through the sea dragon's better eyes, Halcyon could see the ship's name along its bow, the *Migol.*

The *Sanguine* shivered as blast-tube after blast-tube fired its deadly shot off the port side of the dragonship. At these distances, there was no reason to fire all at the same time. There was a better chance to strike the first-rater if each tube waited until it bore on the enemy.

A wall of smoke puffed up in front of the ship, blocking its view of the approaching enemy. As the smoke cleared in the gusty breeze, Halcyon could see that the *Migol's* jib boom was half in the sea, trailing several sets of sail. The jib, staysail, and forestaysail all ripped free and dragged in the water. Ship's crew worked frantically to cut away the half-shattered boom as it drastically slowed the forward motion of the ship.

The two smaller enemy ships quickly tacked to account for the *Sanguine's* direction, but they poorly judged the speed of the dragonship. The *Sanguine* tacked again; ignoring the closer targets of the frigates, it sent the port broadside into the first-rater as the blast-tubes bore on the ship. Over half the shells sailed over the top of the now closer enemy, as the tube crews weren't used to the distance their tubes could cast the new shells. The other half fell into the bow and half-exposed port side of the *Migol.* Plumes of smoke signaled some significant strikes.

Halcyon heard the hatch open behind him. His hand drew his weapon and he turned, all in one motion. He faced the first officer, Dire Wily, not four feet away. Dire was in his battle gear, and the red magical shield pulsed around him. He looked at Halcyon's weapon and sneered, "We seem to be a mite jumpy, Mr. Blithe. Whew, the stench that ice gives off is quite horrible, how do you stand it?"

Halcyon didn't lower his weapon even though he faced a superior officer. "Sir, no sir. I'm not jumpy, just surprised at your being here." He said this last in a shaky voice.

"Boy"—Wily's tone was friendly—"I know how it feels to want to be a part of your first combat. You don't want to see your first battle action within the walls of this room while your mates fight for their lives above deck. We have marines at both hatches; there's no need for you to stand here. I'm ordering you to man the blast-tube with your friends. Now go, that's an order."

"Really, sir." Halcyon couldn't believe his newfound luck. He sheathed his sword and went past Wily to the hatch. Before he opened it, he stopped. He breathed a heavy sigh and recited the first Article of War to himself and Officer Wily. "'No officer, mariner, soldier, or other person of the fleet shall leave their assigned post during combat unless ordered by the captain of the ship or unless extenuating circumstances warrant the abandoning of the post. Such dereliction of duty will be reviewed by a board of court-martial. The penalty for such dereliction is death or other punishment as the court-martial board shall find suitable.' Sorry, sir, you don't know how much I would love to leave this post. I appreciate your offer, sir, but I have to stay here."

"Halcyon, Hal," Dire said, clearly surprised that Halcyon could resist going topside to join the battle. "No one gives a damn about those Articles of War that you are so adept at quoting. Go fire the blast-tubes and enjoy yourself, what?"

To Halcyon's ears, the first officer was only trying to let Halcyon free to do what anyone would wish for, but duty was important, he thought to himself.

"I can't, sir, but thank you very much for your effort on my behalf. I'll stay and guard the heart until I'm relieved. It's the navy way, sir," Halcyon said to the now-unsmiling Dire Wily.

"Blithe, your decision is probably for the best. I don't think you're old enough to know about the navy way, but you do have a wayward way about you, that's for sure. There's really nothing for it but for you and I to dance. Mr. Blithe, draw your steel!"

Suddenly, Commander Wily held a saber in Halcyon's face.

Blithe drew his weapon, doing what he was ordered to do, but still not knowing why he was ordered to do so. Was this some sort of training lesson? Could it be some odd test? Halcyon didn't know what to think.

"Dance, sir?" Halcyon had no idea what the commander was talking about.

"Blithe, sometimes it's hard to believe you come from a family proud of its generations of warriors." Wily's voice took on a deeper timbre and slurred as fangs erupted from his widening mouth. Wily's face and body started changing in front of the amazed Halcyon. Hands gnarled into talons and bones crackled and popped as Wily grew taller. Clothing tore and fell away as flesh took on scales.

"Oh yes, that's much better." Its voice was deep and menacing. "You little humans are such boring creatures. I do so enjoy your politeness. We've none of that in Maleen. Being polite has become sort of a hobby with me. The great dance, boy, life-and-death combat are what I'm talking about. Since you won't be living long enough to gain such experience, let me tell you about the great dance." The thing that was Wily started circling Halcyon. Its larger saber tip constantly pointed at Blithe's chest.

"Fencers have always called the fencing bout the great dance of life. We move back and forth to the beat of our weapons," the creature that was Wily said.

Wily lunged; Halcyon stood his ground and beat the blade away from his chest. Halcyon tried counterattacking, but the monster pulled back in a blur of motion.

"We're dancing now, but you're forced to move to my tune," Wily growled, and stamped his right foot, hoping to draw Halcyon's eyes downward. With the creature's unweaponed, now-clawed hand, it threw a lightning bolt at Halcyon.

The midshipwizard raised his left arm bracer and it absorbed the attack, turning it to dust.

"Your family has been far too generous with their gifts," Wily growled, as the now fully transformed monster stood before Halcyon. A huge, scaly face replaced Wily's human one. The creature's head held four eyes and two slits for noses. Huge fangs protruded from a long muzzle. "We Maleen handle our clutchlings differently from you sickly humans. My birthing female threw me out of the den, ten days after my birth. I survived in the wilds for five years before I was ready to join a clan. No one gave me anything. I took what I wanted." The monster rising out of Dire Wily's body made a feint with its blade that Blithe easily blocked.

Four blazing yellow eyes mocked the midshipwizard's attempt at swordplay.

Absence-of-blade, absence-of-blade, Halcyon thought. He didn't want his sword snapped in half, taking the blows of the obviously stronger creature in front of him. The shapechanger pushed him about the chamber, not intimidated at all by Blithe's attempts at lunge attacks.

"You just aren't strong enough," growled the monster. "Maybe if you lived another hundred years you could have managed to make some of your attacks work against me. Give up, little mortal. Why make this more difficult than it has to be?"

Halcyon went to shout to the marines on the other side of the hatch, and former Wily made a magical gesture. Suddenly the room filled with a light haze. It was almost as if floating feathers filled the area. The thoughts of the creature invaded Blithe's mind.

"There will be no shouting for help. You rise or fall on your own merits. I think we both know how this dance will end. You might have become quite a powerful wizard, human. It's a good thing I caught you before your training made you a danger to my kind." The creature's thoughts were foul things striking Halcyon's mind.

"You are the first one to thwart my efforts. You should be proud

of yourself. On five other dragonships, I was able to destroy each heart in the middle of a battle and escape. I've become a bit of a legend among my kind. Many more of us will now walk among you destroying the things you hold dear." As the creature boasted, it continued its deadly attacks.

Lunge after lunge moved the young midshipwizard about the chamber. Several times Halcyon parried back and made deep hits on the flesh of the monster. Each time the red magical shield absorbed all the damage. Jumping back, Halcyon tried throwing his own lightning spell.

The energy washed over the creature and turned to black dust.

"I was a wizard of power before your famous father was born. You have no skills that can cause me pause. You've been a delightful bit of revenge, but now you really must die." The creature's thoughts filled Halcyon's mind.

Young Blithe was able to feel the intention of the monster as it attacked. He stopped each attack and made a deadly lunge of his own, right at the throat of the monster. The magic of the red shielding spell stopped the blade from penetrating, but the force of the successful attack drove back the monster, as the Drusan shield didn't dull the bruising pain of the thrust.

A huge talon batted Blithe's sword from his grasp. The monster reached out and grabbed Halcyon's throat.

"It's past time to take your life and get on with destroying this ship," the creature thought to Halcyon.

Gray draining magics flowed from the creature's talons to cover Halcyon's entire body. He tried to scream and cast protective magics, but the sound-deadening spell stopped his words. The death magics sucked at his very soul, stronger than the protections placed on his bracers. His hands tore at the massive scaled arm holding him up above the deck.

Unexpectedly, Halcyon dropped from the slack talons. His

back hit the deck. Feet kicking, he kept moving until his head hit the ice of the heart.

The silence spell vanished.

A boarding pike erupted from the chest of the monster, spilling blue gore in all directions.

Halcyon heard Ashe Fallow's voice behind the creature. As it fell to its knees, the man appeared behind the monster.

"There's more than one officer aboard this king's dragonship who can unlock locked hatches, sir! I think you will find that a pike in the hands of an expert can be the deadliest weapon on a king's ship."

The creature's face slammed to the deck when Fallow moved forward and ripped his pike out of the back of the monster.

"You'll also discover, former First Officer Wily, that it's difficult to regenerate a head, even for a shapechanger." With that statement, Ashe used the blade of the pike to chop off the monster's head. "Well, my fine young officer, I thought our saboteur would try something while everyone else was busy."

"You knew Mr. Wily was a traitor?" Halcyon gasped as he rubbed his bruised throat and got up.

"I didn't have a clue. I've been hanging around these parts, by the liver chamber. I thought I would come over here to see how you were doing," Ashe said, smiling at Halcyon.

The *Sanguine* shivered as enemy shells started hitting the port side.

"I had to let it get distracted with you before I could strike. If it had known I was behind it, the battle would have gone a lot differently. Let this experience be another life's lesson for you, Mr. Blithe. If you can't be the most powerful, it's best to have a few tricks up your sleeve. After the creature bested me the other day in drills, I asked our good wizard how to get around the magic of the Drusan shield spell. He told me to coat my pike head in tannin oil. I'm never going on a ship without a barrel full of the stuff from now on."

"So it was just chance that you had the right thing to defeat the monster?" Halcyon, still in shock, didn't want to believe his life stood in the balance because of a smelly root.

"Being prepared is the duty of every officer and crew member. Call it fate, call it luck, but we Lankshire men think the more prepared we are the luckier we get, if you get my meaning," Ashe replied.

Ashe stabbed at the body of the monster. The thing melted on the orlop deck, turning into a mass of blue ooze.

"Nasty business, shapechangers. A smelly mess this has turned into, but it's better smelling it than becoming it. Now, normally I would make you clean this up, Mr. Blithe," Chief Fallow said.

"Aye, Mr. Fallow," Halcyon said.

"We Lankshire men must stick together. After the battle, and by the lack of shells smashing into our *Sanguine's* side, I'm wagering they are all running. I'll have some other poor midshipwizard come down to clean this."

"An excellent thought, Mr. Fallow. I'll continue manning my post until the all clear is sounded," Halcyon said, winking at Ashe.

"Well spoken. We'll make a fighting officer out of you yet. I'll let you report to the captain about this little encounter." Ashe handed Halcyon the blast pike that killed Wily.

Blithe found himself thinking that guard duty in the heart chamber wasn't such a bad duty after all. He would need to work on his defensive spells. Eight-foot-tall, ravening monsters shouldn't be able to kill him easily now that he knew what they were like. He was a Lankshire man, after all. He leaned against the wall of the chamber, suddenly needing the pike to hold himself up.

XX

❧ ❧ ❧

𝕶ing and 𝕮ountry

HIS MAJESTY'S ARTICLES OF WAR: ARTICLE XX

All spies, and all persons whatsoever, who shall come, or be found, in the nature of spies, to bring or deliver any seducing letters or messages from any enemy or rebel, or endeavor to corrupt any captain, officer, mariner, or other in the fleet, to betray his trust, being convicted of any such offense by the sentence of the court-martial, shall be punished with death, or such other punishment as the nature and degree of the offense shall deserve and the court marital shall impose.

Halcyon came up on deck and into the bright sunshine. He looked to the open sea and in the distance noted the last enemy frigate, fleeing under full sail, running with the wind.

The stern of the other frigate was tight against the port side of the *Sanguine*. The frigate's rudder appeared ruined from blast-tube fire.

Tupper ran up to Halcyon, blast-gel soot covering his uniform and face.

"Hal, you should have seen us, it was amazing." The excitement of the action still filled young Tupper. "While marines boarded the enemy first-rater, the frigate started tacking to come around our other side. The port broadside shot away its rudder. We won the fight on the *Migol* and the captain hailed the frigate and made it surrender without firing another shot. The whole thing was brilliant, absolutely brilliant!"

"I'm up here because Chief Fallow told me to report to the captain," Halcyon said, a little nervous. "I'm glad you did well. What of the others, Tupper?"

"They all survived. Mark has a bad shoulder wound, but all the other midshipwizards are alive and well. You better get to the captain. He's on the quarterdeck," Tupper told him, knowing that reporting to the captain took precedence over everything else on board ship.

"Thanks, Tupper, I'll come down and help here when he releases me," Halcyon said as he moved to the stairs leading to the quarterdeck.

Lieutenant Durand was at the bottom of the stairs. "Mr. Blithe, what do you need?" She held out a hand to stop him from going up to the quarterdeck.

"I've been told to report to the captain about the saboteur, ma'am," he told her.

"Really, who was it?" she asked.

"First Officer Wily was a Maleen shapechanger. Chief Fallow and I killed him. Actually it was more the chief than me." Halcyon suddenly found himself uncomfortable at the telling of the encounter. He felt as if he should have done more, now that the action was all over.

"The captain will want to hear what you have to say. There's a line of officers reporting to him on the port side of the quarterdeck. Wait your turn up there, carry on," she ordered, and let him pass.

"Aye, aye, ma'am," he answered as he went up the stairs to the quarterdeck.

Halcyon scanned the deck and mizzen, noting lots of damage. Shot away were the mizzen topgallant and mizzen topsails. The four portside blast-tubes were total wrecks. Half of one of the great wheels controlling the ship stood in splinters. Carpenters were putting on the spare wheel. Other crew and marines were working to clear the damage. The smell of tannin oil filled the area even in the gusty breeze. Crew brushed it on all the wounds of the dragonship's hull.

A short line of men stood in front of the captain's table. Captain Olden's steward gave each reporting crew member a tankard of something. They would take a sip and report.

A much-battered Major Aberdeen, with a huge cut across his cheek and chin, was reporting when Halcyon took a place in the line. By Aberdeen's jovial tone of voice, his spirit was up and he had good things to say. Halcyon was able to hear the tail end of the report.

". . . Andool's blast-tubes had taken the fight out of them. The damage on the upper decks, as you can see from here, was staggering. The crew was beaten, but they didn't quite know it yet, when we boarded the *Migol*," the major said after taking a long pull of his wine. "As we rushed the decks, their quarterdeck filled to overflowing with Maleen marines and Maleen officers. We centered our efforts there during the main course of the battle. The bastards are tough fighters with their backs against the sea wall. I ordered a holding action everywhere else. Once we killed the Maleen officers on the quarterdeck, their command control ended throughout the ship, allowing us to force surrenders. The other decks fell to our blast-pikes and sabers in short order.

"What documents we could find show the *Migol* was fresh out of Malua. We found no dispatches to other enemy fleets or orders for the *Migol*. They must have been thrown overboard before we got to the captain's cabin."

"A few of my marines will be deserving medals when we get back to Ilumin. I'll have a written report for you to read tomorrow. What's left of the enemy crew are all cowed in the ship's hold. There are no Maleen marines or Maleen officers left alive," the major said, now slumping on the captain's table, looking exhausted.

"Steward, get the major a bench to sit on. Excellent work, Major." The captain's words were filled with praise. "We've landed a solid blow this day against the enemy forces. How many marines do you want to send over in the prize crew?"

"I'm thinking fifty marines and a lieutenant major; the *Migol* is a first-rater, after all," the major said.

"Send them over. I'll send Mr. Solvalson for its prize captain, he deserves the task, along with Midshipwizards Surehand and Murdock, ten able seamen, and twenty junior seamen." The captain looked over to the smiling lieutenant who had just unexpectedly become a captain. "Mr. Solvalson, get that ship into the nearest friendly Arcanian port with all speed and wait there for further orders, understood?"

"Aye, aye, sir," Pierce said to his captain. He saluted and almost ran from the quarterdeck.

The major and the captain looked after him.

"Do you remember being that young, Topal?" the captain asked.

"Sure and it seems just a day ago that you and I set foot on the old frigate *Ilumin* not fifteen years past if it's a day," the major said, smiling after the lieutenant.

"Bide with me a moment more, Topal," the captain asked. "I want you to get that cut looked at. Don't go telling me it's just a scratch. You're oozing blood like a stuck pig. I need to hear the surgeon's butcher bill, but Updean is here to report on the frigate and I want your opinion on its disposition."

"Certainly, Captain, I'm completely at your disposal," the major said, still smiling.

Halcyon noticed that the major looked pale. There was a lot of dried and wet blood all over the front of his uniform. The major would be getting stitches, but most of the blood flow from the wound had stopped by now.

The ship's steward handed the surgeon a tankard of wine, and he drank it all in one tipping. The surgeon gave the captain a list of the dead, wounded, and dying.

"We got off lightly this time, Captain," he reported. "We've got twenty-two dead and twice that many with minor wounds. Six more will die before the sun sets. I'm finished with our crew here. By your leave I'll go over with my aides and help with the *Migol's* dying and wounded."

"Of course, Surgeon," the captain said. "They'll appreciate the good treatment and that makes the prize crew's job all the easier. Be back on board before the sun sets. We still have to get to Ordune and that blockade as soon as possible. Well done, Surgeon." The captain stood and shook the surgeon's hand.

"Thank you, sir." The tired surgeon saluted and left.

The steward offered Lieutenant Junior Grade Ivan Updean a tankard.

"Water for me, please," Ivan asked the steward.

Halcyon noticed the captain's glance at that request. The steward was giving the captain water as well.

"Your report, Mr. Updean?" the captain asked.

"At your order," Ivan said, "I took a squad of marines and ship's crew to the Maleen frigate the *Cascade* when she became lashed to our side. The *Sanguine's* broadside sheered away the frigate's rudder. The crew of the frigate was all Drusan sailors. I discovered their Maleen officers were trying to get them to continue the fight. Our size and their helpless condition decided the crew. They killed their Maleen officers and threw them overboard. They surrendered to us and I have repairs started on the rudder. We should be able to have a replacement before nightfall. There's no fight left in them. They seem more than willing to work for Arcania and it's them doing most of the repairs right now."

"Excellent, good work, Mr. Updean," the captain said while rising and shaking Ivan's hand. "Major, how many of your marines should we send over on that prize?"

"I'll send over ten good men with a warrant officer. We've seen lots of these types of defeated crews in the past. With the Maleen gone from the ship, they see Arcania capturing them as a chance at a new life. They won't be giving the prize crew any trouble," the major remarked.

"Mr. Updean, you take command of the *Cascade*." The captain's news stunned Ivan. "I'll send over ten able seamen and Midshipwizards Grunseth and Argo, with Junior Lieutenant Fosentat. That should do you, don't you think?"

"Aye, sir, thank you, sir," Updean said.

Olden rose and shook Updean's hand.

Updean saluted and left.

"Major, now you can get to the surgeon and get that face of yours attended to," the captain ordered.

"Sir, I would feel more comfortable finishing the work on the *Migol*, with your permission," the major asked.

The captain spoke in an irritated tone. "You don't have my permission, sir. I've seen cuts like that kill a man bit by bit. Get yourself to our surgeon before he goes on the *Migol* and to the task of healing. You have good men serving under you; they can get the *Migol* set straight."

The captain again rose and held out his hand to the major. There was no chance for the major to disagree. They shook hands.

"Aye, aye, Captain." The major saluted and left.

The steward handed the ship's carpenter a tankard of rum.

The captain looked after the major's retreating form. "Damn firebrand. I'm glad I don't have an entire crew of that type. He's awesomely efficient in a fight, but has to be told to get out of the rain otherwise, gods protect him." The captain shook his head and made several notes in his log.

An able seaman, the ship's carpenter had come with the captain when he took command of the *Sanguine* several years before. A favorite of Olden's, the much older man could speak to the captain in a different manner from everyone else.

"You did well in this fight, Captain. I'll have most of the damage fixed by tomorrow." The carpenter's tone was more like that of a father to a son than a seaman to his captain. No one else on board would have the courage to critique the actions of the ship's captain.

"Why, thank you, ship's carpenter. I try to keep the king's dragonship of the line in as good a condition as possible, considering the circumstances of my command." The captain's sarcasm made everyone on the quarterdeck smile.

"The ship's sailmaker tells me he's ready to replace the two sails you lost. Three of the blast-tubes on this quarterdeck are total wrecks. I'll replace the carriage of the fourth one tomorrow. The hull punctures are healing nicely and the dragon's main body didn't take any damage, bless its cold, cold heart," the carpenter told his officer.

At the mention of the dragon's heart the captain looked right at Halcyon.

Halcyon looked over to the *Migol* to see that the starboard center section of the ship had taken brutal damage. The hull still smoked from fires started during the battle. It was going to take more than several days to repair all of that.

"Carpenter, what do you think about replacing our lost tubes with Maleen tubes off the first-rater?" the captain asked.

"I wouldn't do it. It's your ship and all, but those iron tubes the Maleen make can't be trusted if you ask me. I could go and look at the tubes on both ships to see if they have any captured Arcanian ones. Those would work for us," the carpenter suggested.

"An excellent thought, do so straightaway," the captain ordered. Olden stood once more and shook the carpenter's hand.

After the ship's carpenter finished reporting, it was Blithe's turn. The steward offered him a tankard of wine and Halcyon asked for water. When he received it, he boldly raised the tankard and said, "To your health, Captain."

The captain waited until Halcyon was through drinking his water. "Thank you for the thought. I'm surprised to see you up here reporting, Mr. Blithe." The captain paused, waiting for Halcyon to speak.

Standing ramrod-straight, Halcyon said, "Sir, First Officer Lieutenant Commander Wily was the saboteur. He was a Maleen shapechanger sent to Arcania to destroy dragonships. He tried again to destroy the heart during the battle. I fought him and Chief Fallow killed him. That's my report, sir." Blithe stood waiting for the captain to respond.

"Durand, get Chief Fallow up here, now!" the captain ordered. There was a scowl on the captain's face.

Olden threw his battle helm down on the table and leaned back in his chair, a perplexed look on his face. "You are just full of surprises, Mr. Blithe, and I'm finding most of them are not pleasant ones. I don't think in all my days in this man's navy I've ever seen an officer like you. I'll tell you one thing, young man. You will either rise to the top like your father or end up blasted to bits in some major combat. Deadly danger to both you and your ship's crew seems to shadow your every step in this man's navy."

Halcyon stood there at attention, not knowing how to respond to the captain's words. "Yes, sir" was all he could utter.

Chief Fallow came on the quarterdeck and saluted the captain.

The captain saluted back.

"Chief," the captain said, still leaning back in his chair and looking irritated, "this young midshipwizard is going to tell us an amazing tale for the second time in my hearing. I'm going to hear more about my first officer being the traitor on board my ship. When he's finished in more detail than I heard the first time," the captain said, emphasizing his last statement and looking straight at Halcyon, "you, Chief Fallow, will then report how you killed an Arcanian officer and I'd better hear important details from you on that court-martialing offense. Mr. Blithe, proceed in detail, if you please."

Just then, Halcyon noticed that there were six marines behind the captain. He hadn't given them any thought before and the reason they might be stationed behind the captain. He now knew what that reason was.

The steward handed the chief a tankard of rum and the chief drained it and asked for another. The steward filled it again without comment, but there was a disapproving look on his face.

The captain's glare spurred Halcyon to start his report again.

"Sir, I was at my post in the heart chamber. Per your command, whenever battle stations sounded my duty station was to be on the orlop deck and in the dragonship's heart chamber," Halcyon said.

"Wait one moment." The captain shouted down to Durand again. "Durand, get Mr. Giantson and Miss Griffon up here on the double," the captain ordered. Olden held his hand up toward Halcyon, meaning him to stop until the other two officers appeared.

Chief Fallow took a drink from his tankard of rum. He smiled and appeared totally relaxed. He grinned at the captain and Blithe, clearly not bothered at all by the captain's irritated glare.

When Giantson and Andool arrived, the captain said, "I want you to hear what Mr. Blithe and then Chief Fallow have to say. Carry on, Mr. Blithe." The captain lowered his hand, waving it for Halcyon to continue.

The added attention of the other officers didn't make Halcyon any less nervous. He drained the last of his tankard, ordered his thoughts for a heartbeat, and began.

"I was at my post in the dragon heart chamber. Quite by accident, I discovered that if I touched the dragon's heart and the ice at the same time, I could see through the sea dragon's eyes in some sort of amazing magical happenstance. I watched the first shots fired from our bow chasers," the nervous Halcyon reported.

"Really," Giantson interrupted.

"Let him finish, Daton. I know you'll have a thousand questions and tests to do later, but for now let's get this story out," the captain ordered.

"As I watched the first successful broadside strike the *Migol*, First Officer Wily entered the heart chamber."

The captain stopped him again. Looking at his second officer, he said, "Andool, for the record I will be reporting that your new shells worked as expected. I just wanted to tell you that as the thought came into my mind."

"Why, thank you, Captain, I was pleased with their service." She graciously smiled at the captain. "My report will reflect your thoughts as well." She looked back to Halcyon, forcing the midshipwizard to continue.

"Before I knew who it was, I drew my weapon and faced him ready for the worst. Commander Wily had cast the Drusan shield about his body, but appeared otherwise normal in his battle gear. He ordered me to go up on deck and join the blast-tube crews in the action." Halcyon stopped for a moment, embarrassed by what he was about to say. "To be quite honest, I almost went. I stopped myself, remembering the first Article of War, and told him I had to stay at my post per your order, Captain."

"Absolutely right and by the Articles, that last was well done," the captain exclaimed, looking more interested now than irritated. He was leaning forward on the table and drinking from his own water glass.

Halcyon gulped several nervous breaths and reached out with his empty tankard for more water.

He continued his tale. "I stood my ground and Mr. Wily became enraged. He began an amazing transformation into some type of hideous monster. I'd heard about shapechangers, to be sure, but the creature chilled me to the bone from the first second it revealed itself. I knew it was a shapechanger from its four eyes. It's the only creature I know of with four.

"At first we fenced, but I was unable to land a telling blow. The Drusan magic kept my edge away from his hide. I couldn't strike it often, as the creature was more skilled than I with a blade. Officer Wily had completely transformed into a monster with four eyes, terrible fangs, and talons for hands. It kept politely talking to me, in Mr. Wily's tone of voice. His shredded clothes hung from its massive body. My magical attacks were nothing to it. The creature claimed to have destroyed five other Arcanian dragon warships.

"When I tried calling for help from the marines on the other side of the hatches, it gestured and filled the chamber with an odd haze. Something like floating feathers filled the area."

Officer Giantson shook his head, clearly knowing about the spell.

Halcyon continued, "My calls for help were totally silenced. The monster started communicating with me in my mind. I don't have words for the terror this inspired in me. Its thoughts were evil and filled with a desire to destroy everything around it. To be very honest it was clearly toying with me. I caused it some pain as I lunged into its throat with my saber point. The shielding spell stopped my point from piercing, but I could feel through the telepathic link that I had badly bruised it.

"The creature rushed me, knocked my saber out of my hand,

and started draining the life out of me. It used some type of magic I've never encountered before. A gray glow touched me through its talons and all the strength left my body. I think I felt the life draining out of my body and into the shapechanger. That's when Chief Fallow took a hand. I never saw him enter the chamber, but thank the gods he did. We couldn't hear anything because of the strange silencing spell that filled the area. Chief Fallow is one of the true heroes of the encounter. His blast-pike somehow pierced the magic of the Drusan shield and struck at the heart of the monster. The chief killed the creature and saved my life and the life of the *Sanguine*, sir."

Halcyon stood at attention, his story finished.

"Chief, what do you have to add to Mr. Blithe's story?" the captain asked.

"Captain, after the first officer bested me in the blast-pike drill, I became a tad irritated at the use of the Drusan shield, if you get my drift," said the chief. "I went to Lieutenant Commander Giantson and asked him how a poor non-magic-using sailor like me could overcome that sort of magic."

Attempts to sound humble were completely lost on the captain. His irritated scowl came back to his face. Chief Fallow lost some of his relaxed slouch and stood straighter in front of his captain, continuing his report.

"I don't like getting beat with my own weapon and that shield magic seemed a mite unfair. The commander was good enough to tell me that dipping my pike in tannin oil would allow the weapon to slip right past the magic as long as the oil wasn't rubbed off the pike in the course of a battle. I tipped my pike in the oil as the drums beat the call to battle stations. I had no idea I'd be using the weapon against Commander Wily.

"I and a couple of the crew stationed ourselves in the liver chamber just to make sure nothing bad happened there."

"That was an excellent thought, Chief, I should have ordered that myself," the captain remarked, the scowl gone again.

The chief continued with his report. As the battle started, "I thought I would check the heart chamber to make sure our Mr. Blithe here was doing well at his post; even though I knew a good Lankshire officer like himself would be where he was ordered."

Halcyon flushed at the praise Ashe sent his way. He stood a little straighter, now allowing himself to smile at the chief's kind words.

"When I opened the hatch," the chief continued, "I saw the boy—I mean, Mr. Blithe—and a Maleen shapechanger in a death struggle. I shouted, trying to distract the monster from killing Mr. Blithe. I failed to distract the creature; words made no sound in the chamber. The shapechanger was holding the midshipwizard up off his feet. There was an evil sort of gray glow over the boy. I could tell there was still fight in him by the way he was struggling in that death grip, but he was getting weaker by the second. I couldn't see any other course of action. I rushed the creature and gave it the best part of my pike into its back. The oil allowed my weapon to slip past the magic shield. I ripped out its chest. I had a brother, he's long dead now, but he told me about fighting Maleen shapechangers when he served with the armies of the Toman before that country fell to the armies of the Maleen. He said you had to chop off a shapechanger's head or they just healed to do their mischief again in a few hours. I took its head and the creature turned into blue mush."

The chief looked at Lieutenant Commander Giantson, clearly relishing his next statement. "You'll be happy to know, Commander Giantson, that I ordered the mess put in a barrel. I knew you'd want to take a look, but it smells pretty high."

The chief came to attention. "That's all I have to say, sir."

"You've both done your duty," the captain told them. "Amazing, simply amazing. Of course I believe both of you, but I have no idea how I'm going to tell the admiralty about all of this." There was a stunned look to the captain's face. "We still need to look into the affair. Giantson, I want you to make a report about that tannin oil. We face lots of enemies with Drusan shields. You will also need to inspect Wily's kit. Use the utmost caution as there might be hidden traps among his things."

"Aye, sir," Giantson replied.

"We're going to have to suggest to the admiralty that there needs to be a way to reveal these shapechangers. The service can't have their best men replaced by these monsters. Commander Giantson and Commander Griffon, you both draw up a report on possible ways to ferret out these monsters. Wily was with the crew for fourteen months. I thought he was brutal, but not a monster."

"Aye, aye, Captain," they both said.

"Mr. Blithe, Chief Fallow, well done, now get back to your duties," the captain ordered. He stood once more and shook both of their hands.

"Aye, aye," Halcyon and Ashe said.

As they left the quarterdeck, Chief Fallow remarked, "No fancy speeches from our captain, just straight to the matter. I like that in an officer. In addition, you never see an officer shake the hand of an enlisted man. That was a noble gesture on his part. You would do well to follow his example." The chief started going belowdecks. Halcyon put his hand on the chief's shoulder.

"I will, Chief, and thanks for saving my life," Halcyon said.

Ashe turned and put out his own hand, shaking Hal's, and said, "I save your life this time, you save mine next time. As you fight with your mates in battle after battle, you'll stop saying thank you. You're just doing what the navy pays you for, after all. You've looked certain death in the eyes, did your best, and survived. Not much will stop you after the experience you just had. I know your father's spirit watches and is proud of you and so am I." The chief went belowdecks.

Halcyon turned to lean against the port railing. Looking at the captured *Migol*, he longed to serve as the captain of such a ship. He looked forward to getting back home and telling his first naval story to his brothers and uncles. After a few more moments, he mentally chided himself for daydreaming on the deck when there was work to do. For a heartbeat, he imagined his father's spirit smiling down on him. He stood straight and saluted into the noon sun, honoring his father and promising to carry the battle to more of the enemy. He'd helped with a small victory for Arcania and his family this day and was pleased with that. There would be more and larger victories if he had anything to say about it.

❧ ❧ ❧

Grog at Four Bells

Halcyon rang the four bells on the quarterdeck, announcing the best time in a seaman's day. Grog and meals were handed out at four bells everywhere on the ship. Today, hours after the battle, the captain had the men assemble on the upper decks for their grog. He stood on the quarterdeck with Second Officer Griffon and Lieutenant Commander Giantson and the rest of the dragonship's officers behind him.

"Crew of the *Sanguine*," the captain roared out, holding a tankard high in the air, "I salute you all!"

The crew on the three decks drank their ration of grog and hailed their captain back with a hearty "Huzzah!"

"A second ration of grog comes to you by my order. Feel free to drink to the bottom of this one. Today you and I captured two prizes. In a few months, when that prize gold comes to us all, I'll drink to your health again."

A cheer rose up once more from the decks.

The lieutenants and midshipwizards standing on the quarterdeck with the rest of the officers threw their hats into the air in celebration.

The sea dragon, sensing the mood of the tiny creatures on its shell, roared in pleasure, spouting gouts of seawater from its throat.

"Although many of you were heroes in the conflict today, there were two crew who performed above and beyond the call of duty," the captain said. "These two have earned themselves high honors. Let me present Midshipwizard Blithe, come forward, sir."

Halcyon walked up in amazement to the side of the captain.

"This young midshipwizard stood his ground and fought his best against a Maleen shapechanger who sought to destroy our *Sanguine*'s heart. I would have you all give him a cheer," the captain ordered.

"Huzzah!" The entire crew shouted its pleasure.

Halcyon just stood there wanting to point out that Chief Fallow did most of the work, but not knowing how to interrupt his captain.

"Using my authority as captain of the *Sanguine*, I'm promoting Mr. Blithe to Midshipwizard Third Class. Well done, sir," the captain said, shaking Halcyon's hand while the crew around him cheered the promotion.

The captain held up his hand, quieting down his crew. "I would also like to take this time to honor one of our marines. The major informs me that yet again, one of his fighters did unusually well battling on the decks of the *Migol*. Would Denna Darkwater please come up here?"

All of the marines cheered one of their own on as she climbed the steps to the quarterdeck. A very red-in-the-face Darkwater came up to her captain and saluted.

The captain spoke loudly enough for the entire ship's crew to hear. "Today I would honor this marine. She is responsible for forcing the captain of the *Migol* to surrender in the heat of the battle. Corporal Darkwater, this ship and crew owe you a debt. I would have you ask something of us this day as a reward for your services."

The entire crew grew quiet, waiting to hear what she would ask for. In the past when the captain made this offer to a crew member, they asked for fresh beef or an extra day of rest for the crew. Denna had something else on her mind.

Corporal Darkwater looked all around and her eyes landed on Halcyon, standing right beside her. "All I want," she said so that everyone could hear, "right here and right now, is a rematch with Midshipwizard Third Class Halcyon Blithe in the blast-pike circle."

The crew cheered its pleasure at the coming spectacle.

The stunned Halcyon hoped there were some bandages left from after the battle as the now-reluctant warrior slowly took his jacket off.